Devian Nikei

SAFETY IN
LOVERS

Rave Reviews for <u>Safety in Lovers</u> by Devian Nikei
5.0 out of 5-star Amazon rating

"**Excellent story...**I kept picking up the book every moment that I got... unexpected twist and turns... Overall I think the book is great and I recommend it."

- **Roni H.**

"**Amazing book...A must read**... This is not just another book about relationships, this book explores the life of a woman, like many..."

- **Allison B.**

"**I'm ready for another book!!!**... Loved this book. I learned some things and angles in regards to love..."

-**Ariel I.**

Subscribe at www.deviancebydevian.com for updates, special offers, upcoming events or to contact author, Devian Nikei

Safety in Lovers

DEVIAN NIKEI

Nikel Novels
Publishing

This book is a work of fiction. Names, characters, places and incidents are products of the author's imagination or are used fictitiously. Any resemblance to actual events or locales or persons, living or dead, is entirely coincidental.

Copyright © 2011 by Devian Nikei

ISBN-13: 978-0692552735
ISBN-10: 0692552731
BISAC: Fiction/Romance/New Adult

Interior design by Devian Nikei

Printed in the U.S.A.

A publication of Nikei Novels Publishing-Charlotte

To order copies and other merchandise or for more information, contact:
website: www.deviancebydevian.com
email: nikeinovels@deviancebydevian.com

Dedication

This book is dedicated both to
the haters and the congratulators,
the dream crushers and the dream weavers;
to my backbiters and my cheerleaders,
for the naysayers and the believers-
You all have contributed to my success
and helped bring out in me my best.
I hope that you never stop doing what you do,
May God continue to bless and keep each of
you.
For all you do,
this book is for you.

Acknowledgements

I would like— first and foremost, to acknowledge the Most High God, who encouraged me from day to day to believe in myself. I thank Him for the gifts of knowledge and wisdom that he freely gave to me— without repentance, so that I could affect my generation without hypocrisy.

I would also like to thank myself because I wouldn't let myself stop until I had written the very best book that I could. I appreciate myself for pushing me to be transparent. Don't know how I would have done this without me.

In addition, I want to specifically acknowledge my niece, Tamecia Sanders, for being my very first reader. Your critiques have helped shape this novel more than any other influence, so I thank you for that.

To Tammie Pew, I give my eternal gratitude because you were a tireless supporter and wonderful friend.

Devian Nikei

Foreword

When I was a young girl, I asked my mother if I was pretty...

After some time, she responded with a considerable amount of nervous determination, "Well baby... you're smart."

But... that was not what I had asked her. As girls grow up, a large part of who they will inevitably become is summed up in that one question. Even as a small child, I understood that. What I had asked my mother was, "Tell me who I am... What is my value?"

Her answer told me who I was and I believed it. Women, like my character Denae and I, are taught that being ugly or dark-skinned or knock-kneed or nappy-headed are flaws and impediments that must be overcome by sheer determination. Women like us cannot rest, nurtured in the arms of a world that loves us, but must instead forge out a place for ourselves by our usefulness to society. We might possibly gain someone's love, if we can somehow prove through our accomplishments and meekness that we have something of value to offer in lieu of a lackluster appearance.

Some women, in their pursuit of value and worth, even go so far as to convince themselves that they don't need love— that respect will suffice. Because love is so elusively inaccessible, they will instead focus on what they can control. Women, clamoring for position, who collect fancy commodities, such as their educational accomplishments, impressive careers and stable finances. Finding solace in success, they create a giant Ice Queen kingdom on top of a frigid, mountainous heart. They believe they have overcome their shortcomings and attained their dreams by the strength of what their hands have wrought.

Denae is that such woman. She believes she is fine and safe in the world that she has created. She has surrounded herself with persons whom she can marginally tolerate. Not having extreme emotions and feelings such as love and passion, help her to feel that she is secure. It is not until the introduction of the character Dennis that she realizes the strange, draining sensation that she has felt on a daily basis— is loneliness.

Denae believes that she is safe in the world because she is alone in it. The way she views herself internally shapes her view of how others see her. Denae finds that her safety is only the product of delusions that she has held about who she really is inside. However, when she encounters Dennis, he ignites in her feelings that she has worked her entire life to suppress. He makes her feel— **beautiful**... and that changes the very core of who she has always believed herself to be. She is unable to continue to live the way she did before that revelation, once she realizes that she is truly beautiful to someone.

Denae, like many women, does not realize the power and influence that ingrained and indoctrinated self-hatred has over her life. It takes someone who Denae can identify with to help her acknowledge the beauty in herself. Finding beauty and worth in Dennis, teaches Denae to recognize it in her own mirror.

When a man makes a woman feel truly loved and beautiful, that awareness ignites an insatiable fire. It completely redefines her life. In this story, Denae finds out just how fragile pride is, when confronted with true love. She finds there is no substitute for it and all attempts at replication in the form of success, power or security are futile.

As I've said before, the character Denae is somewhat autobiographical, but so are all of the other females in the book. I have sprinkled a little of myself and other women, who have shared their experiences with me, into all of them for authenticity. Each one of these personalities possesses some level of insecurities and experiences that I, and other women I know, have had in life.

Just like Denae, once I was truly loved by a man who taught me the art of how to love myself. An art (like cooking) that we don't teach to our children anymore. We make our children compete for love and conform for acceptance. I was a product of that mentality. When a man came into my life, who loved me, just as I was, and found the beauty in me because he knew the beauty he possessed within himself, I instantly tried to test it. I sabotaged that love with insecurity because it shook the foundations of everything that I knew. This man didn't love me because I was smart or successful or had nice legs, it was something that exuded from deep within him and he shared it with me. It was a self-love that he was selfless enough to give to me.

I am glad, however that I learned how to love myself from him before he was gone. That's the beautiful thing about love. It is a seed, not just a present to be enjoyed once and then put on a shelf. No instead, it continues to give life and food to them that cultivate its peaceable fruit.

In this novel, I'll take you and Denae through just a small piece of my journey to a love relationship with myself.

I hope you enjoy reading this story just as much as I did telling it.

PART I

THE PROLOGUE

Safety in Lovers

Alisha, My Solace

"Jamal... I'm pregnant."
"Are you sure?"
"Yeah, I'm..."
"Well, that's great... right. This is what we wanted—"
"The baby may not be... yours."
"What?"

'What?— Not again. I can't believe this,' I thought to myself, as I bellowed boos along with the studio audience.

Once a week, daytime talk show drama is my one descent into sheer ridiculous ignorance. Even people who know me best would probably be surprised to find me sitting here, in pink, footed pajamas, hopping up and down on the couch enjoying "Paternity Secrets Revealed" over a tub of Mint Chocolate Chip ice cream.

"Whose is it, then? Who was you wit'?"

"Tell him! You'd better tell the truth now," I objected aloud, inserting my much-needed advice and wielding a large tablespoon with rabid intensity. 'I mean, really— don't women have anything better to do than sleep with the whole neighborhood, and then parade a processional of men in for paternity testing.'

"*Don't judge! You've obviously got nothing better to do **yourself** than watch it,*" Alisha dissented smugly.

Alisha. That is her name... or what *I* call her.

Some others might call her a "conscience" or a "tiny voice" in the back of your head. I've often heard people refer to her as *something*. For example, *something* just told me that, or *something* said not to go.

"I know that's right," I said, agreeing audibly with Alisha. I have always found that it is easier that way. I have learned through years of trial— but mostly error, that Alisha is usually right.

Alisha— (a' lee' shah): 1. truth, noble; 2. the truthful one, the wise counselor; 3. protected by God.

Pretty nice, right? Being seemingly wiser than me is how she got her name. I was born an only child. My father left before I was old enough to have memories of him. He never wanted any children, so after marrying a childless woman, he relocated to Florida. Might as well have been Cuba, I guessed, if he could have managed that.

My mother, disgraced and destitute, was left slaving to provide for me. Even as a little girl, when I looked into her weary eyes, I could see the desolation of a woman forced to abandon the comfort of a man's arms in exchange for unending maternal duty. Though she never said this, I gathered that I was the cause of the grief that she bore.

I became a recluse of a child. Opting rather to remain enshrouded in an enigmatic world of my own eclectic design, than to develop burdensome relationships. I reasoned— what sanctuary could the outside world offer me? The only two people commissioned with the principal function of loving me were encumbered by my presence.

Creative by nature, I retreated instead to sit alone in my room for hours, lost in and fascinated by the constructs of my own mind— much more exhilarating than the dreary reality in which I lived. Because my mom worked so much, I spent the majority of my time outside of school in the care of the seventy-year old, housing project Candy Lady. The most she ever had to say to me was, "Stay out of the street, little girl," which proved in the future to be famous words to live by. She was a sweet woman, but I perfected the art of being my own entertainment on her front stoop.

My mother would recount to me, of my early years, that I never played much with dolls. I was, however, an illustrious storyteller able to lie— I mean, *spin* a web of elaborate tales to explain even the simplest anomaly, like a missing cookie.

That is how I became aware of Alisha. I guess she was always there, emphatically urging me to tell the truth— insisting that it was the most straightforward route through whatever conundrum I had created. Back in those days, she was more like a feeling or a sensation— a comforting assurance that could quickly transform into a devastating tidal wave of nauseating remorse, if not heeded.

As I matured into teenaged delinquency, she became the distinct voice of resilient opposition, or The Insurgency, as I deemed her. Different from me in almost every way, she even has a strange West Indian accent. It was not until after my quarter-life crisis, following college, that I realized any resistance was futile. All of the advice that Alisha gave came back to haunt and taunt me in those years of educated indigence. Therefore, I conceded to her and even named her to affirm my allegiance.

She became my closest confidant: the one who supplied me with fake aliases and phone numbers for undesirables at nightclubs; alerted me to the infidelities of my lovers; prevented me from the purchase of defective vehicles, and a host of other invaluable favors. Alisha has bestowed on me an unconditional love that I have never experienced elsewhere.

Alisha— my solace, is both empathetic companion and trenchant critic, but over the years, I have come to trust that she minds my best interests.

Well, that's enough about Alisha and enough of this mind-numbing debauchery on my television.

'Is it still considered a talk show, if everybody's screaming?' I contemplated, as the screen clicked off with a buzz.

Devian Nikei

Revelation Elevation

"He came over... again. At night... again. Drunk... ***again***."

Deena is the kind of person who adds dramatic flair to everything she says. It's like she is the chief decorator and designer for a children's television show— lots of bright colors, toothy smiles, and big hair.

Strange woman.

"What's our mantra, huh? ***Self***-respect. Emphasis on the ***self***," I replied indifferently. I couldn't feign enthusiasm for this topic anymore.

'Not again.' I prepared myself for what her pout signified.

Wait for it... wait for it... and... **go**—

"But we've been together for so long. It doesn't seem like ***self***-respect, but ***self***ishness not to be there for him. He's been through so much and I am the only one who understands—"

"*Why do you talk to that woman?*" Alisha interjected.
"I know... I know," I mumbled, responding satisfactorily to both Deena and Alisha. It's just plain sad. Look at what I have become— an affirming, consolatory yes-person to everyone around me, including my own "conscience".

"Denae... Are you listening to me?"
"*No,*" Alisha snarled.
"Yeah, yeah... of course," I answered with a more convincing portrayal of empathy. It didn't matter though. My performance was lost on Deena. She was already back to her regularly scheduled program before I answered. She asks random rhetorical questions like that, from time to time, during her monologues just to break up the monotony.
See— **Dramatic flair.**

By the way, I'm Denae.

Denae— (dee' nay): **1.** mother of Perseus (mythic hero of ancient Greek mythology); **2.** thirsty.

I do not consider Deena and myself to be friends. It is more of a symbiotic relationship imposed on us by the similarity of our names.

"D'ya know what I mean?"
"Oh yeah, girl," I responded instinctively.

Deena and I have no physical attributes in common. She is short, curvaceous and bronze-complexioned, while I am tall, athletic and mocha-colored. However, often being confused for one another has created this bizarre solidarity between us. Usually people call me Deena, more than the other way around, as she is the more popular of the two of us. Her ever-evolving array of hair weaves and a mole, which switches cheeks daily, are much more intriguing characteristics than my customary crinkled up-do and lip gloss.

I get to live out all of my whimsical inventions vicariously through Deena's water cooler depictions of sensuous rendezvous. This chick is more explicit than a romance novel, when at her descriptive best, but lately her blazing vocabulary has been, all but, extinguished by the addition of a certain co-dependent killjoy named— as usual... Derrick (that name must just have bad Juju or something).

Deena's end of the deal is—

"Look girl, you know *I'm* with ya'. Nobody has to understand but you and Derrick."

Tah-dah!

"Hey Deena girl, I've got to finish up this case. You know how the slave driver is and today is deadline."

"Hey Deena girl, you're a case... a real head case!"

A tiny giggle escaped before I could catch it. I couldn't help but chuckle at Alisha's comment.

"Alright, later then," Deena chimed, already disappearing down Cubicle Row.

I know... You're guessing, right?

I'm sure that my astute powers of deduction have led you to presumptions about my occupation. Like just about everyone else in my class, I am not in my field of study. The new millennium met its graduates with abysmal professional prospects and I was no exception. Although I received a Bachelor of Arts degree in Mass Communications (with the hopes of obtaining work in radio broadcasting), I began my career path as a Correctional Officer in the Georgia Department of Corrections for three years. *The Glamorous Life.* Now, after a little additional Criminal Justice coursework, I have transitioned into the Division of Probation and Parole. *Party, all the time.*

Civil service isn't quite my bag, but it pays some of the bills. So for now, I won't complain. It could be worse. Still— if someone had told me five years ago that this is what I'd be doing for a living, I probably would have stepped away to keep from getting struck by the lightning that would follow their words. However, as the years have gone by, I've settled into a routine and found my niche in this profession.

It is my job to discern the motives of men's hearts. I've gotten pretty good at it too. Mostly all of the time, I am right and have, therefore, had very few probationers or parolees to abscond from my custody. I don't hate my job, but I **certainly** do not love it. My sentiment borders on the verge of apathetic indifference. The only notable discontentment that I have with this position is that it lacks any real capacity for professional growth and development. I can't see myself sitting at this desk five years from now, but based upon my progress at this present juncture, I don't see myself anywhere else either.

There is a bright side, however. At least once every day, at some undetermined time, I can look forward to some revelatory epiphany from Alisha that will elevate my consciousness and liberate me from the mundane confinement of my matchbox cubicle. These glad tidings are like tiny, golden nuggets of insight or unexpected love notes from a suitor. I wear them like bejeweled adornments.

Because of these oracles, my acquaintances deem me "wise beyond my years" and "an old soul", believing my keen intuitive abilities to be the product of an extra-sensory perception. However today, in a strange turn of events, my inspiration would find its muse in a different source.

* * *

"Dennison Millsaps?"

"Yes ma'am. People call me Dennis."

"... Mr. Millsaps, it appears that you have satisfied all of the conditions of your probationary sentence—" I paused, skimming over the paperwork again.

Earlier that morning, his file was dropped into my box— one of six probationers that were divided out to me from Jennifer Coaxum's caseload.

Maternity leave— *Oh, happy day*

The profile folder was stamped **COMPLETE**, indicating that this was Mr. Millsaps's final consultation. Even still— I never accept anyone else's work without my own perusal. However, after a detailed examination of the record, everything looked to be in order.

"I just need to collect the remaining balance of your fees, which is seventy-five dollars."

"Yeah, I gotcha." Dennison reached into his jeans pocket. "Here you go," he said, dumping a massive wad of crumpled bills on my desk— mostly singles, which I counted out carefully and with considerable contempt.

I initialed the receipt while he sat in quiet anticipation, glancing around my desk. He was searching— as all others do, for some clue or link into my life outside of the cubicle in which we sat.

Generally, every desk holds some hint that can lead to inferences about the character and values of the occupant: pictures of pets, children or spouses; miscellaneous figurines; various accommodations and plaques, etc. My desk has always puzzled my parolees and probationers. Nothing but office supplies and files, not even a nameplate to distinguish it from any other. Desolate and meticulous, it leaves no conversation starters or icebreakers.

"Sign by all the X's," I indicated with my ink pen before handing over the sheets. Dennison scribbled illegibly on the forms, and then reached them back to me. "So, Mr. Millsaps, now that your *debt to society* has been paid, what do you plan on doing next?"

I leaned back in my seat, checking to ensure that all the signatures were present and jotting down the last few notes required on the paperwork. The customer service clinics that we are coerced into attending every year encourage us to ask such questions:

These questions show a commitment to the rehabilitative process of your clients, establishing trust and resulting in good customer relations.

Criminals?
No, clients.
Convicts!
NO! Customers...
All C-words, I guess.

There is only one reason for my interest in these kinds of inquiries. The answers usually help me determine whether to file the folder to the Records Room or keep it in the divider drawer at the bottom of my desk for quick retrieval.
"Well," Mr. Millsaps began. "I've been working on starting my own HVAC business—"

Typical— Just what the Black community needs... another entre-manure.

I guess I am more like Deena than I thought, because that's as far into his monologue as I got before my mind wandered off. This occupation can really desensitize you to the plight of your fellowman. I wasn't paying considerable attention to Mr. Millsaps. The buzzing flicker of a dying fluorescent bulb overhead presented an aggravating, but albeit welcomed distraction. I was in the middle of counting the number of light flashes per minute, when all of a sudden, there it was...

"What did you just say?" I asked, suspecting that I had heard something twinkle.
"What part?" Dennison wasn't necessarily asking, but soliciting a response that would signify my participation in the conversation.
"The last part," I replied. 'Ha, ha! You missed me,' I gloated to myself, believing that I had dodged his trap.
"I said that doing what I did can only get me what I got. I want what I've never had before, so I'm going to do what I've never done. 'Progress is impossible without change, and those who

cannot change their minds cannot change anything' -George Bernard Shaw."

Damn... he caught me.

Revelation Elevation

It was simple— not five-carats, but not cubic zirconium either.

　　"Well, thank you for your time, Ms.—"
　　"You're welcome, Mr. Millsaps," I offered quickly, slicing the impending question mark off his statement. "Good luck."

Dennison extended his hand.

I extended his file... to the outbox.

Billie's Holiday

"I'm gonna' love you... like nobody's loved you-"

"How do you do it, Billie?'

"Come rain or come shine..."

'You make it sound so I easy,' I lamented softly in my spirit as I gazed at my cocoa reflection in the mirror. I wondered if Billie had ever known what it was like to love a man that didn't love her back. Could she sing this slow jazz ballad with so much soulful confidence in her lover, if she felt the same insecurity that I do?

"Happy together, unhappy together... and won't it be fine."

Here in this introspective place, I can hide from Alisha. Music has that effect. It can drown out her over-protective ranting.

"Days may be cloudy or sunny. We're in and out of the money..."

"Humph," I sighed, scattering all the prickly, straw-like thoughts from my mind with the force of a Big Bad Wolf's puff. I picked up two dissimilar earrings. As I placed them to my ears, I tried to imagine what impression each one would induce. I always choose classic sophistication over fad trends, so back into the jewelry box with the small, dangling disco balls. I placed the thin, gold hoops into my earlobes, then turned slowly around once more in front of the mirror— mostly just to inspect my rear.

It is sheer perfection in this snug black sweater tunic and Lycra leggings ensemble. I topped the whole outfit off with shimmering gold belts, bangles and heels. I finished the careful arrangement of my seemingly disheveled spiral curls and touched up my lip-gloss. I wasn't giving anyone the green light tonight, but I didn't want to display a stoplight either. My look tonight was definitely a flashing yellow signal—

Please do proceed, but slowly.... and with caution.

I know my girls are probably cranking up some club banger shaking their booties and getting all hyped up for a ladies' night out on the town—but not me. If I am going to hang out with those rowdy, half-dressed, hypersexual man-eaters, then I need Billie... Soft, mellow Billie Holiday.

"I'm with youuu... come rain or come shiiine..."

* * *

Known at *The Velvet Lounge*, as Three-Dollar Thirsty Thursday, I come out every week to pay homage to my Trinity of Mixed Drinks. The three M's— Mint Mojito, Mango Margherita, and Mississippi Mudslide.

Can I get a what, what?

"Hey there, lady!" Juniece and Meisha yelled to me, waving as if they were putting out a fire when I entered the front door. We caught up to speed briefly, then checked our coats before strutting out onto the dance floor.

I wouldn't call Juniece, Meisha, Lanelle, and myself friends. Our personalities are far too diverse to form a truly homogenous group. We are instead more like alcoholic enablers. We give each other a reason to socialize, get drunk, and do things we regret without having to worry about one of us posting it up on Facebook the next day. I guess I value loyalty over compatibility in associates.

Lowered Expectations

Juniece Truesdale and Lanelle Motley were suitemates of mine during undergrad at Morris Brown. We didn't quite hit it off— initially. They were more preoccupied with designer clothes and man stalking for sport, while I was at the college on scholarship and, therefore, devoutly committed to my studies and athletics. However, we all began to travel in similar circles after we were all in the same pledge class during our sophomore year. Juniece and Lanelle both crossed over into Alpha Xi Alpha Sorority Inc., and I into Sigma Gamma Beta Sorority Inc., but there was no love lost between us. Each of us held offices within the Pan-Hellenic Council and, on that yard, we were a very close-knit group of Greeks.

We three have stayed in touch over the years. However recently, as of about six months ago, Meisha Christian, a Spelman graduate, has become the latest addition to our brood. She is Lanelle's soror and former co-worker at America's United Bank. I'm still not sure how I feel about this fair-skinned neophyte joining our dark chocolate ranks, but Lanelle does a fine job of keeping *The Princess* in check.

Oh no, here we go... It's way too early for this.

I kept hoping that he was not watching me. I moved to the left... then to the right, just to make certain. Yep, it's official... I got an eye stalker. He's been staring at me since I walked through the door. Whatever... he can get his eyeful, just so long as he doesn't come over here, bothering me when I'm with my girls.

"How you doing, Beautiful?"

Damn!

I could smell him before I even turned around to see him. His cologne was so loud that it was tacky. Call me politically incorrect, but I am not an equal opportunity employer, so not just anybody can apply. First off, he got disqualified for the gold fronts and tiger tattoo on his neck. But if that wasn't enough this guy was so short, he couldn't even look me in the eye—literally. I'm a whole head taller than him in my heels and that just ain't a good look for me. He was *somewhat* handsome in the face with smooth, caramel skin, but obviously too young for me. Every grown man should have at least *one* belt.

"Fine," I replied shortly.

"Now c'mon Ma. Don't be ac'ing like that when a niggah tryin' to get at you."

It would take an elevator for you to get at me, Shorty.

"Look, I'm just chillin' with my girls tonight. I'm not really interested," I stated diplomatically, then turned on my heels, giving him my shoulder.

"I mean you cute—for a dark-skinned chick, but you way too Black to be all stuck up and shit."

Meisha, Juniece and I let out a collective gasp. I didn't mean to allow the shock to show on my face, but his ignorance caught me off guard. I hadn't heard a man, excuse me— boy, say anything that derogatory since my college years, at least not out loud anyway.

"You *need* to be glad somebody willing' to holler at ya' bougie, Black ass."

"Didn't my girl tell your dollar menu ass to step off," Lanelle issued angrily, pointing the tip of her manicured nail in his face.

That's my girl Lanelle. She arrived right on cue. Dependable as ever with her thug-whoadie repellent.

"Oh, *excuse me* then. I ain't know y'all was some dikes."

"If by *dikes*," Lanelle leaned in close. "You mean we more man in the bedroom than you are, then yeah that's us."

Lanelle's insult stung Lil' Thug Whoadie so much that he struggled to find a comeback. "Forget y'all fat, ugly hoes," he conceded quickly with a casual flip of his hand. "I wouldn't fuck none of y'all 'cept the red bone no way," he said, slinking away like a puppy with his tail tucked between his legs.

"Ugh," Lanelle said, holding up her hands in disgust. Deep breath in. She took a moment to find her motivation and get back into character.

Exhale

"Hey, bitches!" Lanelle proclaimed her catch phrase and threw her arms out for a hug. Out of sight, out of mind. We hit the restart button and greeted each other, then carried on as usual, ready to indulge in what we came for—

Alcohol

We took our usual places around the watering hole. Tonight, the bar was abnormally congested. Standing room only. It felt like the trading floor at the New York Stock Exchange. People were throwing up hand signals and tossing money over the counter as if the drinks might run out. The restless din of the customers clamoring for cocktails almost drowned out the hypnotically repetitious *music*.

All of the bartenders were engrossed in their alchemistic art of concocting elixirs underneath the intoxicating effects of red strobe lights. I felt the stress and tension of the week melt away, as I allowed myself to be entranced and mesmerized by the waves of psychedelic potions swirling around in the glasses—

"What can I get for ya', ma'am?" the bartender asked in a deep, rich voice.

Now that's what I'm talkin' 'bout.

'He has great forearms,' I thought to myself, watching him cross them on the counter. They say, "I work hard, but I'm not obsessed." I can tell that a man with forearms like those is doing it for himself and not for me.

I rarely make eye contact with men. Someone once said that it is a sign of low self-esteem... But nope— not in my case; just a lack of interest. I ascertained early on in my life that eye contact equated sexual attraction to most males. Nevertheless, between the voice and the forearms, I figured I would take the plunge. Here I go...

Hello, Hazel eyes

"Ma'am, how can I help—"
"I am **not** a ma'am," I stated, coyly with a smile. Lean in. Elbows on the bar. Look interested.
"Excuse me then, *Miss.*" He smiled back broadly, as he threw a rag over his shoulder.

At least, six feet tall... No missing or discolored teeth.

Ka-ching

"If it's all the same, gorgeous. I'd still like to get something for you. What are you into?"
"*Not you!*" Alisha announced her presence, instantly.

Red Alert

"*Why didn't you stay at home like I told you to? You don't even like these hyenas.*"
'I'm ignoring you, Alisha. Cute guy.'

Since I do not know his name, I will henceforth refer to him as Beefy Bartender, or B.B. for short. B.B. was striking and surprisingly— attractive. He could almost be considered average looking, if it were not for his hazel eyes, which blazed like glowing embers against his smoldering dark, obsidian skin. His facial features were chiseled and distinct, but not extraordinary. His nose was disproportionately large and his forehead revealed deep, expressive creases. His smooth baldhead glistened in the light of the neon signs, but his smile— with perfect, white teeth and dimples nestled at the ends like parentheses— now that was the selling point.

Ding... Pick it up

B.B. had the build of an outdoorsman, robust and brawny. He wore a fitted, black-cotton *Velvet Lounge* t-shirt that hugged his sculpted chest and biceps. His thick, pillowy lips looked as though they could suck the skin right off of your—

"Denae!" Lanelle blasted in my ear.

Face... See, *I* was thinking face. Get your mind out of the gutter.

"What's taking so long, *beetch*?" Lanelle enounced with a Spanish accent. Lanelle is the "big" chick in the clique. Whatever... every troop has one or two. Now don't let the smooth taste fool you. Lanelle gets it in. She doesn't let the weight slow her down. She is a full-figured, cocoa-colored goddess, at least in her own mind anyway. She has a filthy mouth, but an alluringly radiant face, which always comes equipped with a seductive smile.

"I am waiting on my two best friends... Jack and Jose, oooah, oooah. I know you hoes didn't think I came out just to party with y'all." Lanelle makes sure that her personality is just as outrageously colorful as her wardrobe. I just know she was RuPaul in a former life.

"You're going to wish you had stayed home tonight," Alisha piped matter-of-factly.
'Why?' I asked warily.
"You'll see," Alisha replied deviously.

"Here you go, ladies," B.B. shouted, watching me— and only me— intently, as he handed each of us a drink. His fiery eyes seemed to be the source of the heat I felt in my face.
"I can't help but think that you look so familiar," I said, searching his countenance, as I sipped seductively on my cocktail straw. I was drawing a blank. I am so bad with faces due to that whole eye contact thing.

"My name is Dennison... but *you* can call me Dennis." He grinned, as if amused to let me join in on his Reindeer game. I took a loss with the face, however I am dead on when it comes to names and his was not far from my remembrance.

"Mr. Millsaps," I stated flatly. As quickly as it had come, the smile on my face peeled off like old latex paint. My expression was obviously contagious, because B.B.'s— oops— Mr. Millsaps's countenance soured as well.

"*Told ya',*" Alisha vaunted triumphantly.

"Don't tell me you're one of *those* types," Dennison stated acidly. "If I paid my *debt to society*, then what else could I possibly still owe you?

"Three fifty," I retorted coldly.

"What are you talking about?"

"My change," I replied sharply. "Three dollars and fifty cents... please."

Safety in Lovers

PART II

THE PLAYA

Safety in Lovers

Devian Nikei

Strange Bedfellows

"I mean really— I've never met another woman quite like you, Denae."

'Here we go, again.'

"You are *so* beautiful," he whispered, tracing the features of my face with his eyes under the dim light of his bedside lamp. He bit down on his bottom lip before being seized by the sudden urge to kiss me again.

"Really, Ray?" I asked facetiously. "What's *so* beautiful about me?"

"Your eyes. Your smile. Your *body*... Your *booty*," he winked playfully. "You got it all, babe. You're the total package."

"Uh huh." I paused to look at Rayshaun's smile, then started out of his bed.

"What's wrong?" His brow wrinkled, as he pinned me down under his long arm.

"Seriously Ray?" My question stated the obvious.

"Okay— for real, Denae. It's not just physical for me. I love your quirky personality too... and how you're always there for me when I really need you."

Introducing... Rayshaun Bivens.

Tall, sleek, and manicured— Rayshaun is a slice of green-eyed, butterscotch heaven. Well-dressed and well-pressed, Rayshaun is quick-witted and charismatic. He is the type of man that will stay in the yard, so long as you don't put up a fence. He'll wear a fancy collar, but no leash. I have to be careful with him though. He is as slick with his lips as he is with his dick. A girl could fall into a very deceptive trap with a man like him, but I keep our relationship in perspective.

I wouldn't call Rayshaun and myself lovers. To label us that way might imply some intimate affection for each other. We are instead maintenance technicians who service each other at times of mutual convenience.

"But you're gorgeous too and you need to stop acting like you don't know it," he hissed in my ear, as he poked his finger down between my dark chocolate breasts. "Your skin is like silk."

"Alright, that's enough sweet talk for one day, lover boy. You already won the *prize*," I laughed, pressing against his broad, hairless chest. "I gave you the cookies. I don't need the cavities."

"What?... I can't get some warm milk to go with my cookies?" Ray dove down under the covers, burying his face between my thighs. I giggled and then sighed, as his tongue sent a warm tingle up my spine. Before the sigh could turn into a moan, I wiggled away from him, kicking my leg over his head.

"*Gotta'* go," I insisted urgently. I sat up and placed my feet down into my underwear that lay nearby on the floor. Standing up from the bed, I simultaneously stretched my lace thong up over my hips.

"You *gotta'* go?" Ray tugged at my waist, sending me free-falling back into the mound of navy silk sheets. "You're not going anywhere, woman."

He mounted me swiftly. He ran his tongue over my lips, then pulled gently on the bottom one with his teeth. I could feel his manhood stirring between my buttocks, as he wrapped my leg around his narrow waist. His warm body pressed heavy against mine. He felt so good that I almost yielded to him.

"If last night wasn't good enough, then I don't know what to tell you," I said, pushing him aside. I hopped quickly out of the bed before he could grab me again.

Ray laid back amongst the mussed bedding and folded his arms behind his head—watching me, as I dressed. I know he's thinking that his strapping nude body will lure me (as it usually does) back to the bed, but unfortunately for him... not today.

I am taller than the average woman at five foot, nine (and a half) inches. My lofty stature is very forgiving to my figure, causing me to look leaner than my frame would ordinarily allow.

My lovers have told me that I am stunning from the front, but devastating from the back. I'm well proportioned, with a slim waist and voluptuously bountiful hips. Whether intended as compliment or criticism, many have said that I possess an exotic look— a fact that earned me a substantial amount of torment and ridicule as a youth. My slender, black eyes and prominent cheekbones compliment my thin nose and shapely lips. I have a slight gap between my front teeth that— strangely, men often acknowledge as one of my most attractive features. My hair is long, black and natural. Although it reaches well past the bottom of my shoulder blades when straightened, I generally prefer to wear my tresses pulled up into my own version of a curly Afro bun.

"Marry me, Denae," Ray said suddenly, clutching my wrist as I reached down beside the bed for my black high-heel shoes. He brought it to his lips, and then kissed along the inside of my forearm.

For Ray, this remark is becoming a rehearsed slogan. I don't know why some men think you need to hear that to keep giving up free milk. We always go on this way:

'Marry me, Denae...'
'You don't really want that...'
'Yes, I do...'
'No, you don't...'
'Yes, I do...'

Let's try something different today.

"Okay." I said quietly, offering Ray a precarious smirk. The silence, which subsequently filled the room, was so thick and sour that it made the inside of my jaw tingle. Ray's mouth hung open. He looked dumbfounded, as if he'd been smacked and didn't know how to react.

'Pick up your chin, sweetheart.'

"Alrighty, then... See you later, *lil' bunny*," I squeaked playfully like Freddie Brooks from **"A Different World"**, as I placed my thumb on the cleft in his chin.

I dropped down on the edge of the bed and pulled Ray's face to mine, reaching my fingers into the tiny, soft curls at the nape of his neck. I allowed my lips to linger on his. "Thanks for dinner last night. That restaurant was really, very nice."

"Come on now," Ray said, brushing a loose strand of crinkled hair back into the disheveled bun. He kissed my forehead; a kiss so tender that it pinched my heart, causing my eyes to sting suddenly with a start of unexpected tears. A quick bat of my lids stamped out the urge.

"Nothing but the best for my lady." Ray's emerald eyes gazed deeply into mine.

I'm not sure anymore, if I know or care whether he is being sincere with me. If I allowed myself to entertain the thought of his respect for me, I just know I wouldn't be able to lay with him again. I don't know what I'm doing anymore. This doesn't make sense— even to me. All I know is that I enjoy the way he makes me feel when we are together. I guess I am just another bona fide (and satisfied) member of his chicken coop; another link in his chain.

I stepped out onto the cobblestone walkway between the buildings in Ray's community and was jostled by a strong gust of unseasonably warm September wind. For a split second, the draft didn't seem like the external weather. It refreshed me on the inside. More like someone threw open a window in my spirit, allowing a westward breeze to blow across my soul. I buttoned and belted my copper, three-quarter length trench coat against the blasts. There was a faint glimmer of daylight beginning to appear in the early morning sky, as if night was still clinging on to the last of a loving embrace with dawn. A dim, pale luminescence spilled over the rooftops, bathing the cultivated grounds of the development in a silvery brilliance. The first of the fallen autumn leaves rustled past my feet, frolicking and tumbling over each other like playful children, as I strode out to the parking lot.

Tall, old-fashioned lampposts lined the pathway. The wicks were still lit, so I paused underneath their flickering light, to reminisce about the years past, which held such promise.

"What made *you* want to pledge Sigma Tau?" Ray asked me arrogantly, as he rubbed his thin moustache.

That was how it started.

Rayshaun and I met at a Kappa Alpha Phi Fraternity party. He easily caught my attention in the crowd. Rayshaun, a six foot-five power forward on the basketball team, was the only man in the room that I could still look up to in my four-inch high heels. I was attending Morris Brown and Ray was in his final year at Morehouse College.

I was at the function with Alfonso, my boy toy at the time. However, I was the kind of woman who always kept a reserve, so Ray instantly sparked my interest. So awestruck by his gorgeous green eyes, when they locked on mine from across the room, I couldn't find a voice or enough nerve to go over and talk to him. Luckily for me, he took the lead and broke the thick sheets of ice between us by whispering to me in passing to meet him outside.

I allowed a few hour-like minutes to pass before joining him. We stood silently studying each other in the darkness for a few awkward minutes before drumming up some casual conversation, on the quad behind the Kappa house. Although he looked somewhat thuggish, with his long cornrows and diamond solitaire earrings, Rayshaun was highly intellectual— a huge turn on for me. He had a prominent nose and a strong jaw line. His large, teardrop-shaped eyes were hooded with thick, dark brows.

Even through his oversized, crimson sweater, I could tell that he had a lean, muscular physique. He was absolutely gorgeous.

However, as our exchange would reveal— he was also engaged to his high-school sweetheart. With a child in common and six years invested, they were a pretty, solid item. I was thankful that he was so forthcoming with me about his situation. However, back in those days, being a sidepiece was something that I would not so willingly accept. His candid admission wrapped me in a cold, wet blanket and smothered out the fire I felt for him. Needless to say, it would be a few years from that time before any spark between us could be ignited.

I ran— *literally*, into Rayshaun outside of the Java Monkey in late fall, almost four years ago. After we collected our various personal effects, Ray invited me to a replacement cappuccino with a side of conversation. We caught up over steaming cups of latte euphoria. He confided in me that he had just recently finished with a divorce from Treasure— that same high-school sweetheart. During her pregnancy with their second child, Ray found out from a mutual friend that he might not have been the biological father of their first son, Preston. After their daughter, Deity, was born, Ray had a paternity test administered on both of the children, just to find out that he had indeed only fathered the girl.

"I don't blame her," he said, pausing to sip from his cup. "We were so young, and we had some wild times over the years. God knows I've had my share of indiscretions— but I always used protection. I never wanted to bring anything— be it disease or child— back home to my wife. The thought of her putting both of us in jeopardy like that is just over the top. I'm not judgmental or hypocritical, though. I know we were just kids playing love games, but she still should have been honest with me. I'm sure we could have worked through it, but I can't be with somebody who won't tell me the truth," he said with a shrug. "Even to *this* day, she keeps saying that she wasn't with nobody else, like I'm still falling for it or something."

In those first few months with Rayshaun, there was no real love connection between us. He remained in regretful turmoil about whether he made the right decision with Treasure. I was his companion and advisor, but he wrestled with demons, from which I could not rescue him. Ray went in and out, back and forth, round and round on a drama rollercoaster with Treasure.

He still didn't skip a beat though. He seemed hell-bent on making up for all of the bachelor time that he missed during his marriage. Rayshaun dated an assortment of light, bright and (Yes!) even white women— but never for longer than one night. He changed women like underwear.

Other than the occasional, "why didn't you call me back?" (which he politely hung up on), those pigeons didn't even seem to care how he treated them so long as they could be with him. I was thoroughly confused and mystified by the bewitching effect that he had on females. That was, of course... until *I* took a ride on his Carousel.

One evening, the following spring, I came over to his Brownstone. We had a date to go out dancing at *The District*, where he would no doubt pick up some bleach-blonde, caramel complexioned Amazon beauty and leave me with cab fare to get home. But just as I arrived, the night sky opened up heaving torrential rains down on me. Despite the fact that Rayshaun ran, with his umbrella in hand, to meet me at the walkway, I sloshed into his foyer, soaked from head to toe— the damage already done.

Ray refused to allow me any further into his dwelling, until I had been disrobed and dried off. After I emerged from the downstairs bedroom, in his maroon warm-up suit, Ray spread a velvet blanket out on the hardwood floor of his den afront the lambent glow of his gas fireplace. I sat down on the blanket and hugged my knees to my chest. This was the best seat in the house to dry out my hair, which had coiled its way into fuzzy ringlets. Ray had likewise retired his lady-magnet, club wear for a gray, ribbed tank shirt and white silk pajama bottoms.

We talked and laughed, sharing the large pepperoni pizza that Ray had ordered while I was still in the shower. After a while, our chatter settled to a calm, awkward hush. Ray rolled over and stretched out on his back. He folded his almost completely tattooed arms behind his head. I watched his chiseled chest, slowly rise and fall with each breath. I desperately tried to remember that he was one of the best friends I'd ever had, not wanting to destroy our bond with the burning lust that I felt for him in that moment.

"I'm done with high-maintenance girls," Ray declared decisively, as he stared up at the ceiling. "They're just too much trouble." Ray turned back over on his side and propped his head up on his palm. "A fragile, impressionable stud like me could get trapped off with some heart-trampling, gold digger slut... **again**."

We both fell back onto the blanket, kicking and laughing. The firelight flickered and flashed on his body, illuminating the faint pattern of freckles on his cheeks and shoulders.

Years earlier, Ray turned in his long, extravagant braids for a short, curly crop, when he accepted the position of Marketing Analyst at a Sports Management Firm. Instead of his roughneck appeal, he had developed a new sophisticated sexy. He stared at me with intense, translucent eyes, which appeared almost crimson in the light of the fire.

There goes that uncomfortable silence again...

"I think you just need to sleep on it. I'm sure you'll be back to your red-bone, heifer-hoping self in no time," I snickered playfully, poking at his ribs.

Ray grabbed my hand tightly. His face was stoic and expressionless. "Denae, I'm serious. It's taken a long time for me to realize that I'm punishing myself with the women I choose," Ray said, threading his fingers between mine. "I've wasted too much of my time chasing after vain, empty-headed crows who give it up to any man that's got some money. I need some substance in my woman. I want someone who can appreciate me for what's in my head, and not just in my pants. I think I deserve that."

My heart began to race. 'But what exactly *is* in your pants?' I thought, letting my mind wonder, as my eyes roamed down to the bulge between his legs.

'No... Stop... We're just friends,' I kept repeating to myself.

Ray brought the back of my hand to his lips— not kissing but caressing it. His lips were warm and soft on my skin. He turned my open palm towards his face and placed his cheek inside. I instinctively pulled him into my collarbone. I perched my chin on his head and ran my fingers through his thick curls. Ray and I had shared many platonic moments like this one before, but that night, something felt different—and peculiarly intimate. Ray sat back unexpectedly, but before I could speak, he grabbed the back of my neck and pressed his lips on mine.

I wanted to repel myself, suddenly and quickly, as if shocked or maybe even repulsed, but I couldn't-

I couldn't move...

Hell, I couldn't even *breathe.*

My heart began to race. All of the air drained from my lungs, as my chest began to tighten. I wilted into his able arms, which lunged in swiftly to catch the weight of my collapsing body and guide me gently down to the blanket. My head felt heavy. I was drunk with desire. I never conceived that I still possessed such ravenous passion for Rayshaun. Perhaps some child-like infatuation had remained, but nothing more—or so I thought.

But then came **The Kiss**—

That wonderful kiss burst the dam and mighty, rushing currents of pleasure came surging forth, like a flood, covering my body. Rayshaun and I were jumping off the lake pier of curious fascination into a raging ocean of seduction, and we knew it without ever *really* knowing that we knew it.

I rolled over on top of Rayshaun. He ran his hands up my arms and then into my hair, as he pulled me down into another breath-taking kiss. His tongue probed my mouth as his hands continued to explore my body, making their way down to my bottom. He squeezed my fleshy cheeks tightly. I moaned and let my head fall backwards, as he licked along my neck. He wrapped his arms around my back, folding his hands over my shoulders, and crushed me against his chest.

Unexpectedly, the spell of his embrace was broken, just long enough for me to run for cover. Without a word, I untangled myself from Rayshaun's arms and shot up from the floor, grabbing clumsily at the plates and cups, then headed speedily for the kitchen. But—the kitchen proved to be no refuge. Ray caught and cornered me there. He came up from behind, pinning me against the sink, and encircling me with his powerful arms. I inhaled deeply, breathing in his pleasant, subdued fragrance. I could feel his huge erection poking against the small of my back. His breath was hot on my neck, as he slipped the sweatshirt off my shoulder and sank his teeth into my skin. I tensed a little, more from the shock than the pain. I had never been bitten by a lover before... but—

I liked it.

Ray lifted his sweatshirt over my head. A small gasp escaped my lips, when he lightly brushed his palms over my sensitive nipples before giving my plump breasts a squeeze. He kissed a winding path down the middle of my back to the waistband of the sweatpants, then over my buttocks as he pulled them to the floor. I was reeling from the tingly shockwaves that pulsated throughout my limbs, when his lips descended to the backs of my knees.

Ray stood, wrapping one arm around my waist, while the other swept my legs up off the floor. He carried me, folded against his chest like bedding, upstairs to his room, and then tossed me on to the mattress.

Rayshaun clicked on the dim lamp that sat on his nightstand. His bed was enormous and plush, covered with black satin pillows and bed covers. He pressed a button on his remote and the room filled with the romantic stylings of Eric Benet.

"Can't wait 'til I finally found, A Love of My Own..."

"I've never made love in this bed before," Ray confessed sheepishly, as he slid down next to me. He let his fingers glide over each of my thighs. I was still too stunned to speak, as he held my neck and kissed me delicately. "I was saving this for someone special," he said in a low, secretive tone. Ray brushed my tousled hair back from my face and touched his lips to my forehead, then to the bridge of my nose. Suddenly, He stopped and stared at me blankly for a moment.

"Okay, this is weird. Please say something... anything," he whispered with a grin. "Do you want to do this?"

"No. Stooooop!" Alisha shrieked insistently.

"Yes," I breathed, as my entire body surrendered in that one sigh. My femininity throbbed anxiously with the expectation of receiving him.

Rayshaun stood and slowly removed his shirt, revealing tribal tattoos on his chest and stomach that I had never seen before. Rayshaun had more artwork on his skin than on the walls of an art gallery. When he turned to throw his shirt in a chair, I saw the giant, elaborate cross, surrounded by angel wings that covered his back. I guess, underneath the suit, Mr. Bivens—the suave, clean-shaven professional— is still a certifiable roughneck.

Likewise, he surveyed my body for a few seconds before dropping the silk pants to reveal his *impressive* tool, almost ten inches of dark, thick, throbbing meat. Ray reached into the top drawer of his nightstand and pulled out a condom. He slipped the Magnum XL out of its wrapper and rolled it down over his shaft, watching me with eager eyes and licking his lips the entire time.

Then, like a skilled artisan, Rayshaun climbed on top of me and began his craft. He sucked first on my neck, then the inside of my elbow and down to my hips. Ray spread my thighs apart and ran his hands along the inside of them. He reached for my foot and brought it to his mouth. He slid his long, thick tongue over my ankle, and then slowly up to the gold mine. It had been almost two years since my last sexual encounter, so I flinched a bit from the unexpected pleasure, when he tasted me.

"You alright?" he asked laughingly, wiping his lips on the back of his hand.

"Yeah, I'm fine," I whispered lowly, offering him a nervous smile. Rayshaun kissed me again, as if to reassure me that it was the right decision to let him have me. He brushed his lips across my cheek, and then touched the tip of his nose to mine.

"Owww," I cringed, as Rayshaun slowly dipped his magic wand into my honeycomb. He placed his hands on my knees and pressed them further open to relieve the resistance. "What the hell, Rayshaun? I said, 'Owww'," I huffed with a grimace.

"Oh, I apologize, boo." Rayshaun offered mildly, pulling the head of his organ out. He rubbed it over my clitoris, stimulating me so immensely that I forgot about the discomfort. "I thought you could handle the D," he said smiling at me. "But I guess I'll have to take it a little easier on you *this time*."

Rayshaun laid against my chest and slid his hands between the mattress and my bottom. He gripped my buttocks tightly, as he patiently short-stroked his way into nirvana. He pressed his manhood in deeper and harder with each stroke.

We both began to moan in unison, as the slippery flesh yielded to him. My back arched and I grabbed a fistful of bedding, as the pressure mounted. The pinch of pain that I felt under my navel burst like a bubble, releasing a thrilling, tingling sensation that traveled around my pelvis and up my back, when Rayshaun was granted access to the penthouse.

"Oh, Ray!" I exclaimed, hugging his broad shoulders tightly...

After that night, everything changed. The early morning three-mile runs and late night soul bearing stopped. Over the years, we have become like strangers, never saying how we really feel anymore.

Sometimes, I wonder if he loves me.

Sometimes, I wonder if I love him.

After almost four years, I do wonder where this road is leading us.

We do make *strange bedfellows.*

Despite Alisha's disdain for this present arrangement, she is quite fond of Ray and insists that if I would just close up the complimentary dairy farm, Rayshaun might be moved to buy the cow. But I am too selfish for that. I can't play games with him and take that chance. What I have with Ray may not be definite or certain but— at least it's safe. It has taken a long time for us to get to this point. I don't want to complicate our very simple system with schemes and angles.

We operate under a strict "Don't ask, don't tell" policy, however in almost four years, I have never found a female's number in his phone or seen him in the company of any other woman. That's not to say that it doesn't happen—but at the very least, he respects what we have enough not to be obvious with it.

When I call, he answers... no matter what time it is and if I "accidentally" leave articles of clothing at his place, it's never an issue. I can come over unannounced and leave when *I'm* ready.

A lot of people don't even have that kind of confidence in their committed relationships. I know if anything ever changed, Rayshaun would be honest with me and I can live with that. I would rather keep the little part (or should I say big part) of Rayshaun that I get when we're together than gamble on a future that is not promised to anyone... not even those who have true love.

At least, that's what I'll keep telling myself... for now.

Rayshaun's taps revived me from my meditation. I looked up to see him waiting and watching, as he usually does, from his second-story bedroom window. He always remains there until I reach my car. I opened the drivers' side door and climbed inside of my silver Impala. In customary fashion, Ray blew me a kiss on a wave, touching his fingers to the glass, before disappearing behind the curtain.

PART III

THE POET

Devian Nikei

As for Me and My House

"Gentlemen, I don't mean to leave you out this Sunday—"

'Oh, here we go.'

"But we are continuing in our sermon series entitled, 'As for Me and My House' and today is the ladies' turn." The few men in the church gave an approving round of applause, mixed with cheers.

'Of all the Sundays that I could have come' I thought, watching the doors from my typical seat on the back pew.
"We can still leave. They haven't collected the offering yet." Alisha interjected. Although Alisha is more moral and principled than me, she must not be a Christian. *"We've got just enough time to make the breakfast buffet,"* Alisha added eagerly.
I guess I could echo Alisha's sentiment. I did often feel like an interloper in church— kind of like an ex-girlfriend at the wedding.

"Proverbs fourteen and one says, 'Every wise woman... buildeth her house, but the foolish... plucketh it down with her hands.' Ladies, I would challenge each one of you to consider whether you are building a house or destroying one," Bishop Marion Simmons drawled in his heavy Southern accent, as he pointed out into the congregation. He paused and pulled out a satin handkerchief to wipe his lip and brow. "Folks, you will have to excuse the temperature in here. Our air conditioning unit went out yesterday during the Men's Meeting."

"Why yes, Bishop, it does feel like hell in here— effective preaching tactic, sir." Alisha commented playfully.

"We have someone working on it as we speak," he continued.

I spent my hours in church, as I commonly do, writing my weekly agenda and grocery shopping list on the back of a program. I often asked myself, 'Why *do* you show up here?' I know it's not for God, because He is everywhere, and therefore, always with me. Unfortunately for me though— God knows my heart. I am not silly enough to think that He is fooled by this respectable wool, salmon-colored skirt suit. I just as well could have worn nipple clamps and a black, leather thong to church.

I am not depending on these three (or seven) hours on Sundays to determine my eternal destination. I know that I must have a personal relationship with God and a lifestyle, which reflects that intimacy. But— since that's not happening right now— I guess I don't really know anymore why I attend every week. Maybe, I come out of obligation to some social norm ingrained in me from childhood. At this point, it is just a part of my regular routine. Skipping church would be like forgetting to put on deodorant.

"Daughter, we missed you on Wednesday night," the Bishop glared at me like a discerning patriarch. He folded robed arms over his wide, barrel chest. His thick brows furrowed, as he scowled at me.

Bishop Simmons is a middle-aged, pecan-colored man who yet clings to the suburban cul-de-sac of salt-n-pepper hair that still grows on his head. He grabbed me up in a paternal, and somewhat aggressive, bear hug, burying me in the folds of his maroon velvet, pastoral gown. As he released his hold, my feet came to rest back on the floor. Oftentimes, I think that if I did have a father, he would be a lot like this man. I have no basis for comparison, but Bishop Simmons is the first man I've ever known who appears to care for me without any motive.

"I want to see you in that Women's Meeting next Saturday," he said, clenching my hand tightly.

Bishop Simmons greeted a few more parishioners before walking across the small courtyard to meet a baldheaded, blue-collar stranger. I could barely make out the man from that distance, but there he was...

Mr. Millsaps

"What's he doing here?" Alisha inquired discriminately.

"I don't know," I answered in astonishment.

As Bishop Simmons and Mr. Millsaps ended their meeting with an official handshake, I made a beeline—keys in hand—for my car. Unfortunately, my feet couldn't carry me fast enough to keep from being intercepted.

"May God bless you, my sister."

Damn... I mean, darn.

"Same to you, Mr. Millsaps." I kept my eyes on the key ring, as I searched for my car key.

"Look, Miss... um... I still don't even know your name," Dennis stated, almost pleading. I glanced up at him with an indifferent smirk. *"Dang...* you can crack nuts with that look."

Having found the key, I proceeded to unlock the car door.

"Look, I think we got off to the wrong start." Dennison took a step towards me, but I took an automatic step backward.

Occupational hazard

"Let me apologize, I guess my manners are on vacation today."

"Why are you here?" I inquired callously.

"Well, your Bishop called out a contractor for the A/C unit and— voila, here I am," Dennis smiled, waving ridiculous "jazz" hands.

'No, not the smile—anything but that.' I turned my eyes from him and back to the key ring.

Alright

I can't deny my attraction to Mr. Millsaps, but I won't cross that line. It violates too many of my boundaries both on personal and professional levels.

"Well, you're a literal jack of all trades, aren't you?" I retorted sarcastically. "What I meant is that it's Sunday. Isn't it a *sin* to work on the Sabbath?"

The smile, that began to spread slowly across his face, was an indication that he knew I was quizzing him. It was also contagious and I smiled as well.

"There it is. I knew you had it in you." Dennis extended his hand. "I'm Dennison Millsaps, but you can call me Dennis." I accepted his hand, knowing full well that he knew he had me at 'hello.' His hand was strong yet unexpectedly soft. "And you are?"

"Denae Richmond, but *you* can call me Miss Richmond."

"Ooo... crunch," he bellowed childishly into the hand he cupped over his mouth.

Dennis has a charm. It is ethereal, natural and beautiful. He is comfortable in his own skin.

He is... **Real.**

He makes me relax in his presence. A dark prince— regal, yet humble. Besides, he is so sexy that my toes are curling in these heels.

"Look, I wanna' be up front with you." He stepped forward, flashing his amber eyes. "I'm not trying to marry you... yet, but I do want the opportunity to treat you to some refreshment after the inferno you endured in that church. What do you say?"

"I know what you're thinking, Denae, but you can't do this."
'C'mon. You only live once.' I pled with Alisha.
"Everyone who ever said that is dead now. Don't be foolish. Where can this road take you?" Alisha counseled, as only she can. Just when I would have yielded to her, Dennis, sensing my hesitation, intervened. He took my hand in his.

"Hey, I'm more than what's in that folder. Just give me the chance to show you. That's all I want. After that... draw your own conclusion."

I relented, nodding reluctantly.

"Thank you," he beamed like an excited schoolboy. He began to trot away, but stopped suddenly. "Oh yeah, and to answer your question," Dennis continued, turning around to face me. "Jesus said in the book of Matthew, chapter twelve, 'if any of you has a sheep and it falls into a pit on the Sabbath, will you not take hold of it and lift it out? How much more valuable is a man than a sheep. Therefore, it is lawful to do good on the Sabbath," he said, adding a wink to his trademark smile.

* * *

"We could have taken my car," I remarked partially because of my embarrassment at his modest '95 Ford-150, but mostly out of concern for my own safety. As a practice, I never ride with strangers, but Dennis insisted vehemently.

"No woman should **ever** drive a grown man around in *her* car. That's absurd." He laughed, clapping his hands. "My ride may not be glamorous but it's mine and not the bank's."

Dennis traded out his navy work shirt, for a long-sleeved, black cotton, button-down and belted, dark denim jeans. His clothes were neat and fitted—not expensive, but one could tell that he took great pride in his appearance. His attire was simple; however, it brought out to best attributes of his physique. It is rare these days, even in a professional setting, to see a man wear tailored clothing. It was refreshing to be able to take the guesswork out of fantasizing about his body.

"You're a heathen," Alisha said crossly. *"Denae, you need Jesus."*

'Alisha,' I replied wearily. 'We are not going to fight about this anymore. It's just a drink, okay?'

"Yeah, and so was the Kool-Aid at Jonestown. You're only doing this because you've had the same dick for four years and no ring to

show for it." Alisha was spitting venom and I could not stop her. *"If you wanna' make Ray jealous, buy a dildo and stop giving up so much pussy."*

'Whoa, you crossed the line. This conversation is done.'

"Are you hungry?" Dennis asked.

"No!" I answered so defiantly that it was inappropriate for the question.

"Are you okay? You seem irritated or uncomfortable," Dennis studied my face closely.

"I'm fine," I said dismissively. "It's nothing."

"Oh... and just so that you know— I'm not any kind of sex offender."

He smiled.

I didn't.

"Let's change the subject," I said, pulling my glass of ginger ale closer to me. "What do you do for a living... Dennis?" He nodded his approval at my use of his first name.

"Well, the question is, what don't I do for a living? That's why they call it 'a living'. I do what I have to," he offered with a heavy sigh. "However, the short answer is that I have a full time job in HVAC repair and installation. I also work a few nights a week tending bar and..."

"*And?*" I exaggerated the word.

"*And...*" He mocked, "I'm a poet."

"A poet?"

"And ya' didn't even know it," he joked, lifting his glass of spring water to his mouth.

"Let me clear up something for you, right quick. You're corny. If you tell another joke like that, I'm leaving."

My face was expressionless.

Safety in Lovers

"Okay..." I continued. "How does a man, like you, become a poet?"

"A man like *me*... What's that supposed to mean?" Dennis was visibly offended.

"Oh no, you took that the wrong way. What I meant is that you seem like a real man's man, a skilled tradesman— not the kind of guy I would suspect reads— let alone, writes poetry." I clarified.

"Oh—" his face brightened. "You were asking if I'm gay?... No, not at all."

We both laughed, as the server placed a heaping plate of hot wings onto the table. "Now, you sure you don't want anything to eat?" Dennis asked with knitted brows. He seemed to have a genuine concern for my comfort. He was courteous, even chivalrous, like a prince from a medieval time. "You can have some of these wings. They won't eat themselves," he said, dancing the chicken wing across the plate.

'There he goes again.'

I gave him the look— that nutcracker face.

"Don't tell me you're too bougie to eat hot wings. I knew you were a little siddity but I thought you were still Black, "he mumbled.

"I resent that," I puffed, genuinely offended. "I am **not bougie.**"

"Resent it all you want to, but I can hear your stomach growling." He pursed his lips. "Betcha' can't eat just one."

I indulged Dennis and shared his plate. After an hour plus of conversation, I found out that Dennis began writing poetry, as a part of his rehabilitation program, while incarcerated in a Juvenile Detention Center. Dennis confessed, "I was so screwed up. My writings were the only place where I could just say whatever I wanted to and not be judged for it."

He went on to say that he had been convicted of attempted armed robbery and false imprisonment, while he was still a minor. One of his "boys" at the time approached him about holding up the corner store for some fast cash. "I stayed so high in those days that I was down for any and everything." Dennis recounted to me that he didn't even remember what happened that night. "I'm just glad no one got hurt. I could not have lived with that on my conscience." He told me that waking up in a jail cell the next day— and not knowing how he got there, was the most sobering moment of his life.

"I had never been in trouble before. I was a child of privilege," he expounded, leaning back in his chair. According to Dennison's account, both of his parents held Doctorate Degrees and did reputable work in their occupational fields. He grew up in Buckhead and did not want for anything— except his parents' attention. Dennis had one younger, more-talented brother, Stafford. "Stafford was far more focused on his education. While I, on the other hand, was athletic and worked well with my hands, but those traits were not favorable to my parents."

Dennison recalled that he commenced to hang out in the streets, looking for anything that could thrill him out of his lackluster existence. "The streets were exciting. I could reinvent myself there. My skills were considered assets and not liabilities. I made friends quickly, not like at my private school where I was reviled daily for my dark skin and big nose. In the ghetto, they accepted me as I was— there I was celebrated."

Dennison told me that he would put on his school uniform in the morning, leave his house, and then ditch all of his belongings in the crawl space under a neighbor's house, before taking a bus over to Martel Homes. "Doing drugs and robbing people made me feel superior, instead of insignificant. I was a power junky, not a dope fiend. I just did whatever I had to do to fit in."

After the arrest, Dennis's *boy*, a repeat offender— turned on him, in return for a more lenient sentence. He testified for the prosecution at Dennis's trial, declaring that Dennis was the mastermind of the whole operation, and had stolen all of the firearms. "I guess our 'Never would we talk, never would we tell' Goodie Mob oath didn't mean shit when it really came down to it," Dennis offered sarcastically.

Despite all the shenanigans of the District Attorney's Office, Dennis's parents had hired him a masterful attorney, who got the drug and weapons trafficking charges thrown out. Furthermore, none of the victims testified to seeing Dennis with any firearms, so his lawyer also got the kidnapping charges reduced to false imprisonment. Dennison said that he and his parents were devastated when the judge handed down the sentence. "I had never seen my parents cry before. It took going to prison for me to realize how much they actually cared."

Dennison received a ten-to-fifteen years, structured sentence that ended up amounting to five years of confinement and seven years of probation. Dennis continued. "At that point, I figured that I could give the whole education thing a try. My mom wouldn't give it up. She would write to me, saying, 'Son, they can cage your body, but not your mind'." Dennison divulged that he developed a love for poetry, as an escape from the bleak conditions of incarceration. I was astounded to discover that he had published a book of poetry, through the unction and support of his parents, entitled **Khryme Rhymez**. Dennis ended his tale by inviting me to accompany him on some of his spoken word engagements.

"Okay," I interjected. "If you are so passionate about writing, why aren't you pursuing that full-time?"

"Did you like the wings?" Dennis said, gazing into my eyes.

There's that fire in my face again.

"Yes?" I answered inquisitively.

"That's why? I have to eat and provide for myself. Writing is not brain surgery or even HVAC repair, for that matter." Dennis shrugged. "After I was released from prison, I needed steady income and I didn't want to have to ring out my brain every day, forcing myself to create what only God can inspire." His dimples peeked at me, as he sipped on his straw.

I took a second to take him all in... I mean really check him out. He had long, seductive eyelashes that framed his inviting eyes. With a short, neatly trimmed goatee on his chin under his succulent lips, he was truly a vision. I squeezed my thighs together to quell the faint throb between them.

"You're working awfully hard for a single man," I remarked, demurely.

"There you go again... If you have a question— just ask me. No, I don't have any children and I have never been married," he declared matter-of-factly. "I don't want to bring a life into the world until I can provide for it.... And nobody's getting my name until it means something. That's why I work so hard— not for what is, but for what will be." Dennis clasped his hands together with finality, as if to signal the end of the conversation.

"Alright— now you know almost as much about me as I know about myself. So on our next date—"

"This isn't a date," I interposed, sitting forward in my chair.

Dennis paused, looking at me intently.

"On our *next date*," he stressed the words. "I want to learn more about you."

He smiled...

I smiled.

Safety in Lovers

PART IV

THE PROBLEM

Safety in Lovers

Devian Nikei

The Bridge Is Out Up Ahead

"If you're heading southbound on I-285, you can expect delays..."

'Now you tell me!'

"The D.O.T. reports that bridge work is being conducted," the radio announcer continued, *"and you should anticipate detours and closed lanes between..."*

'I should have taken the MARTA,' I scolded myself.

"You may want to leave yourself a few extra minutes for your early morning commute."

'Really now. You think so,' I remarked sarcastically at the radio.

"That's your weather and traffic update. The time is now 8:25."

This morning, I had that feeling when I woke up— late.

I had a feeling that everything that could go wrong today— would go wrong, even before I pushed back the covers. I am usually up long before my alarm clock sounds. I can't stand the terrifying blare of the buzzer, followed by the heart-racing distress of being frightened awake. Once I finally stirred, I quickly realized that I had set my alarm for six-thirty p.m., instead of a.m., and subsequently slept through that entire hour. I knew then that it was the start of a terrible day. This traffic jam only added fuel to the already blazing fire.

'I am officially late,' I told myself, trying to prepare for a crushing blow from the sledgehammer that is my supervisor, Sgt. Mavis Bledsoe.

Sgt. Bledsoe, or "The Dragon" as we *affectionately* call her, is probably the most hateful, frigid she-demon that I have ever met. She inflicts misery and suffering on all who have the unfortunate displeasure of being her professional subordinate. Although she is the darkest-complexioned person in the office, she flaunts her superiority in the fact that she is:

1) married to a Caucasian man
and
2) boss and lord over all of us mere peons.

I came into the office, through the side entrance by the stairwell. I shot a glance over to the "Dragon's" lair, I mean, office that is located at the back of the headquarters.

Coasts clear

I casually meandered through the labyrinth of Cubicle Row, not wanting to be spotted. I walked past desk after desk of the clones that I work with. Not one of them glanced up from their assignments long enough to greet or even notice me, as they rarely ever do. Thus, it's safe to say that I traversed a covert course to my desk without detection.

"Maybe the Dragon got some man's bones caught in her throat and took a sick day." Alisha and I were both chuckling, until I saw the top of Sgt. Bledsoe's frazzled head come bobbing around the corner of my cubicle.

'Oh, no it's a trap.'

Abandon ship! Abandon ship!

"Richmond, can I see you in my office?" Sgt. Bledsoe asked in passing, as she continued through the maze to her office. I rose reluctantly from my desk, like a student sent to the Principal's Office, and trudged down the aisles to her dungeon. "Close the door behind you," she directed in her raspy man-voice, as soon as my foot crossed the threshold.

'This can't be good,' I surmised from her tone.

Open door equals good news. Closed door equals get the flame-retardant jumpsuit. My personnel file was already open on her desk when we sat down.

"This is the third time you have been tardy, Officer Richmond." Sgt. Bledsoe said, watching me over her impossibly thick bifocal lenses. Her short, wiry brown hair looked uncombed, as usual. I have gathered over the years that Sgt. Bledsoe cannot possibly be as old as she looks with her hunchback and dated attire. I reasoned that all the evil she perpetuates must be taking its toll on her. I know she probably can't sleep at night.

"I am going to document this conversation as a corrective counseling in your file. Consider yourself officially warned." Sgt. Bledsoe handed me a form. I signed it, saying nothing at all, even though I was furious.

I have worked in this section for almost three years and have not been late to work in over two years. Let's face it—this witch is just itching for a reason to get on my case. I think she has some sort of dark-skinned arch rivalry thing going with me, as if there's only room for one of us in the division or something.

"That's not the only reason I called you in here, Richmond." My eyebrows rose. I couldn't imagine what else *El Dragon* could want with me. I was already charbroiled enough.

"I was informed that you were seen dining in a restaurant with a former probationer, over the weekend."

Damn, these snitches!

This place is a den of gossiping vipers and one can never know how far their villainy will reach. I never realized how devastating the poisonous slander of the office chatter could be, as I was never the target of their stealthy attacks before today. I wanted to yell out the accusatory question, "Who said it?" but I remained silent because I knew that speaking would only invite the wrath of the Dragon and establish my guilt.

"My understanding is that the probationer in question is no longer in your custody, so there are no formal repercussions for this situation. However, I would like to advise you that circumstances such as these can cast a dubious shadow on how other colleagues perceive your professionalism and judgment." Sgt. Bledsoe clasped her hands together and placed them under her chin. "Richmond, ask yourself this question... 'Where is this road leading me?' and then make sure to pay attention to the signs which indicate that the bridge is out up ahead."

Sgt. Bledsoe paused to glare at me sternly.

This is called... **The Intimidation Stare**.

"You're dismissed, Richmond."

I trotted slowly back to my desk. The wheels in my head were turning, trying to figure out who could have seen me. I wasn't sure whether to be embarrassed or ashamed.

Had I done something wrong?

In my head, I was rehearsing all of the ways that this situation could play out. I was so entirely absorbed in my own internal pandemonium that I barely even recognized the scene developing with me in the starring role. A hush fell over the floor as I walked out of the office. The clicking of keyboard keys. The low ringing of the desk phones. The faint rustling of paperwork. Everything signaled the continuation of business... as usual, however something was different.

As I scanned the office, I noticed that all those eyes, which had offered no acknowledgement when I entered the office this morning, were now focused on me... watching me silently, as I slinked down the aisle to my desk. It didn't bother me as much as it should have. At that point, I realized that I had been the topic of widespread discussion, but one thing that I had learned from being an investigator told me that the snitch would be the one person who couldn't look me directly in the eye. So, I welcomed all of the stares, hoping to flush out the rat. I was careful to dignify each pair of eyes with sufficient eye attention of my own.

"Hey Denae, girl." Deena was sitting on the desk when I returned to my cubicle.

I gave her the look— that nutcracker face.

It worked.

"Ooo, honey chile'," Deena scrunched her face as if some foul odor had crept into the air. "I'll come back later… better yet— tomorrow. Take it easy, babe." Deena slid her immense bottom off my desk and towed it down the aisle.

I busied myself all throughout the day, tending to mundane details that I usually leave to the administrative assistants: making copies, stapling reports, sending out letters—even brewing coffee. The swift passing of hours was the only reward for my exhaustive efforts. No conversation. No hesitation.

I filled my time with uninterrupted labor. I even took lunch at my desk to avoid the break room banter. I puffed a sigh of relief when I looked up to see that my shift had expired. I grabbed my trench coat and headed for the door. However, I left the hectic pace of my job, only to be slammed— once again, by the rush of thoughts I had fought all day to suppress:

-Was it inappropriate to befriend a beautiful, eloquent man like Dennis?

-*Aren't we, P/O's, the same people who encourage our "clients" to believe they can live a normal life, free from the stigma with which society brands felons?*

-*To distance myself from Dennis would be hypocritical, wouldn't it?*

Suddenly— I realized that I sounded just like Deena, using every excuse I could invent to validate a doomed relationship...

Oh shit, just shoot me in the face.

I can't win for losing with this guy. I got into my car and resigned myself to heed the warnings of Bledsoe (icky) as well as Alisha. I had placed the small scrap of paper with Dennis's number scribbled on it in my cup holder. I picked up the paper and tore it sufficiently, before throwing it out of the window.

'So long, Dark Prince.'

Good Mourning, Love

"Dearly beloved, we are gathered here today..."

"To get through this thing, called life," Alisha belted out her best Prince impression. *"Electric word— Life. It means forever and that's a mighty long time."*
'Would you please stop that? It's very inappropriate,' I whispered, inaudibly to Alisha, attempting to remain focused on the minister.

"We mourn the passing of a deeply cherished sister and saint, Mary Ellis Bivens. She will be sorely missed by us all."

This was my first venture out of the house— other than going to work on Sgt. Bledsoe's plantation, in weeks. I had been forgoing Thirsty Thursdays and Sunday services, essaying to avoid Dennis, at all costs. Rayshaun called me late Wednesday night to deliver the somber news that his beloved Maw-maw had passed away.

"Sister Mary has gone on to be with the Lord, yet she leaves behind a legacy of enduring love that transcends the grave."

Maw-maw was as close (if not closer) to me as my own grandmother. Rayshaun's family adopted me, early in our friendship. I had come to attend college in Atlanta, on scholarship, from North Carolina. I matured from a girl to a woman in this city, and therefore chose to stay even after I graduated. I didn't have any relatives in close proximity, so Ray's matriarchal unit came to embrace me as one of their own.
Rayshaun's mother, Rayshelle, took a liking to me from the start. I secretly suspected that it was because I am one of the darkest girls Ray had ever brought home. She insisted that her fondness of me was attributed to my "down-to-earth" nature. However, I imagined that Rayshelle, a lovely mahogany-colored woman, was relieved to have some complexion camaraderie in her home. Ray's family is comprised almost exclusively of cocoa-

colored females, a veritable Hen House. All of the men (including Ray's father) were either estranged, incarcerated, or deceased. It was easy to see how Ray became such a ladies' man: charming, well-mannered, and completely dependent on his mother— the avid enabler.

Weekly, he drops off his laundry and picks up home-cooked meals. I can tell by the way Rayshelle brings me into the kitchen during holiday dinners, to help with the service of the meal, that she is grooming me to compliment her son.

We have become a very close-knit flock, so Maw-maw's death was unexpectedly sudden. And for each of us present, it served as a bitter reminder of the frail uncertainty of life.

Rayshaun picked me up from my apartment in his black Chrysler 300C. He told me that he didn't want to accompany the family on the ride to the church. As flashy and capricious as Ray can be, he longs for normalcy. He loves structure and routines. It makes him feel as though he has control over his life. In the wake of such a humbling event, Ray grasped desperately at any opportunity to exercise his independence. And thus, by choosing the comfort of his familiar car over the alien luxury of the funeral parlor limousine, he regained a sense of dominance in this volatile time.

We rode on, in complete and uninterrupted silence. No music, no words, not even so much as a cough—only the low, droning hum of the engine and the occasional groan of the leather interior, as the car crept slowly towards its destination.

The gloomy sky was cloaked in a murky, ominous cloud cover that seemed to still all the activity of heaven. Even the sun had resigned himself not to light the day, but to spend it in mourning. For miles, we snaked along under a lifeless sky on a seemingly deserted road, lined with groves of naked, barren trees that appeared to be pointing the way with long, skeletal fingers.

Rayshaun was calm and peaceful as he smoothly maneuvered his vehicle into an available parking spot near the entrance door to the chapel vestibule. He opened my door and offered a hand of assistance, as I climbed out of the car. An icy, melancholy chill cooled the air, so I wrapped my gray wool shawl tightly around my shoulders, as we mounted the steps leading up to the church. I watched as the host of Maw-maw's daughters passed by the casket to say their farewells. Some sobbed and others wailed, but the sorrow in the sanctuary was so immense that it moved me to tears— not because of her death but because of their loss. The passing of Maw-maw was the closest that I had ever come to experiencing the bereavement of a loved one.

I was surprised when Ray called, earlier in the week, asking me to accompany him to the funeral. I had not seen or talked to him for some time. Hearing Rayshaun's voice on the phone after midnight, reminded me of the early days in our friendship, when we divulged even our most intimate secrets. He was sobbing something I had never known him to do. The death of his grandmother, a seemingly impenetrable pillar in his life, had caused his foundations to crumble. He was second-guessing himself and all that he held dear.

"Are you seeing someone else?" he asked quietly and completely out-of-the-blue.

"Huh?" The question was unexpected. Rayshaun was in the middle of lamenting about his grandmother when he posed it.

"I haven't heard from you in over two weeks. Denae, that's not like you." The tone of Ray's voice denoted a tinge of anger.

"I've just been really busy at work—"

"Or busy with another man?" Ray interrupted. I was stunned by the sharpness of his question. So much so, that I could not answer it. I stammered and stuttered on the words, which served as an indictment of guilt in Ray's mind. "Look, I don't really want to know. What you do is your own business," his voice softened, as the words spilled out hurriedly.

"Ray, you're the only man I've been with for years."
'Why did I say that?' I condemned myself. 'I might be onto something with this jealousy kick.'

"Look, I told you. I don't really want to know," Ray snipped shortly. "But— I do want to know if you will go to the funeral with me on Saturday."

"Of course, I will."

And so, here I was, sitting beside Rayshaun on the first pew. This is a seat that I have never occupied in a church before. Rayshelle sat on his left. He put a comforting arm around his mother, as she whimpered her way through tearful eulogy given by Maw-maw's eldest daughter, Adelle.

Rayshaun remained constant at his mother's side, her stolid, immovable rock. The funeral service concluded with a heart-felt benediction from the minister. The substantial number of mourners, all clad entirely in black, staggered dismally down the aisle. Their solemn, melancholy faces offered courtly nods to Rayshaun and Rayshelle, as they passed the pew.

Ray and I were the last ones to file down the aisle and out of the sanctuary. He held the door for me and took my hand in his, as we walked out of the church— together

* * *

"Hey everybody, can I please have your attention?"

Rayshaun stood at the head of his mother's dinner table. In a room full of mourners, he was the only one to smile. I almost forgot how Ray could brighten up a room. My encounters with Ray had become such brief and secretive ordeals that I honestly couldn't recall what he looked like in the light. He's like an angel, majestic to behold, in his black three-piece Brioni suit.

Sometimes, it's hard for me to believe that I am graced with such a handsome (and talented) lover. I began to swoon for him, like the first time we met. I was studying his supple lips when startled out of my fantasy by the sound of my name.

"Well, Denae?" Ray said, staring at me with raised eyebrows.

In fact, everyone in the room was looking at me.

What did I miss?... Is it my birthday?

"Well... what, Ray?" I asked shyly, glancing around the room at all of the anxious faces.

"Even though I know this is a sad time for the family, I would like to share with you all the joy that this woman has given me." Ray said addressing the captive audience of his relatives. "Denae, help me turn this day of mourning into a day of celebration by becoming my wife."

I was so terrified with shock that I dropped my fork onto my plate and a loud *clink* rang out. I felt like all the wind had been knocked out of me. I would have pinched myself... if I could move.

Ray navigated his way between the numerous chairs huddled around the long, cherry oak dinner table, and arrived at my seat on the side of the table. He knelt down between his mother and me.

"Damn, I didn't think Rayshaun would crack after only two weeks of pussy pressure. Girl, you a bad mother—"

'Shut up, Alisha.'

Out of his pocket, a small, black-velvet ring box appeared. His jade-colored eyes peered up at me, brimming with anticipation. "Denae, will you..."

I placed my finger over his lips to silence him. "Ray, can I please speak with you, privately?" I whispered in his ear. Ray's mother shot me a concerned and disapproving look, as we exited the dining room.

Once inside the sanctity of Rayshaun's *just-in-case* bedroom, on the second level of his mother's house, I confronted him.

"Ray, what are you doing?" I asked brazenly. I was so distraught that I didn't even realize I was shaking.

"I am proposing ..."

"Why?" I blurted, trying desperately to contain myself.

"How can you ask me that after four years? I didn't spend all these years with you to lose you now."

"Who said anything about leaving. You're paranoid," I yelled louder than I intended to. "How could you just spring this on me, right now... in front of everybody?"

Ray looked puzzled by the question. "Denae, I've been asking you to marry me for a long time?"

"I thought you were joking," I said angrily.

"I would **never** play with something like that," Ray replied assertively with a rare intensity in his eyes.

"Look Denae," Ray ushered me to a seat up on the high, flannel-covered bed. Sitting down beside me, he continued.

"I was the only one who knew that Maw-maw was dying. After her annual checkup last May, she confessed to me that the doctors found a lump in her breast. For months, I took her back and forth to specialist after specialist for series of different tests. She didn't trust anyone else. She said that I was the only one strong enough to carry that burden. The prognosis was bleak. She had several malignant tumors, but the specialists believed that with a double mastectomy and aggressive rounds of chemotherapy, she had at least a slim chance of survival."

Ray began to choke on the words, as he fought back tears. I was not sure if I should or could console him, so I sat in quiet observance, attentive to his every utterance.

"Maw-maw didn't want the treatment. She feared that someone would find out she was sick and cause a panic within the family. I pled with her until she broke down, and told me that she was just too tired to fight. She said that she didn't want..." Ray fell to pieces, releasing a deluge of pinned up tears. I wrapped my arms around his head, as he wept into my bosom. I held him for a little while, until his shoulders ceased to shake. When he finally lifted his head, Ray dabbed hastily at his eyes with his sleeve.

He stood, taking off his suit jacket. Even in his grief, he looked so sleek in his black vest and black dress shirt that hugged his slender waist. Ray loosened his silk, onyx colored tie, as he paced in the room attempting to regain his composure. He unbuttoned the top buttons on his shirt. His eyes were bloodshot from crying and he looked as though he was coming apart from the seams.

"Ray, are you sure this is the best time to talk about this?"

"I need to tell you this. Maw-maw wanted you to know that she was thinking of you as well in her last days." Ray's face became grave and pensive as he continued. "She said that she never wanted to take more than she gave, and that the family would benefit more from her in death than in relentless illness. She told me that she was done with this life." Ray stopped again. His jaw clenched as he mustered the strength to continue. "She said that her only regret was that I didn't have someone to share my burdens with, the way she shared hers with me. She told me, 'Son, life is too short to spend it isolating yourself from giving and receiving love, just to keep from getting hurt. Love Denae for who she is and give her the chance to love you back. Don't keep her at a distance.'"

"Rayshaun," I said softly, rolling cautiously into an intersection of the conversation. "I don't want you with me out of obligation. No one can make that choice for you and you don't owe it to anyone to give up your free will. God doesn't even ask that of us."

"This is my choice. You're the woman that I want," Ray knelt before me, holding both of my hands between his. He lightly kissed my wrists. "Maw-maw could see that. She only helped me to acknowledge what was already there."

At that comment, I became enraged again. "I know you, Ray. I was your friend before all of this. I've seen you smash female after female." I tore my hands away from him. "I was willing to accept not being your first choice. I can even take not being your only choice, but don't degrade me like this."

"What are you talking about?" He raised his pitch, clearly aggravated. "I don't understand you!" Ray was beginning to fume. "I thought that you wanted this. Why did you stay with me for all these years, if you didn't trust me?" Rayshaun raised an eyebrow. "Didn't you know that I wanted to be with you?... Is this some kind of game?"

"You tell me!" I snapped. "Cause that's sure as hell what it seems like. If you love me then why am I the last one to know?" I shrieked. "I have never even seen you look twice at a woman like me in all the time I've known you. You have been hiding me out like a troll for years now."

"I'll be the first to admit that I didn't expect to develop these feelings for you— but I did. I tried to fight it, but not because of how you look. I think you're beautiful, Denae and I tell you that all the time. I didn't hide you. I hid myself from you because I was afraid to have a woman that I could fall so completely in love with..."

Ray's pleading flipped suddenly to wrath. "Wait, why am I explaining myself to you? You weren't even there for me when I needed you. Yeah, I do have issues, but you have a lot of your own too. People can change, Denae. You are not the Judge. It seems to me like you are the one with insecurities about the way you look— not me."

Ray was pointing at me— something that he knows I hate. I pushed his hand down, but Ray grabbed my shoulders. "Look, I'm saying it now, okay?... I love you and I want you. Take it or leave it."

Ray retrieved the box from his pocket and slammed it down on the chest of drawers beside the door. Turning his back to me, he said quietly, "That's for you, if you want it. I've made my choice and now you have to make yours."

Ray threw the door open and it banged loudly against the wall. He rushed out of the room and dashed down the stairs. I followed him out, but stopped at the top of the staircase. Rayshelle appeared at the bottom. She watched her son stomp out of the front door and then slam it closed. Her eyes darted from the front door up to me. She gave me a harsh glare, before storming out angrily after him.

Safety in Lovers

Devian Nikei

Blessing...in Disguise

"You gotta' be out of your damn mind."

"Personally, I think you're doing the right thing. You should have left Ray alone a long time ago."

"You're just a hater, Meisha. You probably want Ray for yourself."

"Well Lanelle, you're just desperate. You will date any clown as long as he takes you to a buffet."

"Okay, skinny bitch! Don't make me cut you. Even E-harmony can't get your ass a date, *Princess*."

"See, I told you... hyenas." Alisha remarked about the grudge match that was brewing in my living room.

"It really is none of *my* business," Juniece started, "but—"

"I'm glad you said that. Why are y'all here again?" I still had my hand on the knob of my open front door.

"This is an intervention," Lanelle said sympathetically, as she brushed past me, leading the pack, into my apartment. "We came to take your loony ass to the Crazy House."

I closed the door— not because they were welcome, but because I was outnumbered.

"We haven't heard from you for a while," Meisha began, "and honey..." she glanced over at Juniece and Lanelle. "We're worried about you."

"With good reason, evidently." Lanelle commented, as she fingered frazzled strands of my unkempt hair.

I closed my purple, terry cloth bathrobe over my pajamas and offered them all a seat, before dropping back down into **Old Faithful**, my green velour recliner. I propped up my pink, bunny-slippered feet, knowing that this discussion was going to be a long one.

"When you didn't return any of my messages... I called Ray," Meisha confessed meekly.

Lanelle and I both whipped our heads and shot her a menacing glare. "Uh-huh. I'll bet you did Meisha," Lanelle said slyly.

Meisha is a bird-framed, honey-colored *Princess*. She carries herself as though she is superior in every setting, but doesn't understand why she can't land a qualified man. She believes that her beauty intimidates men. But the truth is that guys see a high-maintenance, ball breaker and steer clear. I reviled the day that I ever told her about Rayshaun's light-skinned girl fixation. Ever since then, she has gone out of her way to make herself *available* to him. I've let it ride for a long time— but today she is testing my respect for our friendship and desire to remain a free woman.

"Go to hell, Lanelle." Meisha shouted guiltily.

"I'll meet you there." Lanelle mocked, "I thought you were a Christian, Meisha. Even I'm not desperate enough to try a play for my girl's man right in front of her face. Let me find out, bitch."

For someone who didn't know these two well, this would sound very abusive, but this is normal— actually pretty tame for them.

"Anyway," Meisha said, looking defiantly at Lanelle, as she removed her salmon colored sweater jacket. She flipped her multi-toned blonde hair over one shoulder. "This isn't about any of that. It's all about you, girl. Ray told me about the proposal. What are you going to do?"

"I don't know," I shrugged.

"What do you mean, you don't know? You're living the dream, Denae. So why do you look like your best friend just died?" Lanelle asked heading into the kitchen.

"I don't know," I repeated with a tone of irritation.

"Don't you want to marry Ray?" Juniece softly piped in.

"I'm just not sure if that's really what **he** wants," I said sympathetically.

"He asked you, didn't he? I don't know of too many men casually throwing that kind of proposal around these days," Lanelle huffed over her shoulder, as she searched my pantry.

"Ray is divorced, which is proof that he's been wrong before," I stated matter-of-factly.

"A lot has happened in Ray's world lately. I don't think he's in the right mindset to make this kind of decision," Meisha added passively. "I don't blame you for turning him down—"

"I didn't turn him down, Meisha," I replied vehemently. "I simply haven't accepted... yet. We both have some things to think about."

"It is awfully sudden," Juniece concurred.

"You already know where I stand on it," Lanelle puffed, concluding her unsuccessful search. "Say yes," she bellowed in a baritone voice, as she shook her clinched fists. "If you can take the D, then you can take the ring—"

Meisha interrupted, "That's easy for you to say..."

That would have been easy for me to say too. If only I could just say "yes"... but after my cab ride home from Rayshelle's house, I was sure that answer would only cause more problems than it could solve. I tossed and turned on my couch all Saturday night long, then laid in my bed all day Sunday, staring at the two-carat, princess-cut, pink diamond and white gold engagement ring. So overwhelmed with depression, I called out of work for the entire week. My phone rang daily, this or that person— but never Rayshaun.

I was certain that he probably didn't want to see me ever again after the scene I made in front of his family. I couldn't talk to anyone. I couldn't eat anything. I was engrossed in my own misery. I was remorseful for not being there to support Ray during the ordeal with his grandmother. Yet, I still couldn't help feeling that Ray had only proposed to keep me with him. It may have been the fear of being alone or maybe even a need for control that motivated Ray's proposal, but I was certain that love... true love, had not been a contributing factor.

Ray has come to depend on me, like all of the other women in his family, so it's only natural that he would use me to try and fill the gaping hole that his grandmother's death left in his life. Ray needed time— not marriage— to mend his pain.

Then— just to add a huge insult to the injury, I was wracked with guilt over the infatuation that burned inside of me for Dennis. I didn't want to confess or even think it, but the blaze continued to sear my heart no matter how many waves of reason and logic I doused at it. Ray's marriage proposal had only fanned the flames for Dennis, not extinguished them. I needed someone who could love me for who I am and not just for how I make them feel— someone who would be proud to have me. I was beginning to think that maybe Dennis could fit that bill.

The departure from my usual routine, without any disclosure, had alerted people around me that something was wrong. My voice mailbox was full, but my refrigerator was empty... evidently.

"Denae, did you hear me?" Lanelle blared. "You ain't got shit to eat in this place, but a onion and some mustard. No wonder your ass is depressed. You about to perish up in here," she belted out, as she slapped her thigh.

"We've got to get you up out of this house," Juniece said, pulling me off the recliner. She guided me to the bathroom. "We wouldn't be good friends if we left you here like this."

"But, I don't want to go anywhere," I whined, as I shrank away from her.

"Oh, you're going, even if I have to drag you out myself!" Lanelle swelled up. "You know you can't take me lightweight."

I turned and made for the bathroom. Lanelle is always serious when she makes threats like that. She uses us as sparing partners whenever possible. I think she could be training to take the Men's Heavyweight Boxing Championship.

I was sipping my salvation... Mango Margherita, when he walked into our hangout—A place called *Thrive*.

Whom, you ask?

Dennis— that's who.

I felt like a fox caught in a trap, until... a tall, weave-wearing, caramel vixen, stepped through the door behind him. Dennis glanced in my direction, casually at first, but then keenly as he recognized my face.

"How'd he know you'd be here?" Alisha blurted irately.
'He obviously didn't come here looking for me, Alisha.' I remarked, nonchalantly, trying to mask my envy from her.
My girls were all huddled around the table. They chatted away, making their best collaborative effort to heave my spirits up out of the trenches, but all time around me had stilled. I would have thought that my heart had stopped too, if it weren't for the crushing sensation that intensified as they walked past our table.
Dennis and his female companion sat down at a booth behind us. I could feel the heat of his stare on my back. But to turn around would be to succumb to defeat, so I remained absorbed in the drama at my own table.
"He pulled that little thing out, talkin' 'bout, 'You ready?'... I said, 'Fool, are you ready? I think you left your dick out in the car'," Lanelle howled, igniting the table with maniacal cackling.
I gasped suddenly, when he touched my back. Likewise, the laughter at the table trailed off precipitously at the presentation of this dark, sultry intruder.

"Hi ladies. I'm Dennis," he said, placing his hand on the back of my chair. He commanded the attention of the table with his smile.

Damn... The smile. He's got me again.

"Hey... I remember you. The bartender, right?" Lanelle leaned in, looking interested, as she placed her elbows on the table.

She learns from the best— eh.

"Miss Richmond," Dennis turned his focus solely on me. Bending over, he asked quietly, "Could I speak with you for a moment?" His face was so close to mine, I could feel his mint-scented breath on my lips.

I didn't answer.

He didn't care.

"Excuse us, ladies," he said as he took me by the hand.

"Damn, Denae. You can't have 'em all," Lanelle bellowed after us.

* * *

"Blessing. I call her... blessing." Dennis began, in concert with the rhythm of the drum.

The bright spotlight reflected off his smooth head, casting shadows on his face, but his amber eyes continued to radiate a sparkling brilliance through the dark.

"Blessing... in disguise. Because her heart lies. Tells her that she must hide... deep... deep down inside." The guitar strain lingered in the air. "Denies that she's worthwhile, when truly she is sublime."

My lady parts began to throb with each word. I could feel his hands on me, as he gripped the microphone stand. I breathed in every word he expelled like fragrant incense.

"Blessing...*yes*— blessing... in disguise, no doubt. Because her fear won't let her out..." Dennis's voice rumbled throughout the room like thunder. "Cloaked in mysterious beauty. Enshrouded in a design as complex and divine as time. God's blessing . . . in disguise— is revealed in her eyes."

Dennis finished— and so did I. I felt as though the amusement attraction that I was riding on had just come to a stop. Dennis had done more than recite a poem. He had changed the atmosphere and enraptured me in a sensual experience. I applauded lightly along with the audience, as he stepped down off the short platform.

The cozy lounge was dimly lit by tiny lamps that shone up into the crowd's faces, transforming the listeners into an audience of ghostly seraphs hovering over the various tables. Dennis made his way back to our small, circular booth. We sat, silently for some time, covered in darkness.

"Before this week, I hadn't composed a new poem in two years," Dennis said plainly. He put both of his hands on the table in front of him. I couldn't decipher the meaning of the stern expression on his face. "I wanted you to be the first to hear it." Dennis uttered casually.

"I can tell that poetry is your passion," I offered with formal resignation.

"Poetry is merely an expression of passion. I love it, but **it** is not my passion." Dennis replied dismissively.

"Well if not poetry, then what?"

"You—" Dennis's voice was little more than a low vibration. Shifting shadows obscured his entire face—except for his eyes, vivid and inflamed. They shined like two stars in a void, night sky. That pre-existing blaze became an inferno so hot that I began to sweat. "You are my passion, Denae... My muse."

My face was flushed from the heat. I needed some distraction to help stamp out the flames.

"Well, what about *Miss Thing* at the bar? You two looked pretty close."

"Actually, we are very close." Dennis grinned, seemingly to himself as he stirred his drink. "She's my cousin, Celeste." He paused to examine my visage, but I remained as unchanged and expressionless as before, not allowing him the satisfaction of being shocked by the news.

"She was tired of seeing me held up in my house like a hostage, moping over a certain female, who shall remain nameless. So she dragged me out with her."

'Well, isn't that a coincidence . . . or a conspiracy?' I contemplated to myself. Dennis watched me through his golden eyes like a night owl. The intensity of his stare made me uncomfortable.

"Well, Miss Richmond—"

"Don't do that."

"Do what?... I thought this is how you want it."

"Look, if this is going to turn into an inquisition, then you can just take me back to my car, right now." I remarked sharply.

"Alright then," Dennis said, rising from his seat.

Oops... That one backfired.

"Hey," I said softly, placing my hand over his. "I don't want it to be like this."

Dennis lowered himself back down on to the seat. "How do you want it, then?" he asked directly, taking his hand back before folding his arms across his chest.

I paused for consideration. "Hi, my name is Denae Richmond, but you can call me— Denae," I smiled, extending my hand. He wrapped his hand around my fingers and brought my knuckles to his lips. My spine tingled from his kiss, sending a shudder down my legs.

"Denae, I'm not playing a game with you. I can understand why you wouldn't believe me, but—"

"It's not that simple, Dennis." I withdrew my hand from his.

"It's as simple as how you feel. Be real with me. I have been through things that you can't even begin to imagine. You don't have to be phony with me."

"I'm not being phony," I replied defensively.

"If you want to be celebrated and appreciated, then I can handle that, but you gotta' let me know if I have any real chance with you."

Instantly, flashbacks of Ray inundated my thoughts. 'I can't leave things like this between us,' I reflected to myself. Ray has been not just a lover, but also a friend over the years. I felt the heat drain from my body, as a devastating tidal wave of remorse drenched me.

"The truth, Dennis—is that I don't really know what I want, right now."

He grinned widely.

"Thank you, Denae."

"For what?"

"Your honesty. It's admirable and encouraging." Dennis caught me off my guard again. This man is more challenging than a Sudoku puzzle.

"Encouraging?" I inquired with heightened curiosity.

"Yeah. I mean, you must care even just a little bit to be that open and vulnerable with me. It's better than that take-my-number-and-never-call-me trick you pulled the last time."

"Ooo, crunch!" I responded mockingly.

Dennis laughed, lightly, revealing those adorable dimples for the first time in the conversation.

They Smile in Your Face

"Just tell the truth, Rico!"

'What have I just walked into?' I thought.

> "This bitch is crazy. I just came to get my things—"
> "Damn you, Rico—Officer, this niggah' was trying to rob me."
> "Look ma'am," the officer interjected. "I've heard your side.
> Now, I need you to go stand by your door while I talk to this
> gentleman—"
> "Look Officer, I promise, she is the one who told me to come
> over here and get my shit before she burned all of it..."

Ordinarily, Ray's Brownstone community is very quiet and dormant, but tonight all hell must have been loosed. I passed a catastrophic car wreck, just one block from his house, only to arrive here and find the police in his development, as well. I walked up the sidewalk, stepping over pieces of a huge television, obviously dropped from the second story window, as I navigated my way through the carnage of a lover's spat.

After leaving the lounge, I used my ride home to sort out all of the chaos in my spirit. I rolled down my windows and allowed the cool breeze to refresh my soul, as I drove. Once I reached I-85, I involuntarily went north, instead of south to my apartment. I couldn't control the urge to see Ray. I do love him, but his sudden proposal scared me. It shook the foundation of our friendship— and I wasn't prepared for that. I'm not sure if Ray really loves me too, but if he's willing to try, then so am I. This situation makes me nervous, but I would regret it if I let him go.

'I'll make him fall in love with me,' I thought, smiling to myself at the idea of Ray and I getting married. I sat in my car for a short while, gathering my nerve. I uttered a quick prayer, before starting up the walkway.

Now... here I stand outside of his door.

I start to knock.

'No, stop!' I hesitated.
It is very late.
Maybe, I should just wait.
Maybe not

   "You'd better go and get your man," Alisha declared.

Knock-knock
No answer.
Ding, dong

Wait.

Ding-dong. Knock, knock, knock
No answer.

Wait.

Still, no answer.

   'Maybe that's a sign,' I wondered and pondered to myself. I
abandoned my mission, believing that Ray must have stepped
out. 'Probably better this way. I need time to think about what I
want to say . . .'

I began to walk away, but the door cracked and Ray peeked out.

   "Hey," I said sheepishly, turning back to face him.
   "Hey," he responded smoothly, widening the gap in the door.
   "Can we talk?"
   "Right now?" He seemed slightly agitated.

'See, you should have waited,' I reprimanded myself.

"Is it important?" He asked, seemingly distracted, as the argument and blue lights from across the courtyard caught his attention. "What I mean is, can it wait?" Ray returned his bejeweled gaze to my eyes.

"He's so beautiful' I think to myself, surveying his bare chest.

"No, Ray. It can't wait," I said, biting my bottom lip.

Thump

'What was that sound?'

I looked over Ray's shoulder to see a dark, murky figure standing up on the landing in front of his bedroom doorway. I pushed past Ray into the foyer. The form that I observed was the willowy silhouette of a woman.

She is... fair.
She is... blonde.
She is... in his shirt.
She is... Meisha.
She is**... dead.**

I lunged for the staircase in a blind rage.

"Hold on, Denae." Ray grabbed me around my shoulders and waist. He pulled me back and pinned me against the wall.
"Oh, hell no!" I growled out over his shoulder, thrashing against the strength of his restraint. My flats slipped on the hardwood floor, as I strained to get around him.
"Damn it, Denae. You need to calm the hell down."
"Calm down!" I screamed, focusing my attention on him." I'ma kill that bitch!"
Ray dragged me, kicking and screaming, down the hallway, out of his building, and onto the stoop. He closed the door behind us. Once outside, I broke down bawling as the tears came

streaming involuntarily from my eyes and trickling down my cheeks.

"How could you do this, Ray?"

"Do what, Denae?" Ray shouted sharply.

"Ray," I hissed defiantly.

"Denae?" Ray scoffed back at me. I struck his chest, but he caught my hand before I could land a second blow.

"You don't want to do that, Denae," Ray said, glancing in the direction of the flashing lights. He clenched my wrists together until I stopped resisting.

"Let me go!" I screamed, yanking away from him.

"I already did, Denae. I did let you go, alright?" Ray retorted angrily.

At that point, I realized what he meant.

"I can't believe that you would do this."

"Do what, Denae?" Rayshaun stared at me intently. "I can't believe *you*, Dee. Aren't you supposed to be out with some other guy right now?" Ray asked so delicately that his words were like tiny straws on a camel's back.

"Oh, so now you gone believe some shit that skank, Meisha, told you?"

Ray's eyes widened. "If you're going to believe what you want to, then I will too." Ray and I stood there, locked in a hostile stare. No words could express what we felt. I pulled the ring box out of my purse and heaved it at his chest.

"Denae," Ray said, with barely contained rage, as he picked up the box. "You need to leave—**now**." His words stung like a slap, leaving prickly heat in my face. His expression remained unchanged, except for a slight shiver from the cool, winter air.

"Ray," I cried quietly. "How could you?"

"Go home, Denae." Ray stepped back into his building and turned out the light, leaving me out on the stoop, alone in the dark.

I stood there for a few moments, thinking—hoping that Ray would return. I even dropped down, taking a seat on a frigid, concrete step. I made up in my mind that I was going to wait for that trick Meisha and punch her right in the mouth, when she came out of the building. But then, the thought seeped in like noxious gas...

Meisha might not be coming out tonight.

I gagged. I tried to calm my mind, forcing the images out. *She's probably curling up with him, right now.* My stomach rolled over within me. *Yeah, they're finishing what they started before you interrupted . . .* I swallowed hard. I have a very strong constitution. I've only vomited twice in my life and both times were because of a stomach flu that I caught when I was nine. But now, even the idea of them together (gag) made me physically ill. *You know he's giving it to her good. I'll bet she's loving every minute of it.* A dry heave escaped my throat. Eventually my stomach settled down, but the nausea stayed put. After only a few minutes more, the bitter chill in the air drove me up off the stoop. I walked dismally down the walkway back to my car. I glanced up at the second-story of Ray's place before I climbed inside.

The bedroom window was dark, empty and undisturbed.

Devian Nikei

The Magic Touch

"Did he hurt you?"

"What are you talking about?"
"Him—He is the reason why you're here, right?"
"I don't know what you mean."
"C'mon, Denae. It's entirely too late for cat and mouse."
Dennis said, leaning against his front door frame.

After leaving Ray's place, I used my laptop computer to conduct an Offender Database Search and managed to retrieve Dennison Millsaps's last known address. When I pulled up to the modest house, Dennis's truck was parked outside.

The two-story residence seemed a drastic contrast to the meager surroundings of the Clayton County neighborhood. The spacious yard of his manicured corner lot had an assortment of neatly primmed winter shrubbery, which continued to flourish in the dropping temperatures. Various boards of splintered wood siding were removed from the exterior and discarded in an industrial bin on the side of the house. A blue tarp covered the recently re-shingled roof. Dennis's dwelling appeared to be the only building in renovation, clearly divergent from the adjoining community engrossed in a steep decline. I stood at the edge of Dennis's driveway, rationalizing all of the reasons why I should leave. I knew that this was terribly foolish and impulsive, but I needed him tonight—to keep me from going insane and from possibly committing a double homicide.

"I'm here because I *want* to be. After the lounge, I couldn't stop thinking about y—"
"Don't *even* go there." Dennis was visibly irritated. He stepped to the side of the door and motioned for me to come in. "I may be a felon, Denae, but I am not stupid. I know that *he*—whoever *he* is—is the reason why you didn't call, and the reason why you left me after the lounge, and... the reason why you are here now."
I sat down on the small, brown leather sofa. The springs

dug up into my thighs, but I didn't want to offend Dennis by getting up. The living room was humbly decorated but remarkably orderly. There was rigorous remodeling going on inside of the house as well, but the integrity of his organizational efforts were maintained by the immaculate cleanliness of his domicile. Everything had its place—even the dislodged floorboards were arranged into short piles and lined up against the living room wall.

"Did he reject you?"

"Why are you talking about my life like you know me?" I uttered boldly. "I didn't come here for this."

"What did you come here for then?" Dennis asked delicately, his words flowing out over mine. I calmed myself and took my time.

"I just need you tonight," I admitted faintly. "I don't want to be alone. Okay?"

"Is it me that you want or just what I represent?" Dennis paused, rubbing his forehead. "Do you want my heart or my hands, Denae?"

"Both," I said, as I stood up from the sofa.

I stepped over to him and slipped my hands under his sheer brown t-shirt. He shrank away from me, preventing my hands from exploring any further. Dennis turned his back to me, but I persisted. I found the soft dark chocolate skin at the nape of his neck, and brushed my lips over it gently. I reached my arms around his cobra-shaped back and ran my hands over the rugged terrain of his muscular chest.

Dennis turned suddenly and sank his hands into my hair. He dove into a deep, powerful kiss, then came up gasping for air. He pressed my back against the wall. "Denae, this is insane." He puffed, still clutching my head. Dennis's breaths were heavy. I could feel his heart racing against my chest.

"It's as simple as how you feel," I said, quoting him. I realized that I was pulling him into me. My nails dug into the skin on his back, as he devoured my neck with his plump, spongy lips. I could feel his organ stiffening under my navel.

"I don't want this, if you don't mean it." Dennis's amber eyes burned with intensity. I arched my body against his, as my *Venus* began to throb and pulse. Dennis seemed conflicted, yet intoxicated, with passion. I circled around, grazing my buttocks over the expanding mass that swelled within his shorts. He gripped my hips tightly and pressed his pelvis into me.

Without warning, he became exceptionally tender. His lips began to tremble as he lightly kissed the skin behind my ear. Dennis surrendered his control and his resolve dissipated. The confident, self-assured knight transformed into a shy, hesitant novice. His hands were clammy and clumsy, as he pulled off, first, my burgundy turtleneck and then my silk camisole. His fingers were unsure, as they loosened the clasp on my lace front bra, then glided over my rotund breasts.

Next Dennis grabbed the back of my neck forcefully—almost violently, turning me around to face him. He licked down from my collarbone to my bellybutton. My knees weakened, as a deep guttural moan escaped my throat. Dennis gripped the back of my thighs savagely, heaving them up around his waist. I was excited and exhilarated by his capriciously unpredictable love style. He teetered between romantic, adoring paramour and voracious, ravenous beast. I rubbed my hands over his baldhead and sucked on his neck, as he carried me into the kitchen. He sat me down on the counter, pushing my skirt up around my waist. Dennis parted my thighs and pulled off my nylon tights. He ran his tongue from my knee to the band on my satin panties, and then sucked on the wet pathway that he formed. Boy, were those lips just as powerful as they looked.

My body writhed as delightful ripples traveled up my spine. Dennis grabbed both of my breasts and pressed them together in his hands. My nipples hardened as he aroused them by flicking his long, thick tongue quickly over each one. He kissed and caressed my breasts and I, his smooth head.

Dennis stopped abruptly. He stood, pulling my arms from around his neck and backed away from the counter.

"I can't do this, Denae," he said. His entire body shivered as if a cool breeze suddenly swept through the kitchen. "I want you, but not like this. I just... can't.

"Yes, you can," I said, lowering myself from the counter. I unfastened my skirt and slid it down (with my panties) to the floor. I watched his eyes shift down to the thin, strip of hair above my lady lips and then become locked there, glazed over in a trance-like state. I walked seductively over to him and reached down into his gray, jersey shorts, finding the treasure that I sought. His organ, thick and venous, palpitated with the beating of his heart. He went wild, when I vigorously caressed the silky skin of his chubby shaft. He grabbed me under my arms and threw me aggressively over his shoulder, before marching out of the kitchen...

* * *

"If I didn't know better, I would say that somebody's been rocking your world," Lanelle uttered blissfully.

I didn't answer. I just glared at her deviously with squinted eyes, as I sipped, slowly and deliberately, on my large chalice of Mint Mojito.

"Girl, you twinkling like somebody dipped you in fairy dust," Lanelle squeaked. "Who done put the magic touch on you? I know it ain't Ray."

"That's none of ya' business." I smirked.

"Don't trip, bitch. I got the by-line. I know all of your dirt. And just so that you know, I was going to get that slut, Meisha for you, but she's been ducking me. She don't need to sleep, though. I'm gone get her ass. That was some dirty bullsh—"

"Shhh," I put a finger to my lips. Lanelle was getting ready to fly off into Yosemite Sam mode. "Let's not talk about that." I said, waving the thought away.

"Yeah, I guess you're right. I'd much rather hear about that dark, baldheaded Mandingo warrior that's got you gleaming in spite of all this. I bet he screwed the black off your ass, right?"

"I don't kiss and tell, Lanelle."

"I ain't Meisha, okay? You don't have to worry about me trying to test out your merchandise," Lanelle said with pouted lips.

"Well, I ain't gonna' lie. He was pretty tight."

Okay... that was a lie.

The truth of the matter is that it was **over** pretty much before it even got started. Dennis finished the race before the gun went off. I wasn't extremely bothered by it because that let me know that he wasn't a regular at the track—if you know what I mean. But he made up for it over in the *wee* hours of the morning. I woke up to the feeling of his hands fondling me around 4am. He took my body over and over again, satiating me several times before allowing me to retire to my apartment, shortly after dawn.

Dennis was a good lover, but not exceptional. Four years with Rayshaun has spoiled me. However, his sincerity created a different energy than I was used to. Rayshaun is gifted, but Dennis is unpretentious. There's no pressure to finesse with him. We talked and laughed during our session. At times, Dennis laid between my thighs, not even stroking, but just playing with my ears or kissing my neck. He said that being inside of me —being one with me—felt so good that he didn't need to cum. Now I wasn't about to get that carried away. Leaving me unsatisfied is a quick way to get a pink slip from me. However, Dennis did more than enough to stay on staff. Besides, he is so sexy, he barely even had to touch the hot spot to get me off.

In fact, I was beaming over the flowers that he had delivered anonymously to me at work. Since that night, Dennis had spent the entire week surprising me with tiny trinkets of his affection. Love notes tucked into my sun visor that were written to 'you' from 'me', chocolates mailed to me with no return address, etc. I didn't know what it was to be cherished like that by a man.

Dennis was turning my world upside down and showering me with love like a magnificent, real-life snow globe.

But, I couldn't tell Lanelle that. She only cares about juicy sex details.

"I knew it. I knew it!" She shouted, pointing her finger at me. "Those lips looked like they could suck the skin right off of your—"

"Lanelle!" I exclaimed.

"Face... I was gonna' say face, Denae. Get your mind out of the gutter, honey." Lanelle and I exploded into laughter.

"Okay... okay," Lanelle huffed, catching her breath. "I need you to fill in the blanks for me. I know there's some kind of history between you and Shaka Zulu."

"His name is Dennis."

"Whatever. I saw the evil look you gave him, when he handed us our drinks, at *The Velvet Lounge*. It was like he ran over your dog. Then, the next thing I know—there you go strolling out of *Thrive* with him. Something doesn't add up, Denae."

"I don't know what you're talking about Lanelle."

"You do know that I will choke the truth out of you, right?" She made a circular shape with her hands. "Where did you meet him?"

I wasn't eager to disclose Dennis's past to Lanelle, but I knew that if I didn't give into her, a brutal shaking of my shoulders and torso would result.

"I met him at Probation and Parole."

Lanelle gave me a discerning look. "You're not getting wrapped up with your jail bird clientele now, are you Denae?"

"It's not like that," I paused and sighed, before reciting the infamous chicken-head birdcall. "He's different, Nell."

"Okay," Lanelle drawled through tightened lips. "Now, I'm concerned Dee. This guy could do anything to you. He might have some prison disease, or even yet, he could murder you in your sleep. What do you really know about him?"

"Just as much as—if not more than I know about any one of these perverts roaming around freely in this bar," I said, whirling my finger. "Everybody makes mistakes and everyone breaks some law every day, but not everyone gets caught. Some people really can change. You can't just throw people away because they have flaws."

Wow!

The tables in my glass house had officially turned. Here I was playing the role of Deena, and Lanelle was accurately depicting a portrayal of my usual self-righteous indignation and sanctimonious bias. I always thought that I came off as wise and dignified, but now I was finding my conversation to be judgmental and superficial, when the shoe was on the other foot and I was the listener. I also realized that Deena must be a good friend who values my opinion enough to endure such a hypocritical barrage as this. It was amusing and humbling, all at the same time, to find myself defending this relationship. I guess not everything is so black and white after all. Maybe there are gray, or perhaps even diversely colored, areas in this life. One thing is definite—I think I will leave judging other people's relationships to the studio audiences on television.

Lanelle whimpered facetiously and dabbed the corners of her eyes with a black cocktail napkin. "That was touching, Denae. You almost moved me to tears." She fanned me with the napkin. "Girl, you need to be in gospel plays."

"Stop it, heifer." I nudged Lanelle with my elbow.

"Nah, seriously. Inmates are a no-no, honey. I know that Ray let you down but you can't rebound with just anybody." Lanelle's face wrinkled up in a frown, as she shook her head.

"Really Lanelle, I'm just fine. It was only a matter of time before this thing with Ray and me fizzled out. I prepared my heart for this day a long time ago."

"You talking like you done with Ray," Lanelle gasped with genuine astonishment.

"Judging by the way things went down, I think it's Ray who's done with me," I replied dejectedly.

"Denae, I've know you a long time and I have a hard time believing you gone go out like that. You're acting like Ray is some kind of celebrity or something." Lanelle blinked her eyes incredulously. "Yeah, he is a stunner, but you ain't no slob yourself. I've got a news flash for you ... Beautiful, intelligent, take-care-of-home women don't grow on trees these days either and Ray is no stranger to that fact. That's why he's trying to wife you up before someone else does."

"Whatever —"

"I'm telling you the truth, girl. Don't sell yourself short. If Ray is Barak Obama, then you are his Michelle. A man knows his compliment when he sees it and four years show that Ray has found what he is looking for in you," Lanelle paused, then dropped her tone. "I really believe that man loves you."

"Alright—you can stop there," I injected defensively. "You can't go throwing me and Ray's names into sentences with L-words in them. Sharing a bed hardly qualifies as a relationship. Ray is confused and I am **not** going to let him make that my problem."

"Okay fine," Lanelle issued angrily with raised palms. "I know how to pick my battles so I'ma leave this one alone but just be careful. You haven't dated in a while and it's treacherous out here in these single waters. Let me fix you up with one of my friend guys instead."

"Nooo!" I bellowed, waving my hands defensively. "Oh hell no. I am not letting you force me into another blind date."

"Oh c'mon. I only hooked you up once. Dave was a really nice guy."

I gave Lanelle a reprehensible look. "He asked me so many questions, our date was more like a job interview. Besides, he had a little dick. We never would have worked out."

"What?" Lanelle giggled, covering her mouth. "You didn't give him the booty on the first date, did you?"

"No, no, no. I don't spend money on the first date, but I do count it," I said, rubbing my thumb across my fingers. "Girl, he didn't even have enough to buy chewing gum. He couldn't fill my *pocketbook* with what he had in his wallet. Everyone has a line and that's where I draw mine."

"Well, you're letting ex-cons ramble through your *pocketbook* now, aren't you?" Lanelle snapped her fingers. "You're not really feeling this *Donnie* guy?"

"His name . . . is Dennis."

"Whatever," Lanelle said dismissively, raising her eyebrows.

I relented, not wanting to appear any more ridiculous to Lanelle than I already did. I allowed her to believe that she had secured the victory. "No—not really. I guess you're right." I said, biting into a pineapple wedge.

"Look at the bright side," Lanelle flipped her palms upward. "At least you got a good lay out of it. I know them thugs will put a hurting on ya'." Lanelle did a little wiggly dance. "Look, I'd be the last person to tell you that you're wrong," Lanelle flattened her hands out on the table. "But just do me a favor and make sure that you're using protection for your heart... as well as your coochie."

Can You Guess Which Hand?

"There I go, there I go, there I go, there I go..."

Dennis took me out to the *Sweet Auburn Bistro*. The ambiance was chic and contemporary. The main attraction however, was the assortment of divinely ambrosial food on the menu. Every bite of which was truly savory and delicious, from the exquisitely enticing appetizers to the sinfully decadent desserts. Being there made me feel as though I were truly special and important to him.

"I'm sorry that I haven't been able to get up with you this week. I've been *so* busy," Dennis said, smiling at me from across the table. "But I promise, I will do better from now on." Dennis cleaned up rather nicely for the date, sporting a beige corduroy blazer over a sage colored dress shirt with brown slacks. "Thanks for being gracious enough to let me make it up to you with dinner."

"You know I understand that you gotta' get your grind on." I whipped my neck with the words.

"It's a funny thing, but every time I'm near you, I never can behave," the chanteuse's elegant voice hovered in the air.

"I just want you to have nice things, Denae. For the first time, in a long time, I really want to be a better man—the best man that I can be for you. There are so many things I wish I could do."

"You give me a smile and I'm wrapped up in your magic..."

"You've already done so much, Dennis. You don't have to go out of your way to impress me. I'm not that kind of woman," I said ardently, wanting to convince him of my authenticity. I already felt a bit embarrassed because of the way he was bombarding me with gifts. I didn't know how to take his benevolence. I wasn't sure what his angle could be.

"Well I figured this dinner would be a good start to my amends." Dennis said, cutting into his steak.

"Start?" I exclaimed. "I'd say the flowers were the start. This dinner is the icing on the cake."

An uncomfortable expression came over Dennis's face. "Denae, that's the second time you've said something to me about some flowers." Dennis looked genuinely baffled. "Did I supposedly send you flowers, or something?"

What?

I was taken completely aback. Now, I was thoroughly confused. If Dennis wasn't responsible for the flowers—then who was? Furthermore, if he hadn't sent the flowers, were the notes and candies from this secret admirer, as well?

Uh-oh. I've said too much. I needed a Twix moment.

"Oh… the flowers probably came from the staff at work, since I was out so long. I probably just lost the card, or something like that—" I was rambling too fast to catch myself. Dennis paused in mid-bite, staring at me with a raised brow.

"Okay," he announced slowly. "I can tell you one thing. You deserve all of the good that I can give and I'm gonna' make sure that you get it. That's just the kind of man that I am."

"Obviously, he's not the kind of man to send love notes and chocolates in the mail. I told you this was a bad idea," Alisha perceptively interjected.

'Alisha, you are not invited to this dinner,' I internally proclaimed.

"Are you sure that you are invited yourself? This could be another hoax from your anonymous lover. You really got punked."

"Denae, is something wrong?" Dennis interrupted my inner mayhem with the soothing rumble of his velvety voice.

"No. Nothing's wrong. Everything is perfect." I smiled and leaned in. Elbows on the table. Look interested.

I had to resort back to my pimp tool kit. After all, I had left the table, and for that matter—the building. I was off, in my mind, to all the places that this mystery could take me. It didn't take long for my exploration to find its desired destination—

Rayshaun

"Nothing but the best for my lady," Dennis mouthed the words, but Ray's voice resonated in my head. I felt like running out of the restaurant screaming, but I stayed bolted to my seat out of respect for Dennis. After all —I could be wrong. That's not even Rayshaun's style, but...

What other explanation could there be?

I centered my focus and applied myself to enjoying the delectable meal. Dennis was no Rayshaun, but he shouldn't have to be. Rayshaun in many ways was just as flawed as Dennis. However, Dennis makes me feel individually special and unique. He flaunts me around like his most prized possession. He wants me to be his woman and not just his concubine. But unlike Rayshaun, Dennis is equally as interested in my well-being and happiness as his own.

At least, that's what I'll keep telling myself... for now.

* * *

"Okay, Ray. Now it's gone too far."

Ray stood in the doorway of his place with a smile—that *prize*-winning smile—on his face.

Another week had gone by. My mysterious wooer was stepping up his game with antics that ranged from the endearing to the embarrassing: such as sending a singing telegram to belt out "Forever My Lady" at my office and stashing an engraved, sterling jewelry box filled with candy necklaces in the planter box on my patio porch—just to name a few. After I found an enormous stuffed animal strapped into the backseat of my Impala, I figured it was worth the risk of possible humiliation to investigate Rayshaun as a possible suspect.

"If I knew the life-sized panda bear was all it took to get you over here, I would have sent him first," he declared smugly.

After heaving the bear out of the car and up the walkway on my back, I couldn't assemble enough might to haul the bear inside of Ray's Brownstone, so I left him out on the stoop and went inside.

"So *you* are the one that's responsible for all of this?"

"Who else would be?" Ray's eyes twinkled with exhilaration. He was thoroughly enjoying my vexation. "Is there something you want to tell me, Denae?"

"No... What I do now is none of your business."

Ray rolled his eyes. "I meant, thank you. I think *thank you* would be an appropriate response." Ray paused for a reply, but he didn't get one. "Well, I've got something else for you, Denae." Ray extended two closed fists towards me. "Can you guess which hand?" he asked playfully.

I didn't know how to take Ray's behavior. He was lighthearted and mischievous, just like in the beginning, before that first illicit night. This was how I came to love him, but I couldn't let my guard down now. Ray had gone too far and even he could see his wrong— but it's too late.

"Stop it, Ray."

"Stop what?"

"Stop acting like nothing happened."

"Why don't *you* stop acting like something *did* happen." Ray paused again, then whispered tenderly, "Unless there's something you have to tell me, sweetheart."

"Look, Meisha may have backstabbed me, but I am not into that. Whatever you two have going on, I don't want any part of it."

"Whoa, whoa. That's where you're wrong. I don't have **anything** going on with Meisha."

"Ray, I've seen you kick that game to those dim-witted, hard-up females you deal with, but I'm not slow," I said defensively with my arms crossed over my chest.

"Awww, sweetie," Ray pinched my cheeks. I pulled away from his touch. "You're *so* sexy when you're mad." His eyes displayed a hint of the yearning that we always feel when we are near each other.

"Come here." Ray sat down on his cream loveseat. He patted the cushion next to him, beckoning me to come. I sat on the sofa instead. "I'm going to tell you the whole ridiculous story, then you can decide for yourself what you want to believe."

"I really don't want to know what happened, Ray." I said, dismissively.

"Well you're going to hear this." Ray's tone was forceful. "I worked too hard getting you over here for it to go down like that."

Rayshaun told me that Meisha showed up at his door, after leaving Lanelle and Juniece at *Thrive*. "I wouldn't have let her in, but she swore that she was having car trouble and needed to use my phone to call for roadside assistance."

"She has a cell phone." I replied intently, tapping on his forehead.

"It was inconveniently—or maybe conveniently—dead, according to Meisha," Ray said, brushing my fingers away.

He continued on to say that he let her in and she made a "phone call". Ray said that they struck up random conversation while she waited. He asked Meisha how I had been. She disclosed to him that she had been with me that night and that I had left with some dude named Dennis. "At first, I was upset but then I remembered —this is *Meisha*, so I suspended judgment." Ray lingered on the comment for a minute, searching my face for any expression changes.

I continued to gaze at him as blankly as before.

He resumed his tale, recounting that next she pulled a Steve Urkel klutz move and spilled a whole cup of soda on her blouse and pants.

"Do you *really* expect me to believe that, Ray?"

"Believe what you want to, Denae. I can only tell you what actually happened."

"I saw her coming out of your bedroom—*Our* special place..." I couldn't mask the heartache in my voice.

"Yeah," Ray said, scratching his head. "I saw that too. I think that was some extra show she put on just for you, cause when I answered the door, she was sitting on the couch. She was never in that room with me, and she was out of the door like forty-two seconds after you left... After a stunt like that, I practically threw her triflin' ass out."

"I stayed on that stoop for a good minute and Meisha didn't come back out."

"Now c'mon. I wasn't gone send her out into a lion's den like that and then have to come bail you out of jail," Ray waved his hand dismissively. "Besides, you shouldn't be fighting in your condition."

"What do you mean by—*my condition*?" I inquired with suspicious eyes.

"You mean, you really still don't know?" Rayshaun answered my question with one of his own.

I raised my eyebrows with a wag of my head. Rayshaun studied me with narrowed eyes, then opened his mouth. Only a breath came out before he closed it back.

"I'm just surprised that you don't know by now that you are emotionally unstable," he said with a sarcastic grin.

"Anyway—no sooner than you left, Meisha was on her way out too. Believe what I say." Ray leaned over the arm of the sofa to kiss me. With my lightning-fast, cat-like reflexes, I dodged his lips like bullets in "The Matrix".

"Come on, Denae," he whined. "You can't still be mad about this. I didn't do anything wrong."

"Then what's with all of the gifts?"

"They're because I miss you... and because you deserve them. I want to finally show you how I feel about you." Ray took my hand. "I didn't sex Meisha. I wouldn't do that to you."

"Why didn't you tell me all of this before?" The devastating tidal wave of nauseating remorse came crashing down on the shore of my heart.

"Would it have made a difference? You obviously don't trust me and you already weren't talking to me. Besides... I was angry with you."

"Angry with **me**?" I puffed.

"Uh... yeah." Ray asserted brazenly. "I can't believe you would even think that I could do some shit like that. Even in my whore days, I didn't smash girlfriends. Besides, Meisha is not my type. She's a high-maintenance, ball breaker. I wouldn't hit that with some other guy's dick."

Case and point

"Okay, now it's your turn?" Ray asked calmly, placing his chin in his palm and his elbow on his knee. "Who's Dennis?"

"I don't want to talk about that." I responded passively.

Ray walked over and sat down on the sofa beside me. "I knew you'd say that." Ray brought his arms down over my head, and embraced me. "It doesn't matter anyway. He's not me."

"That's for damn sure," Alisha cooed.

Ray's arms surrounded me in comfort—the kind that can only come from a lover who has charted the entire continent of your mind, body and soul. He knows me. I'm still not sure what I mean to him but I know what he means to me... **Total Ecstasy.** I didn't resist his advance, even though I wanted to. Damn, did I want to. But his hold dissolved my willpower.

"Whatever happened, it's all my fault anyway." Ray whispered in my ear. "I shouldn't have let you get away from me." His warm breath on my neck was like a match to a wick, igniting my desire for him.

'Wait... What did he just say?'

"What did he just say?... That pussy pressure must be a bitch. It's gone completely to his head."

"You had four years, Ray... Four *long* years to show me what I meant to you." Tears began to stream down my face. I wasn't upset. I was just disappointed— and mostly in myself.

"I know, baby. You're right. I fucked up and I'm *so* sorry." Ray kissed my cheeks. "Just give me the chance to win you back. I'm a changed man. Start over with me. Please forgive me, Denae."

My heart broke and I began to cry— to sob even. He held me against his chest, lifting my legs up into his lap. I curled up in the fetal position, like a child. We stayed that way for quite some time while he comforted me.

"You still didn't guess which hand?"

"What are you talking about?"

Ray extended his closed fists again.

I touched the left hand.

Ray opened an empty hand.

I tapped the right hand.

He opened another empty hand.

"What's that supposed to mean, Ray?" I giggled through the tears, wiping away the drops that hung from the tip of my nose.

"It means that you got me." He placed both of his hands on my face and pressed his forehead to mine. He closed his eyes and his expression turned solemn. "I'm yours, Denae." He kissed me more tenderly than I could ever remember. He pecked a few more, tiny kisses on my tear-streaked cheeks, before looking me in my eyes.

"Okay now, c'mon. Let's go get Dennis." Ray declared, patting my legs.

I stared at Ray apprehensively.

"Dennis... That's the bear's name."

* * *

I already know what you're thinking, so I will answer all of your questions in order of importance:

Yes, I did give Ray some action. (C'mon, he earned it.)

Yes, it was great—indescribably mind-blowing to be exact.

No, I won't stop seeing Dennis... for now.

Yes, I am in completely over my head.

No, I don't have any idea who or what I really want.

Yes, I am afraid that I could lose them both.

I think that about covers it.

Now, to hell with it—

May the best man win.

PART V

THE PROPHECY

Safety in Lovers

Devian Nikei

Self-Fulfilled Prophecy

"See, y'all don't seem to understand—"

'Okay, here we go again.'

"I was on my way to the urinalysis appointment, but my girl went into labor."

"Mr. St. James, it's your responsibility to make sure that you report for all of your appointments. Those are the terms of your probation."

"Hey, I'm doing the best I can. I'm a man—not some kind of machine."

"Mr. St. James, this is the third consecutive time that you have missed urinalysis."

"But I been here for all my consults. I always let you know what's going on. I got a job. I'm paying my restitution. What else can I do?"

"Unfortunately, I have no choice but to terminate your probation."

"I can't go back to jail. Damn man, my girl just had a baby."

We might have a fighter on our hands.

You would be surprised to find out how many brawls have taken place right here in our seemingly serene office. We all love to fight, but only when provoked and necessary to compel compliance—of course. It's a pastime that brings excitement and satisfaction to our sometimes unfulfilling profession. It's great exercise and a wonderful stress reliever, both for us and the instigator. Don't let the news and television shows fool you, confrontations are almost always a two-way street.

No one gets as much action as Ludlow though. Mr. St. James is one of my neighbor, Officer Davis Ludlow's probationers. This case is probably going to end as many have before. Davis is a waifish, blond-haired white guy. He's a dreamboat—if you're into that sort of thing. But Davis gets tried the most often by the probationers out of all of us because of his pleasant appearance and demeanor. That White boy can scrap though. He is a grappler. Davis is into all that Krav Maga, Ultimate Fighter stuff, when he's not fighting crime for the Division of Probation and Parole. Mr. St. James didn't know it—but he was about to meet his match, if he bucked. Ordinarily, I would be poised and positioned directly behind the probationer's chair, should we have to *"subdue"* and *"restrain"* him, before returning him to the custody of the County Jail. However, today was different. I resigned my position to Officer Smythe, a robust, stocky milk chocolate colored ex-Marine. Officer Ludlow asked his assistance with the consult after my declination.

"Still not feeling quite yourself, Richmond?" Ludlow inquired, peeking over the top of our cubicle divider.

"Nah. I'm fine, Davis. I'll just pass on the action today. I've got a lot of work to catch up on. The last thing I need is another Use of Force Report."

"I know what you mean. Internal Affairs is going to start investigating me, if I keep tying all these guys up into knots," he huffed, offering a strangely amiable smile.

Okay, here's the truth—

I'm *late...*

No... not late for work again.

The *other* kind of late, and very late at that. I haven't missed a period since I was fifteen years old and even then, the doctors attributed the cessation of menstruation to athletics. Unless television remote presses qualify as strenuous physical activity, this could be a big problem.

I kept telling myself that it was just stress, after all I've had more than my usual share in the past few weeks. But week after week, the visitor never came. Even Rayshaun is beginning to notice that something is different. Lately, he has been completely insatiable, ascribing his enthusiasm to my new "thickness." I have become undisputedly curvy and tender to the touch.

'It can't be,' I kept telling myself.

I am almost thirty years old and never had even one slip up. The baby daddy drama has always been reserved for my television set. How could *I*—of all people—be experiencing this spectacle in my own life?

"*It's called **self-fulfilled prophecy***. *Deep down inside, you wanted this. That's why you forgot to take…*" Alisha began, rattling off her professional diagnosis.

'That's enough. I didn't ask for your psychoanalysis, Alisha.'

"*My psychoanalysis would've kept you out of this mess. Don't get mad at me because you shattered your own glass house with those big stones you've been throwing around.*"

I decided that honesty would be the best policy. I would tell both Rayshaun and Dennis the truth—you know, that whole practice what you preach philosophy. I deliberated on that idea for a few days, but then I appealed to my own better judgment and overturned the decision. I chose instead to keep the situation a secret until I could sort out this whole chaotic ordeal.

* * *

"Okay," Dennis started.

"What's *your* passion, Denae? If you could do anything you wanted, what would you do?" He raised the thick sponge, drenching my shoulders in soft, cascading water.

This is what I love about Dennis.

He told me last week to leave this day open. "Plan nothing and expect nothing but to be pampered by your man," was all he would say. Because Dennis works so much, we see each other regularly, but not often—maybe only once or twice a week. This was the first day that we woke up in each other's arms, with the prospect of waking up the next day—still together. We passed the day occupied in various imaginative, craft-like activities: canvas painting at the museum, flower-jewelry design at the

Botanical Gardens, cloud interpretation during our winter picnic in the park, and so on. It was so liberating. I felt like we were Bohemian hippies, completely unencumbered by space and time.

"That one looks like a giraffe," I declared, pointing up at the gray sky.

"Not a chance, it looks like a fire truck with the ladder raised," Dennis said, placing a grape in my mouth. "Okay, that one—" he said turning his eyes back to the clouds, "looks like a... rocket ship."

"Nope, you're absolutely wrong."

"Can I have my own opinion, here? This ain't Rorschach's ink blot test," he smiled. "What do you say then?"

I whispered in his ear.

"See, that's your problem. You've got a dirty mind." Dennis mushed my face. "Where's your imagination? You said the same thing about that banana cloud a few minutes ago."

We would have been content to remain oblivious to the hour, had it not been for the temperature dropping, as the daylight began to fade in the sky.

"Let me take you home," he murmured quietly to me, as he placed his thick, brown scarf around my neck and rested the pink Camellia blossom wreath that he made on my head.

When we arrived at his house, he placed the large oil painting he composed of me on an easel. The mural of my profile and silhouette extending up from a blooming black rose reflected the very essence of my image. I studied the painting while Dennis prepared the "surprise" he planned for me. The portrait was an accurate representation of me in every way; full of doubt and hope, dark yet beautiful. Each brushstroke was like an ode to the love he felt for me. I was amazed to witness what a gifted artist he was. I turned from admiring the painting to wandering around his house. I had never spent very much time there so on this occasion, I took the opportunity to do some investigative exploration.

Dennis's home should have an **"Under Construction"** sign posted on the door, but I have respect for the fact that he is a home improvement do-it-yourselfer. Everywhere there was evidence of his desire to elevate the status of his living arrangements. Dennis recounted to me that the house had been left to him by his late uncle. After paying the back taxes, he was able to purchase the house for next to nothing. Dennis appreciated the value and security of home ownership, but this property also gave him the ability to practice other hobbies that he enjoyed, like spackling and molding. There were some exposed beams in the walls, but the house was structurally sound. I found it captivating to observe what breathtaking feats he could accomplish from week to week.

"Okay, it's ready," Dennis beamed. "Close your eyes." He took my hand and led me up the stairway. I realized, at that moment, that I had never been to the upstairs floor before. Suddenly, Dennis swept me off of my feet, and then placed them down on cool floor tiles. "You can open your eyes now."

My eyes adjusted to the dim room, illuminated only by candlelight. We were in the bathroom. The bathroom—next to the bedroom—is my most favorite place in a house. It is the place of cleansing and renewal. I probably spend more time in mine, than I do anywhere else in my apartment.

Dennis set the ambiance perfectly for a night of passion. Stepping into his lavatory was like stepping into a portal to another dimension. The wide space was completely renovated. There were sterling fixtures with pearl inlay and crown molding around the ceiling. The onyx and bone colored, marble tile created eccentric patterns on the floor and walls. In the corner, there was a grand shower, enclosed completely in glass, with dual showerheads suspended from the ceiling like a chandelier. The centerpiece of the room was an enormous, four-legged vintage bathtub full of warm, fragrant water with floating rose petals. Dennis also transformed himself into a nude spa attendant complete with a brawny, hairy chest and my canary yellow robe on one arm.

"I guess I really don't know." I uttered, allowing Dennis to lather my body. "I've spent so much time trying to suppress my passions and impulses that I'm completely out of touch with what excites me." The shimmer of the candlelight danced in his eyes, as he watched me.

"There has to be something that drives you. If you didn't have any responsibilities or concerns, what would you most want to fill your hours with?" Dennis dribbled water down my arm, creating a tiny puddle in my elbow.

"When I was a girl, I loved clothing design and fashion. The only dolls I played with were paper dolls. I would draw my own patterns and then cut them out to dress my dolls."

"Why didn't you follow your dream?"

"I don't have time for that Dennis. Besides you are one to talk."

"Hey, I surround myself and fill my days doing the things that I love, even if it doesn't pay the bills. If you can waste all of your energy at a job, fulfilling someone else's ambition, then you can certainly carve out time to further few of your own." Dennis embarked on a trail of soft kisses that began behind my jawbone and made its way out to my shoulder.

"It's not that simple, Dennis," I replied in a hushed voice.

"It is that simple. No one is going to remember you for the job you did, or the possessions you had, but for the way you lived your life—good or bad. That's all that matters once you leave this earth. You've got this one life— so enjoy some of it."

"You sound like a new-age Zen master."

"Seriously, life without hope and aspiration turns people into machines or beasts. The machines become integrated into the establishment while the 'animals' are cast out and caged for the purpose of being conformed to the standard."

I gazed stoically at Dennis over my shoulder.

He smiled and let the conversation go with a tiny squeeze on my neck. He allowed his fingertips trace the swirling design of the tattoo on my back that span between my shoulder blades.

"I always find it strange that I'm the cop and you're the ex-con, but I'm the one with the tattoos."

"Not really, if you know me," Dennis whispered into my ear.

"What do you mean?"

"I'm not who you think I am," he growled lowly. I turned back around to study his face because I found his tone disturbing. "I'm not a thug. I'm not that guy. I don't knock anybody for scarring up their skin but I just don't feel the need to do it. I've got enough scars on the inside. I'd be the most tatted up man on the planet, if people could see them all."

"I don't think it's that serious. It's just decoration... more of an accessory like a bracelet or earrings."

"Yeah, but you can't take off a tattoo or switch it out if you want something else later on. Everyone I know who has tattoos have stories behind them. I don't want to be bound to my past like that and I don't like to call attention to myself. I think God made me fine the way I am. I got no need to add or take away from myself." Dennis shrugged dismissively. "I'm good on the whole tattoo thing."

"Why does everything have to be a cause with you," I said laughingly. "I feel like I'm dating Huey P. Newton or something."

"Nah, I'm not that guy either. I'm just principled that's all. My views don't govern anyone else's life but mine. I live the way I do to save myself a lot of headache. You have to know what you stand for in order to keep this life from swallowing you up. It would benefit you to be more like me."

"I don't need any pointers from you on how to live my life," I replied heatedly.

"I'm sorry, Denae," Dennis stated swiftly for my appeasement. "I didn't mean for you to take it that way. What I'm saying is that I hate to see you so stressed out. It's not good for the baby."

Damn... I mean, crap... Shit, shit, shit.

How could he know?

"Baby, what baby?" I blurted out.

"Denae, you can hide your feelings from me, but the cat is out of the bag on this one." Dennis pinched my chin. "Babe, you're glowing like a jack-o-lantern and eating like a mule. Besides, you forgot to flush the vomit that you left in my toilet last week."

I smacked my forehead. I could not find any words, though I diligently searched for them. My thoughts were scattering like roaches when the lights turn on.

"Denae, why didn't you tell me?" He stroked my cheek with the back of his hand.

"I wasn't sure myself. It still hasn't been confirmed." I started to rise out of the tub. Dennis gently pulled me back down into the water and hugged me to his chest.

"Well, we can confirm it, tonight. There's a twenty-four-hour drugstore right down the street."

"No, Dennis. I don't want to do this with you right now." I hesitated, dreading the words that would follow.

"It... I mean, the baby... might not even be yours."

'Oh, damn you, daytime melodrama.'

The words sound scripted even when very much authentic.

"Denae, I know that I was an unscheduled interruption in your life when we met, but from tonight on I want us to be upfront with each other. I want it to be official. I'm already completely committed to you, and now, with the baby coming..."

"Didn't you hear me? . . . This may not—"

Dennis clasped his hand over my mouth. "You're my baby. So if my baby's having a baby, then that baby is my baby, too."

I felt dizzy and faint. I wasn't sure if it was the pregnancy or my betrayal that was the source of the sinking feeling in my stomach.

"Honey, I don't feel well." I muttered the words lowly. Dennis lifted me up out of the water and carried me to the adjoining upstairs bedroom. It was equally as exquisite as the bathroom. There were sheer, chocolate-colored curtains hanging from the bay windows. The room was painted a faint turquoise (my favorite) color, with a paisley-patterned chocolate border around the top and bottom of the walls.

"I finished this room for you, yesterday. You deserve to sleep in luxury." Dennis said, as he wrapped my robe around my shoulders. "Do you like it?"

"It's wonderful Dennis."

Dennis pulled back the checkered, brown and turquoise bedspread. As I laid back, he lifted my feet into the bed and tucked me in. "You lay here and rest. Don't worry about anything. I'm going to the store and I will be right back." He pecked tiny, anxious kisses all over my face. "Do you need me to bring you anything back?... Some ice cream and pickles," he said jokingly, as he toweled off and slipped into his gray sweatpants. I shook my head. The thought of food made me nauseous all over again.

"Okay, then just relax and I'll be right back." He pulled on a matching hoodie and disappeared from the room.

Relax, huh?

'That's easier said than done,' I thought as I laid, unnerved and disquieted, in his soft, downy bed. It had all been fun and games up until now. At this moment, a life that had nothing to do with this madness was beginning to form inside of me.

What would I tell Ray?

Should I tell Ray?

It was always so easy to judge other people in this position from an aloof, detached moral high horse. Now again, here I am discovering for myself that nothing is ever really just black and white. Sometimes, I guess maybe there are gray or, perhaps even, diversely colored areas in this life. That sinking feeling consumed me again, before I plunged off into a light, fretful sleep.

* * *

I awoke with a start.

I wasn't sure exactly what had roused me out of my sleep, until the phone rang again. I didn't know whether to answer the call or not. It was still dark outside, so I wasn't sure how long I had been knocked out. After what seemed like a thousand more rings, I staggered downstairs and located the phone.

"Hello . . ."

"Sorry to bother you at this hour, ma'am," a burly, official voice came through the receiver. "May I speak with Denae Richmond?"

"This is she," I answered apprehensively.

"Miss Richmond, this is Detective Ronald Blazing. I need you to come down to the Police Precinct on Fair Street."

"What matter is this pertaining to?"

I had been summoned down to the precinct many times before, in reference to this parolee or that probationer, but how would they know to look for me here?

"We need to ask you some questions pertaining to Mr. Dennison Millsaps."

"What is this questioning in reference to?"

"Ma'am," he interjected sharply. "If you would please just come on down, we can discuss this at the station."

My mind raced through the possibilities, seemingly all at once.

Had something happen to Dennis? . . . Did he do something illegal?

Right at that moment, I began to realize that I didn't know Dennis nearly as well as I wanted to believe that I did. I wanted to imagine that the two of us could exist apart from the rest of the world— free from the past and hopeful for the future. But the fact remained that I didn't know any of his family or friends and none of his hangouts, habits, or vices. Dennis is a felon and ex-drug addict, by his own admission. I didn't even concern myself with what other details he may have omitted. I felt ashamed of myself as I drove out in the middle of the night.

Could I be connected with some criminal activity that I wasn't even aware of?

This affair has gone too far, and now I most likely have a child to think of. The confusion dust was starting to settle. I didn't know how my conduct would affect Rayshaun, but by the time I reached the station, I had decided that my relationship with Dennis was over.

* * *

As I sat in the OBGYN office, my mind was so preoccupied with activity that I didn't hear the nurse when she called my name.

Just days prior, I was at the police headquarters being questioned by detectives—some of which I had been professionally acquainted with before the incident. I could feel their eyes on me—judging me. I was seen as another weak female officer who had become smitten with a criminal, forsaking her duty to protect the community. It is **extremely** difficult for a woman to earn respect in this male-dominated field, and now I had violated the trust. I knew I would hear about this at work once the paparazzi snitches were done spreading propaganda. Not to mention the fact that this pregnancy would add raging hellfire to the blaze of gossip.

Dennis was apprehended as a "person of interest" in a home invasion robbery case that took place earlier that night in his neighborhood. According to Dennis, he had not even turned the corner when the police pulled him over. The officers told him that he fit the suspect description given by the victims and took him in to be interrogated by the detectives. Dennis submitted and went voluntarily down to the precinct. Evidently, he gave an account for his whereabouts, which included me as an alibi.

When I arrived at the station, Dennis was being detained in a holding cell. Maybe it shouldn't have, but seeing him caged up like an animal changed my perception of him. The detectives informed me that they had an eyewitness who identified Dennis, in a line-up, as the assailant in the robbery. Only my statement could exonerate him. I signed an affidavit declaring that Dennis had spent the entire day with me up until the minutes before he was picked up by the police. The detectives took my statement and thanked me for my cooperation with their investigation.

The absolute truth is that there was no way Dennis could have broken into a house and robbed anyone that day. He was definitely being falsely accused. However deep down, I knew that the investigators believed I was vouching for a thieving hoodlum. Dennis could not understand my aggravation at the situation, since he was innocent. Dennis believed that I should be glad to help him right an injustice and strike a blow at the system. I let him relish his victory and didn't rain on his civil rights parade by saying that—to them, he was still nothing more than a criminal with a crooked cop accomplice. To them, he was still deep in the pit of degradation and had only pulled me down with him. Deep inside, I felt he knew that anyway and maybe that was okay—for him. But for me—to be linked with the likes of his element, on an intimate level, had crossed over and created strife in my professional life . . . and those are two things that I never mixed—business and pleasure.

"Ms. Richmond," the doctor began. "You are definitely pregnant."

My sigh was an indication of both relief and despair. I was glad to know that the baby was fine but mortified by what the pregnancy signified.

"The baby appears to be developing well at this point. However, I am unable to determine the baby's gestational age based on the information you gave." The doctor motioned for me to lie back on the examination table. "According to the approximate LMP—last menstrual period information that you supplied, you should be about twelve or so weeks pregnant. However according to the fetal developmental chart, you could actually be a little further along." The physician stretched the measuring tape from the bottom of my breastbone down to my pelvic bone. "I cannot be even somewhat certain until we perform an initial ultrasound."

Dr. Kukreja paused as an uneasy look came over her face. Dr. Kukreja is a lovely East Indian woman. She has smooth skin the color of sienna and intense dark eyes. With her shiny, chin-length hair, I thought that she resembled the pictures of Cleopatra that I have seen. She came highly recommended by my primary doctor. My referring physician described her as courteous, but comprehensive, so I knew that she would leave no stone unturned. A fact that caused her to make this statement—

"I read your chart and found that the medical history information for the father of the child was omitted."

"That's a long story, Dr. Kukreja," I said passively.

"And not an uncommon one," she reassured me. "However, I must urge you to resolve as much of the matter as possible, for the sake of this child. Should any unforeseen complications arise, that medical history could become pertinent information."

After a thorough pelvic exam, Dr. Kukreja removed her gloves and helped me to a seated position. "Well, Mom. I will get you scheduled for the ultrasound. Get lots of rest and keep a well-balanced, nutritious diet. Remember you are not eating for two. You are eating what's best for you. I am writing you a script for prenatal vitamins. I will see you in about four weeks."

Dr. Kukreja disappeared behind the door and I disappeared behind my shame. Over fourteen weeks meant that the child definitely belonged to Rayshaun. However, twelve weeks or less meant spin the Wheel of Paternity. It felt like my whole world was crushed in that instant, then...

I felt them—The Butterflies.

My baby was making its presence known and for the first time, the thought of him or her made me smile.

PART VI

THE PROMISE

Safety in Lovers

And Baby Makes Four

"So, what are you going to name the baby?"

"Oh, come on. She's not thinking of baby names yet. She probably wants to find out the sex of the baby first, right?"

'Oh here we go.' They are talking about me like I am not in the room, again.

"She probably can't even think straight with all the morning sickness and hormone changes."

I had been banished—exiled to the Chicken Run. The department modified my duties because of the pregnancy. I had to work with the pigeons in Administration and Records. I was now reduced to the clerical and secretarial tasks that I found to be the most burdensome of all the chores assigned to the house Negroes. I almost missed Sgt. Bledsoe's plantation work compared to this reality show gone wrong.

Deena was elated. Now that I was officially in her section, she could keep me filled in on every unsavory detail of her Shakespearian tragic comedy of a life. The only upside to this extradition was that they were extremely compassionate and understanding about my excessive bathroom breaks and spasmodic vomiting. The downside is—

"Well do you?" Curtis beamed at me.

"Do I what?" The irritation of being snatched out of my meditation showed.

"Do you have any names picked out?"

"I really haven't thought about it yet, Curtis."

More like Curtisha. Curtis Jones fits in almost seamlessly with the ladies. A petite cashew-colored "girl", Curtis is the gossip anchor of the Administration block. He wore the collar of his fuchsia blouse flipped up, with a gray tweed vest and pants suit. His processed hair, dyed Beijing Black, laid down in thick, shiny waves on his head. Curtis has no idea how uncomfortable he makes me with his probing questions. He sat there glaring at me like Sally Jesse Raphael, with one fist cocked under his chin.

'Is he wearing eyeliner?'

"Alright then," I slurred awkwardly, as I left my desk to copy some files.

Throughout the day, I sat tuning out the din of clucking that constantly ensued around me. Every minute—no second to quitting time ticked down painfully slow. When the "buzzer" rang, I jetted out of the office, keys in hand, desperately seeking the comfortable quiet of my Impala. I jumped anxiously into the driver's seat and sank into its cool, leathery embrace.

Tap, tap

I was startled by the light rapping on my car window. Dennis's eyes were blazing embers in his head. Not angry, but not pleasant either. I lowered the window, but only about an inch.

"Don't do that, Dennis. You almost scared me to death. You could have been a car jacker or—"

"I'm sorry, but I need to talk to you and you won't return any of my phone calls."

"I've been busy," I replied flatly.

"Not this... *again*. Denae, you can't just shut me out—" Dennis placed both of his hands on the car door and leaned in.

"I wish that you hadn't come to my job. It's not the place for this." I glanced past Dennis at the flock of onlookers that had gathered nearby in the parking lot.

"Are you ashamed of me, Denae?" Dennis asked, watching the ground as he spoke.

"What?" the question felt more like a stinging accusation. "I... I—"

I... couldn't say anything more. Dennis had hit a nerve with his question and we both felt the pain. His jaw clenched, as he returned his gaze to my face. Dennis smacked the door before striding quickly away from my car.

* * *

I would never want any child to grow up the way that I did.

Being fatherless, on daddy/daughter days in school and church was a humiliation that I wouldn't wish on my most despised enemy. Out of respect for the child I carried, I decided to go make amends with Dennis. He could very well be the father and I did not want our relationship to hinder his presence in the baby's life. Many men would be M.I.A. at just the mention of a pregnancy, so I could respect his commitment to fatherhood.

Knock-knock

No answer

All of the windows in Dennis's house were dark. I felt the sickly, ominous sensation of déjà vu. I could not endure another Rayshaun scene in my already unbalanced emotional condition. I was turning to leave when I heard his voice through the door.

"What do you want, Denae?"
"I just want to talk." I held my face close to the door.
"So talk," he retorted blandly.
"I can't talk to you through a door. Dennis, this is juvenile."
"So is not knowing who your baby's father is."
His comment stung. A slow intensifying flame leapt up from the middle of my chest. I opened my mouth to unleash it, but then I stopped myself and turned instead to leave. Shortly, the front door flung open.
"Denae!" he called after me.

I didn't stop.

Dennis hopped across his yard and seized me in his arms. "I apologize. That was low."

"Let me go, Dennis." I said calmly, not wanting to struggle with him.

Dennis continued to hold me tightly to him, his arms wrapped firmly around my chest, pinning my arms underneath. "I just wanted to hurt you, like you hurt me, but that was wrong."

"I accept your apology." I responded gently. Dennis breathed heavily into the scarf that I wore around my neck. His hold loosened and he circled around to face me.

"Denae, I know it's too soon, but I love you so much. It's making me crazy. I'm losing my mind." Dennis rubbed his hands over his head. "I'm losing myself." I could see his breath as he spoke, his lips shivering from the cold.

"Let's go inside," I quietly whispered.

Dennis closed the door behind us, as I sat down on the couch. He stood by the door, arms crossed, staring at me. I dropped my gaze down to my gloved hands folded neatly over my lap.

"Well—" Dennis said crossly.

"*Well*—" I mocked sarcastically.

"Do you want to take off your coat and hat?"

"This is not that kind of visit Dennis," I said, not raising my eyes.

"Then what kind of visit is it? What do you want, Denae?" His eyes showed his bridled anger. "Do you even know?"

"Yes," I answered directly. "I want a healthy child and I want its father to be in its life."

"So is this what it comes down to? I thought you of all people would be better than this."

'What does that mean?' I contemplated to myself. 'You of all people,' the words resounded in my mind. I wasn't sure if it was offensive or not, so I dismissed the comment.

"You know what it is to be the runner-up. You know how it feels to be dedicated to someone who denies you. How can you inflict that same misery on someone else, just because they have the audacity to love you back?"

"There's no one in this room but you and me, Dennis." I pointed at him, trying to maintain a low tone. I don't know what my stress tolerance is anymore, so I attempted to be as civil as possible. "This isn't about anyone else. The reasons why we can't be together are ours alone."

"And what are they, Denae—the reasons, I mean? Nothing has changed about me since we met. You always knew what you had in me. How can you turn your back on me now—after everything?" Dennis dropped his arms. "Yes, I do have two strikes against me in society. Yes, sometimes it's hard even for me to live with the mistakes that I've made. I wouldn't want to drag anyone else through the struggles that I face, but I'll be damned before I let you treat me like anything other than the good ass man that I know I am. I deserve to receive the same love and devotion that I have shown."

"I wouldn't refute that. You are a wonderful, articulate man worthy of all the love that this life can bring you—"

"Don't patronize me, Denae. I've been nothing but real with you. If you want to leave, you can do it, but don't give me that consolation bullshit."

I knew it was time for me to leave. I could feel that knot in my stomach, which signals that I need to eat or puke— one of the two.

"You don't look so good," Dennis approached me. "Can I get you something?" He instantly fell back into his nurturing role.

"No, I'm fine. Just a little tired is all."

"You can lay down upstairs." Dennis continued, attempting (unsuccessfully) to sound nonchalant. "I won't bother you. I'll stay downstairs."

"You don't have to do that, Dennis. I'll be fine." I nodded my head, trying to stave off the vomit. "Seriously, I'm fine." I croaked. I stood to leave, but ran instead to the downstairs bathroom.

I heaved into the toilet. My stomach felt as though it was being wrung out like a wet washcloth. By the time I finished offering my sacrifices to the Porcelain god, my head was pounding painfully. I slumped down to the floor, clinging to the base of the toilet. As revolting as this may sound, its coolness soothed the fire that burned in my cheeks.

Dennis stood in the doorway, looking both delighted and disgusted.

"That's it. You're not going anywhere," Dennis said laughingly. He unfurled my vomit-splattered scarf from around my neck and slid my gray, baker-boy cap off my head. "I couldn't forgive myself if anything happened to you. You're going to stay here tonight."

"No... I... gotta... go." I tried to protest between the gags. I spun around to clench the commode again. I hate this part— all that's left to throw up is the stomach acid.

Dennis returned to the bathroom with a cool, damp rag. He dabbed my forehead, and then my lips when he was sufficiently sure that it was safe to do so.

I had come to officially break it off with Dennis and he had come to rescue me. I felt so conflicted. I couldn't imagine what I had done to earn such kindness from this man, but I also couldn't surrender to it either. He was so wonderful, yet so marred.

"Tell me, what can I get for you?" Dennis sat beside me on the bathroom floor, patting my back.

"Actually," I paused. "I'd really like some ginger ale and something to eat."

We both grinned widely.

"Okay, we'll get something to eat right after you brush those teeth." Dennis snickered as he reached for the pink toothbrush— my toothbrush.

Safety in Lovers

Devian Nikei

A Change Gone Come

'Our Father, who art in heaven,' I began my prayers, as usual.

'Hallowed be thy name. Thy kingdom come...' I knelt piously at my bedside; hands clasped together, head bowed. It is very early in the morning— not even a hint of the daybreak to come. The moonlight was the only illumination in the room. 'Lord, you know my heart. I repent of any harm that I have or may cause. My desire is to do your will and I can feel the change coming. I appreciate all of the ways that you bless me in spite of myself. Lord, I thank you and I love you. In Jesus name,' I paused to reflect, momentarily. "Amen."

I rose up from the floor. All of my muscles ached from my workout yesterday afternoon. I looked at the clock before getting into the shower— 4:15 a.m. I let the warm water run vigorously over my head and shoulders before lathering. I knew I had to hurry. I have to make this meeting before the sun comes up.

This is the last time.

I want all of this behind me. Denae and the baby have awakened something in me. I realize that I can't be with her and continue to live this way. I don't want to deceive her anymore. She works in Law Enforcement. If she knew that I was hustling, what little chance I have left to win her would be gone. I have been fortunate— hell miraculously lucky, up until now. My secret is still safe... but for how much longer?

When the police pulled me over that night, I was carrying a small delivery in my truck. The cops, however, weren't after that. They were looking for a thief, not a dealer, so they didn't open my toolbox during the vehicle search. That's why I submitted so easily and just went to the station with them. I didn't want to get all amped up about my innocence and blow my cover.

Denae doesn't know what I'm up to and I want to keep it that way. I love her and I want a better life for us, not to mention this baby—

My first child.

I almost smiled to think of it, but the rushing water brought me back to the issue at hand. I couldn't be soft, not right now. This was the big one. The deal to end all deals. I was done with slinging dope. This money was the last of what I needed to start my own Heating and Air Conditioning enterprise. I had the business licenses, bonding, and investors. I had receipts from all of my contracting "jobs" and several *customer* recommendations to cover all of the funds that I generated.

This time I left nothing to chance. I wasn't that same shermhead kid, from back in the day. I took the time to better myself and develop a full-proof plan. I used the first of my drug money to acquire my HVAC certification, then took a technician position within a local company. I learned the business from the ground up and developed into a sophisticated businessman, both on the job and in the streets.

My first order of business was to hire an attorney and an accountant. Their advice and supervision has helped to keep my affairs organized— and legitimate— at least on paper anyway. I never intended to make this hustle a permanent occupation. I became part of an intricate organization through prison contacts. My associates and I are all part of a loose conglomerate of enterprises. All of the companies involved are cover agencies for different facets of the operation. Some businesses are suppliers, while others are distributors and still others, launderers. The infrastructure is very complex, but I don't really care. All I do is drive and once I get my money up— I'm out. The less I know, the better. That's the way I see it.

I've kept it low key all of these years, denied myself the finer things, all so that I could throw everyone off the trail. Now it's my time. I have the woman that I want and things can only get better from here. Denae is my one and only weakness. I splurge all my affection on her. She is a gift from God, validating that He still loves me—that I am not beyond redemption. It hurts me that she can't see what she means to me, but I know that if she gives me the chance, I will die trying to show her.

I was feeling oddly optimistic in light of it all, but one thing—one meeting— stood between me and my dreams. I promised the Lord that if Denae came back, then I was done for good. My goals weren't unreasonable. I didn't desire to be a millionaire, I just wanted enough money to give my family a secure future.

I can still recall how hard I tried in the beginning to go straight. It just seemed as though I was damned if I did and damned if I didn't. If I put on an application that I was a felon, then I wouldn't get the job. After a while, I started to omit that information on forms. It still didn't profit any, until I finally landed a decent job, working as a shift leader at a regional sporting goods retailer. It still wasn't up to my standards and the pay wasn't that hot, but at least I was employed. I worked at that store for over a year. I never came in late and I never called out sick—not even one day. However, the very same day that I was promoted to Customer Service Manager, they found out about my prior convictions and fired me on the spot.

After that, I slaved on menial day laboring jobs only to collect mere pennies at the end of a backbreaking shift. For almost three years, I could barely afford to sustain myself and pay my probation fees. I begged and borrowed until I almost resorted to stealing again.

I couldn't live that way, with my destiny in someone else's hands. I only hope that God and Denae can understand that, and forgive me for what I have to do. Before leaving the bedroom, I stopped to watch Denae sleep. 'She's so beautiful,' I said to myself. I pulled the jersey sheets up over her shoulder before bending to kiss her cheek. I trotted downstairs and opened the safe that I installed inside the wall behind the mural of Denae. I grabbed my Glock from beneath the stacks of cash and secured it against the small of my back. I covered my head from the cold with a blue skullcap and threw on my black leather jacket before walking out into the dark, quiet chill of the early winter morning.

The stars were the only company out at this time of morning. This is our meeting time. The cops change shifts at five-thirty and mostly all the criminals have crashed by this time. No one is stirring except the law-abiding citizens, or at least that's the conventional assumption. I drove silently down the street. The only sound was the rumble of the truck engine.

I ride alone.

Most dealers have an entourage. They see it as a safety precaution. I see it as a liability. Too many cooks or "snitches" is always a recipe for trouble. I never deal with anyone that doesn't have just as much to lose as I do. I am what you call a *mule*. I just move the product. I don't buy it and I don't sell it. I don't ever carry large sums of cash on me at any time. All of my transactions are handled in advance through "contracts", if you will. Every deal I complete appears in my ledger as a freelance HVAC job. Deposits are made into my business account, by my "customers", then I get all of my delivery details (pick-ups and drop-offs) on pre-paid cell phones. Unfortunately for me, I had already been compensated for this contract before Denae showed up last night.

Right now, she is naked and asleep in my bed, but...

I am obligated.

She is on her way to believing that I am who I say I am, but...

I am on my way into an affluent Alpharetta neighborhood to make a drop.

I have tried ever so desperately to give Denae all of me that I could, so that she would never search for the things that I was hiding from her. I have never been so vulnerable and open to loving a woman so completely. I have to reconcile these two conflicting personas, so that I can live a full and honest life with her and this child.

I tried to push all thoughts of her from my mind as I arrived at my destination. I pulled into the driveway and took a deep breath before turning off the engine. I stared up at the lavish estate.

'Soon,' I thought contentedly to myself, as I surveyed the grounds.

Mr. Salinas is the owner of an upscale Latin restaurant chain. He is one of my regular "clients". His air conditioner or furnace goes out routinely, at least once a month to be exact. Mr. Salinas is a hot-tempered, Salvadorian widower who found that a sure way to keep his house full of young, beautiful women is to throw exorbitant parties, treating all of his guests to party "favors" and gift "bags". I could tell early on that Mr. Salinas was simply trying to numb some pain by sniffing lines of cocaine off the thighs of twenty-something blondes. I could identify with that loneliness. It was the very same void that I tried to fill with dope and violence in my youth. My job, however, was not to commiserate with Mr. Salinas, but to accommodate him.

* * *

All's well that ends well.

I "repaired" Mr. Salinas's unit and bid him farewell. He told me that my departure saddened him. He always said that he had respect and admiration for my business savvy. Mr. Salinas liked me and allowed me to deliver directly to his home because he recognized that I was well-educated and mannerly, not the typical drug dealer stereotype. He also knew that I didn't dabble in the product. What was ordered is what was delivered. Sometimes, I even tied up loose ends for him around his home— landscaping or painting—and nothing ever went missing.

Once last summer, he actually really did need me to service his air conditioning unit—all for an extra charge, of course, but it was a good way to pick up supplementary cash. I delivered to Mr. Salinas's home for about a year, before he trusted me enough to allow me into the inner sanctum of his life.

One day, while I was repairing the hole he made in his wall with a champagne bottle, he confided in me that he had lost his wife and only daughter in a car accident. Mr. Salinas fell asleep at the wheel and careened into a telephone pole. Only he survived the wreck. His wife was thrown from the front seat, and his eleven-year old daughter suffered such severe blunt force trauma to her head that her brain swelled. She remained in a coma for five days before the injuries took their toll on her body and she died. Mr. Salinas told me that he had not slept a full night without nightmares until the first time that he smoked a blunt laced with heroin.

"I took every kind of prescription sedative known to man," Mr. Salinas sighed. "Nothing any doctor ever gave me helped and most of it caused me to be so depressed that I wanted to pour the whole bottle down my throat."

Mr. Salinas told me that he wished he had died in the crash along with his family. "For many years, I felt like I had died, until heroin gave me my life back." Mr. Salinas let out a rich laugh. "I bet I sound like some strung out junkie making excuses for my addiction, huh?"

"You sound like a human, Mr. Salinas," I said empathetically, patting his shoulder. "Besides, I'm not the one to judge. I am the hustler—remember?"

Mr. Salinas was the first legitimate investor that I acquired. The fact that he was willing to be professionally linked with me, while knowing what my side endeavors were, boosted my confidence to pursue this project. However, *that* lifestyle officially ended with *that* delivery and I am now a certifiably changed man —

An entrepreneur.

* * *

I stopped my truck outside of the corner gas station by my house.

  I wanted to grab some orange juice. Denae's appetite has picked up tremendously, so I wanted to have breakfast ready for her before she woke up. Willie James, the proprietor, was at the counter as he usually is, unless his "no-good" son, Juney, is there. You could steal the whole store out from under Juney's nose.

  "Sup, Willie?" I threw up my hand and pulled off my cap in his store. I was always very respectful to him, even though the entire neighborhood treated him like the wino they knew him to be. I even locked up the store and drove him home one night, after I found him slumped over the counter in a drunken stupor. He was like the intoxicated grandfather that I never had. I invested money in my own company under his name so that I could siphon a few stacks back into his store every once in a while. I knew what it felt like to have everyone, including yourself, give up on you. The way I see it, we are all going to live until we die, so every day is another chance to improve.

  A few minutes after I arrived, Terrence Thigpin walked into the store, equipped with a forest green hoodie and brown backpack. His eyes were glazed over and he looked as though he was on autopilot. Everyone in the neighborhood called him, "Tigger" (or "Tig"—for short) because of the scars on his face and his high-yellow complexion. He was an exceptionally gifted rapper and lyricist, but the ghetto broke him, as it did so many youths before. He and I didn't come from the same world. Clayton County is a long way from Buckhead, socially not geographically speaking, but I had been that same guy not even ten years ago. I knew he was there to steal something but as long as he kept it inconspicuous, Willie James would turn a blind eye.

  Tig roamed languidly up and down the snack aisle. He browsed over the selections then placed a bag of chips into his fatigue jacket pocket. Something still wasn't right though. Tig didn't scurry out of the door. He continued to rove, almost pace, in the aisle. His aimless gaze turned into focused—but conflicted, determination. I wasn't sure if Tig was aware of my presence or not. I stood in front of the cases containing milk and juice, silently observing the reflection of the scene in the glass. My banging days were long behind me, but I still had enough streetwise to know that something was about to go down.

Tig walked casually up to the counter. "Give me the money, old fool." Tig swiftly pulled out his pistol. I crept cautiously towards the front of the store, crouching down to conceal myself within the aisle. "Damn, man. You hard of hearing. Get the register open." Tig pointed the barrel straight at Willie's head. Both men were trembling. I couldn't tell which was more afraid.

"NOW!" Tig screamed out, but Willie James was frozen in place, paralyzed by fear.

"Hey, Tig."

He spun around wildly. "Niggah, who the hell are you?" Tig aimed the gun towards me, as he glanced back over to Willie, who was still shaking. "I don't know you, man."

Tig's face was covered in sheer apathetic hatred. All of his muscles tensed with aggression. I began to imagine that this was how I must have looked that night, over ten years ago. The sun was coming up and light was spilling in through the storefront windows.

"Hey, Tig. You don't have to do it like this, man. If you need something, I'm sure Wills here will help you out—"

"Don't fucking talk to me like you know me, mane. You don't know shit about me."

"You're right. I don't know you," I said with a dismissive shrug. "But you don't know me either," I challenged with narrowed eyes. "I have been in the same place you are right now."

As I spoke, Willie James thawed out enough to move. He began to reach under the counter.

"Don't fucking move, old man!" Tig swung the gun back towards Willie James. Tig's hands shook furiously, as sweat dripped down his face.

"Tig," I interjected softly, trying to divert his attention.

"Ay, man this ain't no afterschool special. You can save your damn pep talk." I looked into Tig's eyes. He wasn't high. He was sober and extremely dangerous. His stone-cold stare portrayed reckless abandon. Tig pulled the hood off his head.

"As a matter of fact," Tig came towards me with the gun still raised towards Willie James. "Get your damn hands up, mane." Tig circled around behind me, where he could monitor both Willie James and me. He kept the gun aimed right over my shoulder, with Willie in the sights. "Since you wanna' be Captain Save-A-Wino, let me see what you holding."

Tig commenced to patting me down. He plunged his hand into my jeans pocket, only to collect about eleven dollars and change.

See—I never carry cash, and this is the reason why.

"Niggah, that's all your broke ass got?" Tig continued to pat. "Alright. That's more like it." He dug the ring box that I had been carrying all week, out of my other pocket. He used his chin to flip the case open. Tig carefully scrutinized the three-carat diamond ring. "This shit is beautiful," Tig said facetiously, in a distinguished tone. She must be a really bad bitch. Now I see why your ass is broke, but I guess she won't be getting this today," Tig mocked, dropping the box into his jacket pocket.

I didn't speak or budge an inch. I couldn't think of Denae right then. I got more than enough money to replace the ring. I was hoping instead that Tig wouldn't discover the piece secured against my back.

Damn, no such luck.

His hand ran over it, just as he was concluding his search. "You the damn police, ain't you? You a fucking cop?" Tig dug the gun's barrel into the back of my head. My nerves got the best me and my knees buckled.

Damn it, Dennis. Man up.

My heart pounded painfully inside of my chest. I took in a deep breath and exhaled slowly, attempting to contain myself. My thoughts escaped me, fleeing to the darkest of places. Then, an image of Dena flashed into my mind and sucked me into its vortex. I envisioned her, lying in my bed. Hair disheveled. The morning sun illuminating her smooth, dark skin. Denae was as radiant as an ebony angel, as she rolled over to search the pillow for me right about . . . now—

Pow

Darkness engulfed me. I felt a sense of tingly numbness all over my body. I wasn't sure if my eyes were open or closed. All I knew, for certain, is that I had hit the ground. The tile floor underneath my face was cool. The blood that ran down the back of my head was warm. I laid there, listless and semiconscious, amid the contradictory sensations that were beginning to return to me.

A bright ring, an outline of light, encircled the dark, and seemingly dense cloud that obscured my sight. My vision seeped in, foggy and hazy at first, as images and shapes came into view. Tig's voice became audible again. First, muffled sounds amongst a loud ringing noise. Then, slowly, I could perceive the distinct words.

"I told your punk ass to get down on the ground." Tig stood above me, with a gun in each hand. "You ain't gone get the drop on me today, bitch-ass, pig niggah."

I felt the back of my head. Tig pistol-whipped me. I remained on the floor. My courage drained from me just as the blood from that wound. All I wanted in that moment was to return to her.

'Oh, Denae, what have I done?' I asked, myself.

If I had only stayed there, in the bed with her, I wouldn't be here right now.

Damn . . . Karma.

The bell that hung suspended from the front door jingled as a fair-skinned stranger entered the door. An expression of unbridled amazement spread over Tig's face, as his Catch-22 turned into a Catch-23, right before his eyes.

"Don't move!" Tig barked at the tall, green-eyed professional.

I had never seen this guy around the neighborhood before and I could tell by his polished appearance that he was a long way from home. This fresh, freckled-faced pretty boy wouldn't last a minute here.

"Look," he started apprehensively. "I don't know what's going on here." He displayed his open palms to pacify Tig, who was now holding both guns on him. "I just stopped in for directions, but I can walk right back out of here. I won't tell anyone anything—"

"You ain't going nowhere, Red Man." Tig replied intently. Tig was playing a game of Glock eeney, meeney, miney, moe as he pointed the muzzles from each one of us to the other. He was visibly overwhelmed by the predicament. From the floor, I watched the newcomer closely. He shifted his weight from foot to foot. I could tell he was an athlete, but I wasn't sure if he was going to run or fight.

Whoosh... Flap

A pile of magazines slid to the floor as Willie James dove under the counter.

Bang

A shot rang out. The lofty intruder lunged at Tig. He grabbed Tig, only to find that he had met his pint-sized match. The tackle impeded Tig, but didn't level him, as the stranger seemed to have hoped. My gun slid loose from Tig's grasp as the two of them struggled over the other one. The man elbowed Tig in the chin and they both fell to the floor. I leaped to seize the Glock... or so I thought. Try as I might, my legs would not cooperate with my will. I scuffled across the floor, dragging my body on my forearms and elbows. I stretched out my arm, and reached for the gun. The tips of my fingers brushed against the grip.

I got it.

Bang

Bang

Bang

I didn't feel any pain, just the sensation of falling from a high place, even though I was already on the ground. I couldn't catch my breath. But then, here comes the darkness again—

A pitch black net rushed up quickly to catch me.

"Denae."

* * *

"Police are combing the area, hoping to apprehend the wounded assailant in a convenience store shooting of two local men early this morning..."

I awoke abruptly.

'Man, I hate alarm clocks!' I raged internally, as I rubbed my head. I took several deep breaths in, to slow the pace of my racing heart.

"Police report that both men were rushed to Southern Regional Medical Center. At last report, both victims are listed in critical condition. Police describe the suspect as a black male, approximately five-nine—"

I reached out, letting my hand slam down on the clock radio.

'That thing is loud enough to wake the dead.'

Bright sunlight poured in through the windows, stinging my eyes as I pulled the covers down off my head. I rolled over to find that Dennis was not at my side, but that's not necessarily surprising. Dennis is usually a very early bird. I was exhausted after the barf-athon last night, so I slept in late. My head throbbed with pain. 'Maybe I need something to eat.' I pondered. The whole pregnancy thing had turned my mind and body into a challenging conundrum. I could never be sure how I would respond to stress, scents, or activities. I was even too nauseous to make love to Dennis last night. After a soothing, warm oil massage to relax the tension in my shoulders, he spent the remainder of the evening kissing and caressing my belly between my vomit breaks.

'If you're sick all day and night, how can they still call it *morning sickness*?' I considered the thought while I laid in the bed.

"Hey, Dennis!... Dennis?" I yelled out, but only silence answered back.

'Maybe, he got called out for a job?'

It was a Saturday, so I didn't have anywhere in particular to be. But for Dennis, who stayed "on call" during the weekends, Saturday was his busiest workday. I moved to sit up in the bed. "Owww," I winced, falling back into the pillow, as hot dagger-like pains shot through my head.

"Something is wrong," Alisha buzzed in. She had made herself very scarce lately. No doubt, she was offended and hiding out somewhere sulking about it.

"Duh, ya' think," I replied sarcastically, as I clutched my head.

"Not that. It's something else." Alisha's tone indicated her panic. When I threw back the covers, I saw it —

Blood smeared on my thighs and on the sheets.

"Oh God. No... no," I gasped, holding the round pouch that had developed under my navel.

"Get to the hospital now," Alisha bellowed.

I pulled on my robe and staggered to my feet. I wobbled as I took unsure steps forward. I steadied myself against the wall and carefully shuffled my feet across the floor. But then, before I could establish my footing, darkness engulfed me and I fell forward into oblivion...

Safety in Lovers

Chances Are...

"How is she?"

"Well, she's fine. She's stable."

"How long has she been out?"

"A few hours now. She was barely conscious when she arrived, but once she came to, she began raving uncontrollably, so the ER attendants sedated her."

"But what could have happened to her?"

"It's hard to say exactly what caused her to pass out. It's likely a combination of dehydration, exhaustion and stress. Her iron levels are extremely low... anemic even. But overall her vitals and blood work look fine. I want to keep her overnight for observation just as a precaution because of the fall she took. Then tomorrow she can —"

"What about the baby?" I croaked out, interrupting the doctor.

"Oh, there she is." The doctor remarked cheerfully, as they stepped over to my bedside.

"What... *baby*?" Rayshelle snapped.

Silence

The doctor was the first to break it. "Well, Ms. Richmond, I am Dr. Aiyagu," he started in a docile tone, sensing the tension between Rayshelle and me. "The baby is perfectly fine. The heartbeat is strong." The doctor explained in a heavy accent, probably something African.

"I have some questions for the obstetrician, whenever I can speak with him or her." I whispered. My throat was so parched, I could barely force out the words.

"Actually, I am the obstetrician on staff today." The voice of the small, raven-colored man boomed as he spoke.

"What exactly happened?" I struggled to a seated position.

"I don't know all of the details, but you were ambulated here after one of your neighbors found you lying outside of your front door. I was called to the E.R. after the doctor's initial examination revealed that you were pregnant. They stitched up the lacerations on your lip and brow—"

"Excuse me, doctor. I don't mean to be rude but I don't care about anything but this baby. Could you please cut to the chase?"

"We ran extensive tests, including an ultrasound, which confirmed that there were no signs of distress or trauma incurred by the baby."

I sighed, as relief flooded my body. Then suddenly, terror seized my mind once again. "I remember something." I felt the panic rising up in me. "Before I came here, I was bleeding from my vagina. Are you sure that everything is okay with the baby?"

"We did notice some minor hemorrhaging but it is unrelated to the pregnancy. More than likely it is a symptom of your iron deficiency. Although it is uncommon for a mother as far along as you are to bleed, it is not unheard of. Some women do still have menstrual bleeding even into their second trimester."

"Second trimester?"

"Yes. We determined the gestational age of your son to be about twenty weeks— give or take a week or two."

"It's a boy," I whispered, stunned and astounded.

"I apologize. Did you not know the sex of your baby?"

"That's fine," I replied faintly, as a wave of bewildering dizziness washed over me. I felt so lightheaded that I gently laid back against the pillows.

The ultrasound had confirmed it— this was undoubtedly Rayshaun's child. I could feel the baby moving in my belly for the first time. As much as I wanted to lose myself in the joy of this momentous occasion, I was agonizing over much more detrimental thoughts.

"Denae, you're pregnant?" Rayshelle asked. I wasn't sure if she was astonished or appalled.

"Why are you here, Rayshelle?" I asked gingerly.

"They called me, Denae," she replied.

"She was listed as your emergency contact, Ms. Richmond." The doctor interceded, only to find that his comment was not welcomed.

"I meant to change that," I said lowly, shooting Rayshelle a cold glare before allowing my eyes to drift off to the window, as I turned my head away from them both.

"Don't get an attitude with me, *Miss* Denae." Rayshelle mumbled out of her tensed lips. "Sass me again, little girl, and see what's gonna' happen to you."

A tiny giggle escaped my lips before I could catch it with my hand. Whenever Rayshelle talks like that, it's her way of making fun.

"I don't care if you are pregnant, I can still punch you in the face."

The doctor, however, was not amused by her humor. "I'm going to leave you now, Ms. Richmond. Any further questions, the nurse should be able to answer them for you. Make sure to follow up with your regular physician."

Rayshelle crossed the room and took a seat in the armchair beside the window.

"I didn't think you wanted to see me again." I whispered passively, with my eyes still fixed on the window.

"Well, listen to this, *Miss* Denae. I love you like one of my own. If you need me, then I am here. Whatever you and Ray got going on between the two of you is none of my business. If you and me got any rift between us, then *you* put it there, because I always treated you like flesh and blood, girl."

"Yes, ma'am." I answered sheepishly. Ms. Bivens could instantly cut me down to size, making me feel like a little girl who got caught stealing cookies from the jar. She didn't intimidate me, but she made sure to stay at the top of the respect hierarchy— the Alpha mama of the pack.

"You think I haven't been right where you are? I know that you and Ray love each other—"

I rolled my eyes followed by my body, as I turned away from her again.

"Sugar, you're just scared. You can try to run Ray off with that act, but you don't faze me, honey... Humph," Rayshelle snorted. "Both of y'all think because you got good jobs, nice cars and houses, that you grown. Can't nobody tell neither one of y'all a damn thing. You're both still babies who don't know shit."

'Oh, here we go again.'

"Rayshelle, I appreciate you coming down here to check on me and everything, but could you save the lecture for another day?"

"No, you gonna' hear it today, *Miss* Denae." Rayshelle rolled her eyes followed by her neck. "You look like you're in need of a good dose of wisdom straight from the horse's mouth. You think you know everything, but you don't know pain like I know pain. Rayshaun's daddy hurt me something awful. I didn't think that I could ever love again. I guess it hurt me so bad, because I never figured he would have done what he did on account of him being a White man and all."

"Wait a minute... Rayshaun's father is White?"

"Yeah... You couldn't tell to look at him?"

"Not necessarily. I wouldn't have assumed that." I searched for the right words. "I guess what I mean is that I never thought that *you* would date outside of your race."

"I think I understand what you mean. Times were different back then. It definitely wasn't the norm, but it did happen occasionally."

Rayshelle commenced to tell her story, "Let me see. I met Ray's father at the bus stop, when we were both only nineteen years old. He was a tall, *handsome* White guy, named Shaun Toler. Shaun had dark, brunette hair and these gorgeous green eyes. He reminded me of John Travolta. I called him *Big* Shaun, but I don't need to tell you why?"

Rayshelle giggled to herself, as I gave her a reprehensible glare.

"I was *so* in love with him. I had never been with a White man before and he was so different from any other boyfriend that I had in the past. I guess sometimes, we tend to judge people by the way they look. I'll admit it. I believed that Shaun would be a better man to me just because he was White. He was very intelligent, romantic and attentive to my every need. Back then we thought what we had was love, but we were so young. I know better now. It was probably just a fascination, more curiosity than anything else. It may have even been a little bit of rebellion. Our families didn't like the relationship, but we didn't care— we thought that love could fix everything in our world. We were together for over two glorious years, before I got pregnant."

"At first, Shaun was happy. We talked about marriage, but when he told his parents, they threw him out of their house. They told him that no 'nigger mutt puppy' would ever be a part of the Toler family. I could tell that hurt Shaun deeply, but he seemed even more determined to make *our* family work. We got a small, one-bedroom apartment together. Shaun got a job in a furniture mill and I had a part-time waitressing gig, after my nursing classes at the Community College. For a while, it seemed like everything was going to be okay."

Rayshelle sighed heavily. "Then more and more over time, he began to withdraw from me. He started staying out all night, smoking and drinking— something that he never did because of his Christian upbringing. The bottom fell out when he lost his job. He went into a *deep* depression. I was about nine months pregnant then. Rayshaun was due any day, so I thought that the baby would bring us back together." Rayshelle shook her head, and then stared off into space.

"I guess I didn't know just how bad it really was. I was in our tiny kitchenette fixing dinner one night, when Big Shaun says, 'Darling, I'm out of smokes, I'll be back in a little while.' He kissed me, before he slipped out the door." Rayshelle seemed to be searching around with her eyes for something invisible in the air above our heads. "Shaun didn't come home that night, but I didn't think anything of it. I finally started to worry after about three days passed and no word from him. I called the police stations and hospitals to make sure that nothing bad happened, but there was no trace of him anywhere. I went into labor that same week. Shaun's parents had a listed number, so I called them. His father answered the phone and said that Shaun was staying with them and wanted nothing to do with my 'jungle baby'. He politely asked me to never contact his son again."

Rayshelle covered her face with her hands. Her shoulders began to shake. I couldn't tell whether she was laughing or crying until she raised her head, patting away a few tears with a tissue from her purse.

"Ray and I bumped into Shaun at the grocery store when Ray was about five years old. He had two little blonde girls with him; one maybe four and the other one, two. He looked right through us like we weren't even there. I never told Rayshaun about it because I didn't want him to hate his daddy. I guess somewhere in the back of my mind, I always hoped that Shaun would one day want to meet his son. But after that, I told Ray that his daddy had died, because that day in my heart he did. The times I had with Shaun are still some of the best years of my life. I wouldn't do it any differently if I could. I got an immaculate son out of the whole deal, but the break up from Shaun left my heart utterly destroyed. I found out, in the end that being White, didn't make Shaun any better or even different from any other man. He was still human, and just as capable of all the same dirty double-crossing as any other man I had known."

"After he left, I was afraid to trust any man ever again. I let a lot of very good men go, for this or that reason, but it wasn't them. It was me. I didn't want to let anyone get that close to me again." Rayshelle touched her chest. "I never married. That was wrong and selfish of me to do. Because of my fears, my son grew up without a good father figure and that is something that every boy needs. I know my son. I know the man that I raised. I taught him a lot of good life lessons, but how to cook... and be a good man— those are two things he could never pick up from me. He has made some serious mistakes and suffered a great deal of hurt, trying to figure out on his own what it means to be a man. That's most of the reason he stayed with that tramp, Treasure, for all those years. I don't think he ever *really* loved her, but she was his first so he didn't want to leave her the way his father left him and me. After she got pregnant, he was as good as locked down. I kept telling him that she was no good for him, but he wouldn't listen. By the time he decided to get off of that rollercoaster with her, he was ruined. It hurt him dearly to find out that Preston wasn't his son... Which anybody could have told him that. Hell, a blind man could see that boy wasn't no kin to us. Don't get me wrong, we love him and everything, but come on now..."

Rayshelle began rambling on the way she does, then caught herself. "Anyhow, I saw history repeating itself with my child. Ray became a fortress after the divorce, he wouldn't let any of us in, but girl you broke him down. If you walk away now, Ray might lose his faith in love, all over again. Inside of all that hurt, he is a strong, beautiful man and it pains me to see him like this. I know that he wasn't always the best to you, but it wasn't because he didn't love you. It was because he didn't know how. I can't say that I would blame you if you wanted to pass on him. I know you don't want your heart broken either, but—" Rayshelle paused, reflecting on something that was obviously too personal for her to share. When she found the right words, she began again. "Just give him a little more time to redeem himself in your eyes. If you could just be patient with him, you will see that he truly loves you. He's a good man, Denae."

"I can't take this right now," I mumbled, wiping away the tears that had begun their descent down my cheeks.

"Does Ray know that you're pregnant?" she asked plainly.

"No. Why should he?"

Rayshelle raised one eyebrow.

"Look," I licked my dry lips, trying to prepare for the abrasive words. "This isn't Ray's baby."

Rayshelle came to the edge of the bed. Her face was surprisingly gentle. "What does that matter? You and Ray aren't married. He's already taking care of a child that isn't his. He will forgive you if you tell him the truth. He will love you and this child."

"Stop it, okay."

"I know you love him, too. You should tell—"

"Stop it. Just stop it, Rayshelle!" I shrieked. "Did you come all the way down here to check on me or to vouch for Ray? He's a grown man. He can speak for himself. You can't fix this for him."

Rayshelle took a moment to compose herself. Her face showed the immense effort that she was exerting to taper her wrath. "Denae, I was already here with Ray when I got the phone call about you," she said in a low, mechanical tone.

"Why? What's wrong with Ray?"

"Look sugar, you need to get some rest. Now is not a good time to give you this kind of news. I'm going to come pick you up tomorrow. We'll talk about it after they discharge you."

"You've already said everything you wanted to say without any regard for my condition. So go ahead, ask the cat for your tongue back and spit it out." Rayshelle and I have enough love between us to act as anti-venom for all the vile things that we say to each other.

"Rayshaun was shot earlier this morning."

"What?" I gasped. My chest started to burn as I choked on painful breaths.

"He's fine. He's perfectly fine, Denae," she reassured me. "He came out of surgery about a half-hour ago and he is resting in a recovery room a few floors down. The doctors say that he's doing very well."

"What happened?"

"I haven't had a chance to talk to him yet, but I will tell you what I know. He was on his way to some workshop or something in Clayton County, when he stopped into a convenience store.

Some thug came in to rob the place, and started shooting people. I always tell him to stay out of those parts of town..."

Rayshelle's voice trailed off. I couldn't hear her anymore. Her lips were moving, but the sound of my own heartbeat drowned her out. I began to sob uncontrollably. I was overwhelmed by the guilty feeling that God must be judging me, convicting me for my actions. The fact that Ray was shot this morning— just blocks away from where I laid, with his child, in another man's bed— seemed more like a condemnation of sin, than a coincidence. I never even considered that my conduct would cost the people around me so much.

"I knew I shouldn't have told you." Rayshelle handed me some tissues from the bedside table. "You okay, sweetheart?"

"Yes," I blabbed out between sniffles. "I'm fine." I calmed myself quickly. I knew that Rayshelle had no idea of the remorse that was drowning me right before her eyes. I couldn't be certain, but I was beginning to believe that Ray must have gone there to look for me.

'Why else would Ray be in Clayton County?' I pondered.

"Well, look on the bright side. They say Ray and that Dennis Millison guy are like heroes or something—"

"What did you say?"

"I said that Ray is a hero—"

"No, you said a name. Who else was involved?"

"Some Dennis or Donnie character. I don't know." Rayshelle was staring at me inquisitively. I saw the wheels turning in her head, as she studied the shocked expression on my face. "Do you know him?" Rayshelle asked.

"No . . . No, of course not. It's just the investigator in me— occupational hazard, I guess." I shrugged the comment off casually.

"We can go and visit with Ray after you're discharged tomorrow." Rayshelle said cheerfully, rubbing my leg.

"Hey, no offense Rayshelle but I am not ready to see him yet."

Rage flashed in her eyes. "What?... My son almost lost his life and you don't even want to—" Rayshelle held her tongue. She gulped slowly as if trying to extinguish a blaze stirring up from her gut.

"I just don't think it would be a good idea... considering the situation."

"That's fine, Denae," she said with a tone of resignation. "Perfectly fine, if all you care about is yourself. I'll be back in the morning to pick you up. But for now, I am going back downstairs with my son. *I want* to be there when he wakes up," she emphasized. Rayshelle gathered her jacket and pocketbook from the armchair before clopping swiftly out of the room.

* * *

I spent the entire evening essaying to find out as much about the shooting as I could.

I became a scavenger for details, collecting tidbits from the television news reports to the hushed conversations of nurses at the station right outside of my door. To my astonishment, from what facts I could gather, both Rayshaun and Dennison were shot at the Gas-n-Go, earlier that morning. The gunman had also been shot by Dennis. The police apprehended him hours later, bleeding profusely, just blocks away from the scene of the crime.

Ray had surgery to remove a bullet from his shoulder and he was recovering fine. Dennis, on the other hand, was in a much graver situation. I couldn't get a comprehensive picture of his condition, but I overheard it said, "Chances are... he won't last the night".

Many of the medical staff did not believe that Dennis could survive to the next day. I tried to convince my charge nurse to allow me out of my bed to go see him, but he insisted that the doctor's orders be followed to the letter. I tried, a couple times, to sneak out of the room, but I was caught by a nurse before I could get down the hallway. They told me that the physicians would reevaluate me in the morning and at that time, I should be permitted to walk, but in the meanwhile, bed rest was the order.

I agonized all night long.

What if tomorrow is too late?

I couldn't help but see this turn of events as a divine judgment against me. The two men I cared for were both gunned down in the same instant. How am I supposed to take this? It feels so surreal. What are the chances that something like this could even happen?

Yet, it did happen

I felt so helpless. Trapped in my own black widow's web, which threatened the lives of two men who challenged me to love not only them, but also myself. They both taught me something I never knew before—that I was worthy of being adored.

I delved deep into myself, needing to purge my spirit of all the hurt that had imprisoned me. 'Why have I remained the quintessential *outsider* looking in?' Just an observer, even in my own life— watching everything, but never really experiencing anything. I treated everyone else like a stranger when it was my own self that I had estranged. All of the recent events had caused me to realize that I didn't really know myself at all. I cycled back in my mind, through all of the memories, to the place where my faith and hope was lost, then replaced with mistrust and unbelief...

I was molested several times as a girl by my mother's various revolving boyfriends. Some of them were sleazy, "come and sit on my lap" smooth talkers with candy in hand. Others were aggressive drunkards who believed that they were entitled to the *package deal*, if they were expected to help provide for me. After a while, I began to think that something was wrong with me. *Why did these men keep touching me?* I thought it was my fault, so I wore baggy clothes and became even more detached and independent than any child should ever be—exposed too young and grown too fast. Soon, even the one relationship that I did put my confidence in was shattered.

My mother did have poor judgment in men but her number one priority was always my protection. That is, until she met Vaughn Mitchell.

I was about seventeen, when he came into our lives. Vaughn was in his mid-fifties — a tall, toffee-colored man with blue-gray eyes. He was well built for his age and wore a pharaoh-like beard with a gray streak in his wavy, shoulder-length hair. An ornate man, he always wore elaborate rings on his fingers from the pointer to the pinky. Vaughn was a pleasant, even-tempered man— cultured, cultivated and worldly. Mama felt that she had hit the mother lode with him. Although Vaughn lived at home with his wife, he routinely lavished my mother with gifts, out-of-town trips and tons of affection. Although he made me somewhat uncomfortable with his slimy, used-car salesman demeanor, I had never seen her happier. I reserved my judgment about Vaughn, wanting my mother to experience all the bliss that my birth had deprived her of.

My mother was my best friend. So when one of her men got fresh with me, I always let her know. With Vaughn, it was different. I kept it to myself the first few times that he accidentally "brushed" my bottom. I didn't want to continue to be the reason why my mother had to remain alone or with men that didn't truly please her. So when his brush turned into a pinch, then the pinch to a grab, I decided, for the first time, to take matters into my own hands.

I confronted Vaughn.

"I think it's very inappropriate for you to disrespect my mama this way."

"Girl, what are you talking 'bout?"

"You know what I'm talking about," I replied calmly. Vaughn put his glass down on the end table and sat forward on the sofa.

"Well, what you plan to do about it?" He said, licking his lips as he stroked his beard. Vaughn surveyed my entire body, toe to chest before looking me directly in the eyes.

"If it stops now, then it ends here. If it continues, then I'll have to tell her."

Vaughn burst into hearty laughter. His shoulders shook as he doubled over. He slapped his knee and wiped his eyes, as he huffed out the last of his amusement.

"I'd better stop playing with your boney, Black ass. You taking this shit too personal." Vaughn stood up from the sofa. His shirt fell open, exposing his hairy chest. He walked up close to me and grabbed a handful of his crotch. "Trust me little girl, you ain't grown enough to handle a man like me, but if you ever need someone to make a woman out of you. Ya' know... teach you a thing or two, then you know where to find me."

Vaughn's commentary was insulting and offensive. It left a bad taste in my mouth, but I believed that I had said enough to make my protest known. At least— that is—until I got home from work the following evening:

My mother met me in the driveway. "Denae, what the hell are you trying to do?" she hissed sharply.

"What Ma? What did I do?"

"Vaughn told me that you were coming on to him."

"I don't know what that asshole told you, but—"

"You will not talk to me like that. You will respect me and Vaughn."

"What?" I howled. "That bastard's been coming on to me."

"Denae, it's the same story every time I find somebody decent. Don't you want me to be happy?" Tears began to stream down my mother's face. "I can't bring your daddy back. I would think that you are over that by now. You're almost grown."

"Mama, this has nothing to do with that. I swear Vaughn has been touching me for months now."

"That little bitch is lying. I don't want no chap." Vaughn called from the porch.

"Go in the house!" my mom yelled back at him. "Let me handle this."

Vaughn stared directly at me. He had a slight amusement in his eyes as he threw back the vodka in his glass. Satisfied with the havoc he caused, he stepped quietly back into the house.

"It's always been just you and me. I didn't tell you this time because I didn't want to hurt you, but he is trying to come between us." I pled with my mother, holding her hands in mine.

"I think I'm starting to see what's going on here," my mother nodded compassionately. "You're jealous, Denae. All these men can't possibly want you. You just ain't that damn special. You've been coming on to my men, then blowing the whistle so that I would get rid of them. You want to keep me all to yourself." A look of disgust came over my mother's face.

"Okay... Now you're losing it. You done let the dick go to your head."

My mother struck me dead in the mouth. I could taste the blood that spilled over my tongue. I staggered back for a second, astonished by the strength of the blow.

"I know you ain't no damn virgin, Denae, but I'm not going to have no competition up in my house. If you grown enough to have all that damn mouth and straddle my men, then get your hot ass out of my house."

So that's what I did.

I stayed with my aunt for three days, until she talked my mom into taking me back in the house. My mom and I had a long discussion. We laughed. We cried. We hugged. It seemed as though all of the hurt and offense could be mended and reconciled until she dropped the bomb that she was going to continue to date Vaughn. I knew that I only had eight months until I went off to college, so I made myself extremely scarce. School, work and the library became my home. I only came to the house to sleep, shower and change. In those days, I excelled even more in my studies and was a model employee willing to work late shifts even on school nights. My guard was never down. My defenses were always up. However, that didn't stop Vaughn from planning his attack.

Life was good for the next six months. I had even developed a steady relationship with a blond-haired, blue-eyed White boy named, David Lee. He was only a few years older than me, but the first guy I ever dated who had his own place. Most nights, I stayed over at his apartment. My mother didn't seem to mind so much, as the arrangement gave her more time and less tension with Vaughn. Then one night, David and I had an argument. It was late, so I had no other alternative than to return home. To my relief, when I arrived the entire house was dark and the driveway was empty. I came in, pulled off my jeans and crashed into my bed. That was the first night I left the padlock on my bedroom door unsecured since I had installed it months prior. But that night I wasn't concerned with locks. I was a million miles away and oblivious to the world until...

I woke suddenly—

I wasn't sure what stirred me, until I smelled his scent, pungent and musky, in my room. I heard the lock snap on my door. Vaughn was walking towards me and I could hear him unbuckling his belt.

"What are you doing in here?" I said, bolting up in my bed. I was still somewhat confused and had not completely gathered my bearings.

"I came to get what I want," he declared smoothly. His bass voice made the skin on the back of my neck crawl. In the silvery light, I could not see his face, only the outline of his figure. He was within inches of my face before I could make out the cylindrical object. Vaughn stood over me stroking, as it grew in his hand.

"Open your mouth, little girl. I got some candy for you."

"Stop—" I cried out, but Vaughn clasped his giant hand over my face and heaved my head into the mirror headboard. The glass splintered but didn't break, leaving a dull ache at the base of my head, as stars appeared before my eyes.

"You need to calm your ass down and act like a lady." Vaughn pressed his knee into my chest, pinning me to the bed. He crushed me under his weight, as he reached down into my underwear. I felt his long nails scraping the tender flesh, as he poked his fingers inside of me, and then brought the syrup to his lips.

"Mmm, tastes good," he hissed. I could feel my breastbone pop from the pressure. My breaths shortened to shallow panting. "I don't like it rough, okay. So, if you promise to play nice, I will let you up."

I nodded my head. I could see the saliva glistening on his lips, as a slow smile appeared. "Just relax. You're gonna' love this. Can't no young boys make you feel like I can." He pulled up my nightshirt and then he placed a knee on each of my elbows. He ran the head of his penis up between my breasts and then over my chin and cheeks. "Don't bite," he whispered, pulling my jaw open.

I zoned completely out. It was as though I went into standby mode. My body went limp and numb, as I detached from all of my senses.

"That's *good*. That's a *good* girl," he chanted soothingly, as he cupped the back of my head. I felt as though I had drifted away, my soul hovering just above my head while my body stayed cemented to the bed. Time slowed and coagulated, seeping into all of my orifices like a thick, sludgy substance that began to suffocate me.

But then suddenly— like a hand reaching in to save me out of deep water, I revived long enough to realize that Vaughn had stopped to remove his shirt. While his arms were still trapped within the sleeves and his face covered, I mustered all of my strength and threw him backwards off the bed. He shrieked as he hit the ground. I jumped swiftly to my feet, clutching the key that hung on the chain around

my neck. I keyed the padlock and flung the door open, but before I could run down the hallway, Vaughn grabbed my ankles. I teetered forward and smashed down, chin-first, against the hardwood floor. I bit through my tongue and was blinded by the tears that instantly filled my eyes. Vaughn jumped on my back and wrapped his massive hands around my neck.

"Ma, Ma!" I yelled out, but only strained gasps escaped my mouth. My mother was passed out on the couch, only a few feet from where I was being tortured. I was closed to fainting when a foggy memory drifted into my head like a dream.

"You okay?" Mom said, helping Vaughn up off the floor.

"Yeah," Vaughn grunted. "This hip ain't been right since the replacement..."

I reared back and dug my elbow into his right hip. Vaughn groaned, then toppled to the floor. As we both climbed to our feet, Vaughn grabbed me in a tight bear hug from behind. For me, athletics had always been a form of recreation, not competition, but now it was a matter of survival—

I dropped down and gathered all of my leg power to drive him backwards into the wall. He slumped to the floor as a portrait frame smashed down on his head. I began screaming incoherent words at him, most of which I can't remember to the day. As I repeatedly jousted my heel into his hip joint, he writhed in pain from each blow.

I stood over Vaughn, weltering in victory when—

Whap!

My mother attacked me from behind, striking me across my back with a metal rod. She wacked me several more times, slicing the skin on my arms and shoulders, before I could wrestle the rod out of her hands.

"What are you doing?" I hollered at her. "Are you out of your mind?"

"This is my house and you are not going to run my company off."

"Ma, he attacked me." I dabbed my hands in the blood that flowed from the gash in my chin to show her.

"Damn you, Denae." My mother lunged at me. She grabbed my nightshirt and hurled me to the floor. She smelled as though she had gone swimming in a gin pool. She was so inebriated that she lost her balance and fell back against the wall.

"Come on bitch." She slurred the challenge, as she stood clutching a shoe in her hand.

"I don't want to have to hurt you, Ma— but I will."

"Is that a threat or a promise?"

She seized me and we tussled vigorously. My mom snatched up a handful of my hair and began to beat me in the face with the heel of the shoe. I pressed my forearm firmly against her throat, worked my foot up between us and kicked her off of me. I sent her careening across the coffee table.

She laid on the floor for a few minutes. I felt guilt flood over me, as I watched her struggle to her feet. However, the dread quickly reverted back to adrenaline, when she flew towards me in savage fury.

Then something unexpected happened—

Vaughn stepped in to intercept and restrain her. "Stop, Saydhe. Stop it now," he commanded. "Let her go." My mom strained against him like a wild beast caught in a trap. Her Farrah Fawcett wig hung off the back of her head. Make-up mixed with blood was smeared all over her face, rendering her almost unrecognizable. However, it was not only her appearance that disfigured her. My mother, Saydhe, was a picturesque light-brown skinned vixen with large, lovely doe eyes. She had often been compared to Diana Ross. Growing up, I was continually disappointed by the fact that I did not look anything like her. People even asked if I was her child. My features always seemed so common and ordinary in comparison with hers, but for the first time in all the time that I'd known her, I didn't envy her. My mother was as ugly to me as I had often been to myself.

"Fuck you!" she raged.
"Fuck you."
"No! Fuck *you*, **bitch**."

Vaughn's defense began to collapse. "Denae, you had better go," he stated calmly, glaring at me with icy blue eyes over my mother's shoulder.

"You ain't no damn good." My mother continued to hurl insults at my back. "You on drugs, ain't you slut?" I went to put on my jacket and jeans. Saydhe— as I would refer to her henceforth now and forever, Amen— stood in my bedroom doorway puffing, drooling, and bleeding. "This man don't want you," she drawled on. "Your own damn daddy didn't even want you." She spat out the words as though they tasted disgusting. "Ain't nobody ever gonna' love yo' old, ugly, Black ass."

I remained silent, as I laced up my tennis shoes.

"Leave her siddity ass alone. She ain't worth the energy." Vaughn added from his seat on the living room sofa, as he pressed a handkerchief against a cut over his eye.

"Sho' you right, Vaughn," Saydhe chimed jovially. I brushed past Saydhe, throwing her off balance. She reached out to brace herself and caught on to my hood. She tightened her grip, gagging me and drawing my face to hers.

"I should've aborted you— just flushed you down a toilet like ya' daddy wanted me to."

I yanked my hood out of her hands and trudged out into the darkness. I started to jump into my hatchback, when Saydhe called out, "Where you think you going in *my car*?"

I had paid every car note, tax bill, insurance premium, maintenance cost (you name it) for that car without so much as even one-penny's worth of assistance, but it became *her* car whenever all other means of social control failed. I launched the keys into the neighbor's yard and trekked off down the street.

It's funny how you can always stay over at your friends' houses, until you get into trouble. Then everyone treats you like the plague. "My momma said you can't stay" or "we gone be out of town all this month" was all I heard on the phone that night. I called every friend, relative and associate whose number I had, but the news spread through the grapevine faster than my fingers could dial. After the initial string of no's, only busy signals, answering machines, and endless ringing followed. I promised myself, as I curled up to sleep at the CATS transit station that would be the last night that I would ever trust anyone else with my heart.

I spent the last two months of my senior year, living in a shelter. Three times a week, I was required to sit in on support groups. I listened to stories (somewhat similar to my own) of abuse, fatherlessness, violence, and almost always—molestation. The rehabilitative benefits of these meetings continued to be lost on me though. Because, you see, I was nothing like these women. I wasn't a prostituting crack fiend. I didn't have psychological problems. I still attended school, worked at night, participated in team sports and tutored preschool children. I didn't grow up poor in the hood. I had nothing in common with them. At least, that's what I thought. I created a space— a tiny, dark closet— for all of the rage, hurt and disappointment that I felt. I threw all of my pain inside, bolted the door and destroyed the key. I believed I was as well-adjusted as (or maybe even more than) any other teenager. Alisha was the only one who stayed by my side through it all.

A few days after the police found me sleeping in the transit center and took me to the shelter, Saydhe came looking for me at my school. She pled with me, saying that she had no recollection of the events of that night.

"I thought you were staying over at David's, until I called and he said you two broke up."

"Yep."

"Are you okay?"

"Yep."

"Will you please come back home?"

"Nope."

She tipped my chin up to see the gooey wound underneath. "Well at least make you a doctor's appointment. You need to get that gash stitched up or it's going to leave a nasty scar..."

'And that's just what it did.' I thought, rubbing the smooth keloid skin, as I laid in the hospital bed. That day left more than just the small boomerang-shaped blemish under my chin, it left a soul-shaped hole in my heart.

Breaking Up Is Hard to Do

I spent the entire night in the hospital conducting a comprehensive self-inventory.

I couldn't sleep. Somewhere around midnight, the fluorescent bulb of the night lamp in my room began to buzz and flicker. I tossed and turned, daunted by thoughts that I could not repress. The baby, whom I was becoming acquainted with as a sensation of indigestion, kept me company. Thoughts of him drove me to search my soul for all of the pain that had caused me to be incapable of giving and receiving *real* love for all of these years. Rayshelle was right. I was the prison guard of my own confinement facility—not anyone else.

Not any one of the traumatic events, rejections or failures, which I could dredge up at the drop of a hat, had defined me—only I could do that. I guess one too many of those "ugly-little-Black-girl's" must have hit the mark and left a scar so deep and hideous that I began to define myself by it. It's so bizarre how the experiences that propel us on to success are the same ones that destroy us, eating us alive from the inside out.

I came to realize that somewhere along the way, I started to believe and empower the lies that pressured me into living up (or down, in most cases) to whatever expectations other people had of me. Everything about my life, from my job to my lifestyle, was a product of trying to prove a point to everyone else but myself.

In the midst of the profound wreckage, I was finally able to locate my closet. However, since I had no key (or clue how) to get back into it, I had to pull out a large fireman's axe and break down the door. I permitted all of the pinned up animosity, resentment and grief to spill out on to the floor.

Tears flowed like a river, as I found not only things that I despised, but also tons of things that I cherished were locked up together inside of that closet. I was surprised to see how much love I had lost, trashed even, to keep space available for my expanding closet of calamity. I pulled out a match and torched everything that I had exposed, deciding that I would start over fresh. I watched the entire closet go up in flames. I wouldn't wait for anyone else to give me a second chance. Instead, I would give myself the first chance to live. I finally realized that I, and my child, deserved that chance. I couldn't be a loving mother to him, if I couldn't be a forgiving friend to myself.

An interesting thing happened though. After the smoke cleared, I found that one man was still standing there, amid the ashes in my mind. One sole survivor of the inferno. One man that I had chosen without knowing that I did. One man that I truly loved without regard to his past. The confusion was finally gone and all that remained now was the apprehension—the question of whether he could accept me if I let him into my newly renovated walk-in closet.

Does he truly love me too?

I know that I will be more careful to decorate this space with only beautiful things, but will he want to share this space with me?

"Congratulations, grasshopper." Alisha said, interrupting my deliberation.

'Hey,' I mused.

"Welcome back. I love what you've done with the place."
A warm sensation, like a hug, engulfed me.

'Welcome back to you. You're the one that's been incognito,' I replied introspectively.

"Never that. I am always with you Denae, but you lost yourself and your whole damn mind, girl. I couldn't help you." Alisha chuckled. *"But I'm proud of you, because you did this one all by yourself, and I couldn't have done it better myself. You must have finally learned something from the **Master**,"* she vaunted.

'Yeah, yeah. It feels good too. I didn't know I was holding so much inside.'

"Yeah girl. It was all a big mess up in there. I had to get GPS navigation just to find you in all that drama." We giggled together.

"But this is just the beginning of your love affair with yourself. Once you get to know yourself the way I do, you will find out why so many people love you so very much."

"So many people?"

"Yeah... You've been missing out on a lot with that whole self-defamation thing you've been doing. God loves you and so do so many more people than you think. You are so very precious, Denae... So what do we do now?"

'Oh, so I get to do the honors? You giving me a drivers' license, now?'

"More like a learners' permit, but I think you've earned the right to be the co-captain of your own destiny."

'Gee, thanks.' I said mockingly.

"Ya' know. I do what I can."

* * *

Over into the evening, on the second day, I was discharged from the hospital.

Rayshelle brought me some clothes from home earlier that morning, but they advised her that it would be quite a few hours before my release, so she left. I didn't call her back. Instead, I asked Lanelle to come and get me.

During my bed rest incarceration, I learned from nurses that Dennis had survived the night and was doing much better than expected. He was stabilized and taken out of ICU. His condition was downgraded from critical to serious, and he was progressing very well.

Once I finished signing all of my hospital discharge papers "in blood", I went down to Dennis's room. He was laying there looking almost lifeless. There were so many monitors and IV's hooked up to him, all beeping, ticking and clicking in rhythm. I stood at the door, unsure of whether to enter or not.

"He's doing much better," a familiar voice spoke from behind me. I turned to see him. His emerald eyes were level with mine.

I couldn't speak.

What should I say?

"You look beautiful and well-rested," he continued. "How's the baby?"

Silence

"Rayshelle told you that I was here in the hospital, didn't she?" A puzzled look came over Ray's face. "I didn't know you were here. I just came to visit Dennis." I searched Ray's face. I wasn't sure if he was being facetious or not. Ray's right arm was in a sling. The bulky bandages were visible through his long-sleeved navy t-shirt. His curly hair was glossy and he wore flannel pajama pants with brown leather slippers. I couldn't believe that Ray was GQ'd up even for a hospital stay.

I looked away from him, returning my eyes to Dennis. Ray placed his left hand on my chin and turned my face back to his. "You didn't answer me," he said, touching the stitches over my brow.

"How else would you know about the baby, if Rayshelle didn't tell you?" I asked accusingly.

"Now c'mon, Denae. I've been making love to you for years. I *know* your body and I could tell that something was up. I knew that you were pregnant a long time ago, probably before you did."

I closed my eyes. I almost couldn't take it anymore, standing there between the two of them.

"I'll tell you what else I know." His hand dropped from my face and ran down over my belly. "I know that baby is mine."

I gave Ray a blazing look, before swatting his hand away.

"You don't know that, not for sure."

"Yes, I do... You were pregnant even before Maw-maw died. Up until then, you were all over me every day."

"If you know so much, why didn't you say anything before now?" I lashed out in a hushed voice.

"At first, I didn't say anything because I wasn't completely sure. But after that, I knew that if I said anything about the baby, you would think that was why I wanted to marry you."

"Well... is it?"

"Do you want me to be honest?" Ray asked with one eyebrow raised.

I raised both of my eyebrows, signifying an affirmation.

"Yeah," he wheezed, "but that was only a little part of it." I began to walk away, but Ray gripped my elbow tightly. "Don't go. Just hear me out." He drew me back to him. This pregnancy has taken all of the fight out of me, so I complied with his pull.

"I was going to propose anyway. I've had that ring for almost a year now. I was just waiting until the time was right. I was waiting on you."

"Waiting on me!" I blared out before I could contain it.

"Shhh." Ray glanced down the hallway. "Yeah, Denae. I know you're not ready for marriage. You don't trust me, or anybody else for that matter, but I reconsidered once I knew for sure that you were pregnant." Ray stepped closer to me. "I never made a big deal about it before because I thought that the pressure would drive you away. You seemed so comfortable with keeping things the way they were, so I didn't want to push for more and then lose you."

I was mortified by his words. This whole time I thought that he was in control and calling all the shots—that he wanted to keep the relationship open, but now, here he was flipping the script on me.

"When I saw our relationship slipping away, I hoped that proposing marriage would bring you back— but it didn't. The whole thing backfired, but I never wanted any of this. All I wanted was you. I love you, Denae." Ray placed his hand on the doorframe beside my shoulder. "My heart made that decision for me the first night that I was inside of you and nothing I do can change it." He leaned over to kiss me, but I turned my face away.

Ray's tone changed from gentle to bitter. "I'm sorry if that's inconvenient for you, but I don't know what else to tell you, Denae. I don't know what, or should I say *who*, you want."

"What's that supposed to mean?" I snapped angrily.

"Look I know what you've been up to, Dee." Ray glanced over at Dennis. "After he got shot, he was delirious. I put pressure on his wound while we waited for the paramedics to come. Dennis mumbled your name over and over again until he lost consciousness." Ray rubbed his hand over his mouth. He looked as though he said something that shocked him.

"I have to know," I started. "Is that why you were there?... Did you come to confront him?... Did you follow me?"

"Wow," Ray's eyes widened with amazement. "You're awfully conceited, aren't you?... And I thought I was bad." Ray scratched the back of his head and turned away from me. I thought he was going to leave, but then he turned back to face me.

"Did I **ever** question you, Denae?"

I shook my head.

"Whenever you came to me, was I there for you?"

I nodded slowly.

"I can't believe that you are this self-centered. Not everything has to revolve around you, Dee. I have a group of at-risk youths that I tutor in Math **every** Saturday morning, at the Main Library in Clayton County. I stopped at that convenience store to get them some candy like I always do."

In four years, I have seldom seen Ray get this angry. His eyes blazed as he continued to explain. "I'm only here now because I thought that Dennis might be awake, so I could thank him for saving my life." I felt my heart plummet down into my stomach as he spoke. "How can you know so little about me after all this time. I'm not that kind of man, Denae. He and I can't settle this. Only **you** can. You're the only one out of the three of us who still hasn't made up your mind."

Ray was absolutely right. The realization hit me like a brick and it was actually quite painful.

"I've already made my decision." I responded flatly and said no more. A look of acquiescence came over Rayshaun. His hands dropped dejectedly to his sides and his eyes moistened.

"Look if Dennis wakes up, can you tell him that I came by to see him." Ray turned and glided casually down the hallway and around the corner.

I brought my attention back to Dennis, still lying motionless. The charge nurse came to the door.

"Are you family?" she blared.

"Well I'm his—"

"Cuz' only family is allowed up here—"

"Yes," Dennis huffed. "She's family." The words seemed to be a tremendous strain for him. His eyes remained closed and his brows were furrowed.

"I'm sorry. Come on in then, Mrs. Millsaps." The nurse said presumptively. Dennis turned his head to see me and gave a grimace that was supposed to be a smile.

"Mr. Millsaps?" the nurse said, as she checked the large gauze bandage on his chest.

"Dennis... please," he whispered.

"Okay, Dennis. How's your pain? Do you need anything right now?"

Dennis gave her a slow thumbs up. Then the hand sign for okay.

"Is he alright?" I asked.

"Yep. He's the best patient we got." The stubby, red-haired nurse talked so inappropriately loud— like we were hearing impaired or something. "Isn't that right, Dennis?"

He gave her the thumbs up again.

"I'm talking about his condition," I looked at her name badge. "Pam."

"Oh, he's doing **real** good. He took a hot one to the chest, but the doctors decided that since the bullet didn't pierce any major organs, they're gonna' just leave it on in there." The nurse made me want to choke her. She was talking about Dennis like he was a fun craft project. "Barring any infection, he should be out of here and back to himself in no time. He can't walk right now though, on account of that nasty bump on the back of his head. The doctor's say that's temporary and he should regain the use of his legs, after a little while. Still though, he's a big fellah so you'd better be prepared to have somebody help you with him."

Dennis touched the nurse's arm.

"Water . . . please."

"I gotcha' there, Dennis. Give me a few minutes and I'll be back with a pitcher for you. Okay?" Her shrill voice still rang in the air, even after she left the room.

"Thanks," I sighed, pulling the chair up to his bedside. Dennis poked out his bottom lip and threw up his thumb with a nod.

"How ya' doing?" I whispered softly.

"I've... had worse... days," he labored out the breaths. "I... missed... you."

"I'm here now. I was upstairs, myself."

Dennis pointed at me, then made the okay sign.

"Yeah, I'm fine now. I was in pretty bad shape and didn't know it though. This baby almost knocked me on my ass."

Dennis patted his stomach, then made the okay sign.

"Yeah, the baby's really good and strong too."

Dennis pointed to himself.

"Yeah, just like you."

He grimaced a smile again. Dennis reached his hand over to my face. I gently grabbed his hand and placed my cheek inside. A painful expression came over his face.

"Did I hurt you?" I whispered, placing his hand back on the bed.

Dennis shook his head.

"For . . . give . . . me" The words took his breath away and he laid there panting. I reached over into the bedside dresser and found a small notepad. I gave Dennis a pen. He began to scribble away instantly. He didn't seem completely comfortable with writing either, but it was better than talking and he obviously had something that he desperately wanted to say.

He wrote:

> I made you and God a
> promise but I didn't
> keep my word.
> Can you forgive me?

Dennis tore off the sheet and handed it to me. I read it.

"Forgive what, Dennis? You're a wonderful man and you've been nothing but good to me."

> I knew that I wouldn't get
> away with it. I knew that God
> would punish me.
> I'm sorry for being so
> selfish and not thinking
> about you and the baby

"Honey, God did not do this. This was the act of some thug maniac."

> Be not deceived.
> God is not mocked.
> For whatsoever a
> man soweth,
> that shall he also reap

Dennis scratched away like a madman. I wasn't sure if he was completely lucid, because I didn't know what he was referring to, but it all sounded so cryptic.

> I wish I had more time
> to show Him that
> I deserve you.

"What are you talking about Dennis. You're not going anywhere. The doctors say you are going to be fine."

> It was our love for you
> that saved us both, but your
> heart will decide our fate.

"I'm not sure I know what this means," I paused. I knew couldn't tell Dennis everything about Rayshaun, the baby and my decision. It just wasn't the right time for that discussion. Dennis shook his head, and then smiled. His dimples showed and the painful expression left his face. He gazed at me lovingly.

> Do you love him?

I didn't ask who, because I knew that would be offensive and unnecessary.

"Yes... Yes, I do love him."

> I didn't keep my part
> of the bargain. You don't owe
> me anything but to go on
> from here and enjoy your life.

"What do you keep talking about, Dennis?" I insisted.

> I hope that you never know,
> so that you can always
> keep what we had,
> because it's the realest thing
> I ever gave anybody.
> Loving you has made me believe
> that I could be good again.

After I read the sheet, I didn't know how to respond to it.

> Did I make you happy?

"Yes... very." A tear dropped down on the paper. Dennis frowned and shook his head, as he wiped my cheek with his thumb.

I took the notepad and pen from Dennis.

I wrote:

> You taught me how to love

I handed the pad back.

Dennis read it and smiled. He blinked back tears, and pointed at me then back to himself.
"Okay, okay." I waved my hands. "That's enough of all this morbid talk. You'll be fine. I'll be back tomorrow with some things you need and we'll discuss all of this when you get better."

Dennis gave me the thumbs up. As I got up to leave, he touched my hand. He quickly jotted down a note and folded it up. He handed me the tiny square of paper. I started to open it, but Dennis tapped my leg.
He wagged his pointer finger. "Not... yet," he moaned.
"When?"
"You'll... know.

I kissed Dennis's stubbly head. He brought the back of my hand to his chapped lips, and pressed it firmly. "I love... you." he winced with the words.

"Rest now. I promise I will be back." I returned the notepad and pen to the drawer, then placed the square in my jeans pocket. "I love you too, Dennis."

His eyes began to glaze over and his lids lowered, as he fell asleep.

PART VII

THE PURPOSE

Safety in Lovers

So Long, Dark Prince

Dennis died on a Friday.

Almost one week after the shooting, he was discharged from the Hospital and died on the sidewalk outside.

Prior to Friday, I spent every day at his bedside. We talked often, and even though I knew there were always questions right on the tip of his tongue, he never asked them.

We read poems to each other.
We watched T.V.
We played cards.
We talked about our past— but never the future.

Dennis had many visitors during the week—Rayshaun, Willie James, Mr. Salinas and a host of other neighborhood residents. I didn't know how influential Dennis was in his community. His mother, Simone, arrived Tuesday morning. She and his father were at a conference in Washington D.C. and didn't get word about the shooting until Sunday night.

Because Dennison's father, Dennis, was there as an engineering consultant on the Energy Conservation Committee, the decision was made that Simone, a Pulitzer prize winning writer and professor of Liberal Arts and African American studies at Emory University, would travel alone back to Atlanta to be Dennis. Simone, a petite, sable-skinned sophisticate in couture clothing, donned an identical pair of intense amber eyes as her son. I never imagined that someone as modest as Dennis would have such distinguished parents.

Simone glared at me with disdain when we met initially. My earthy, casual appearance and civil service occupation didn't meet her standards for courtship with her son. However, I grew on her once she learned that I was college-educated. Dennis never revealed to her that I was pregnant, and I was glad. I left her alone with her son all day on Tuesday, but she and I consented thereafter to take alternating, overlapping shifts. The doctors advised us on Thursday that Dennis had made sufficient progress to leave the hospital on Friday. Simone and I used the entire day to ready her house for Dennis's stay. She turned her downstairs office into a bedroom for him so that he would not have to scale any stairs or be left unattended in the guesthouse. Dennis had regained some feeling in his legs, but could not yet walk completely under his own strength.

Friday morning, the nurses allowed me to assist them in getting Dennis dressed. They put him in a wheelchair and proceeded to take him out to the car. He had developed a bit of a nosebleed that morning, but insisted that it was nothing to be concerned about.

"I feel good and strong." Dennis declared. "I'll be fine, Ma." He reassured her. He laughed and smiled a lot that morning. Other than the occasional wince or grunt, one would almost think that he was back to himself. Simone and I stood on the sidewalk, in front of the Emergency Room entrance, with Dennis and the nurse, while waiting for Rayshaun to pull his car around. Without any warning, Dennis slumped over in the wheelchair. The nurse attempted to rouse him, but when he remained unresponsive, she pulled him back inside of the hospital.

Simone is probably the most austere, reserved woman that I have ever met. Her countenance is like steel— rarely revealing any emotions. But when the orderlies threw Dennis on a gurney and rushed him into surgery, she wailed incoherently. "What's wrong with him? Tell me something!" was all I could decipher. I sat as calmly as I could, for the sake of everyone, as she and Rayshaun paced in the waiting room.

When the doctor entered the family waiting room, his expression said it all. Simone broke down, collapsing to the floor before he ever spoke one word. Rayshaun collected her up and held her close while the doctor delivered the news that an aneurysm in Dennis's brain ruptured before they could locate it.

"He bled out within seconds and there was nothing else we could do," the doctor said solemnly.

Simone bawled on Ray's shoulder. She yanked on his leather jacket, as she yelled, "Why?... How could this happen?" Simone cried out to God, and even beat at Rayshaun's chest, but he refused to let her go. He held her tightly until her hysterical raving tired to a whimper.

It was all so unsettling to watch. I was being affected in more ways than one— not just as Dennis's lover, but also as a parent. No mother ever thinks that she will bury her own child and as I felt the activity of my own son within me, I was consumed with grief.

I left the room to find a quiet corner for my tears away from the scene. I slid to the floor and allowed the sobs to overtake me. I'm not sure how long I was there before Rayshaun appeared over me.

"Are you gonna' be alright?" He asked gently, as he dropped down on the floor beside me. His eyes were full of nothing but unfeigned compassion. I didn't speak. I just allowed my head to find his shoulder. "Simone's sister is coming to get her. Do you need me to take you home?" Rayshaun wrapped his arm around my shoulders.

"Yeah, I do." I replied benignly. "I have something that I need to do."

Something about my tone must have raised an alert in Rayshaun. "I don't think you should be alone tonight." He said, pinching my chin. I could tell that Rayshaun's motive was purely innocent concern for my well-being. "Do you want me to call Lanelle?"

These days had showed me that I didn't really know him. I had unfairly created a persona for Ray that was formed out of my own perceptions of his actions and not his true character. I never knew he had such a vast capacity to care for other people. I had judged him as egotistical and self-centered from the moment I met him and even that assumption was based more on his appearance than his attitude.

I had been disgruntled and angry all of my life, believing that I was being judged because of my looks, my hair... my complexion, only to find that I was a perpetuator of the same prejudices. I never even gave myself the chance to get to know Rayshaun for who he really was. I never gave him a chance either. I expected him to disappoint me and acted accordingly. It was me who was self-centered and I never even knew it.

I wanted to beg his forgiveness and confess to him that I loved him— that it was him I chose that night. It was always him and only him that I truly desired. I longed to tell him that his past didn't matter to me anymore and that I was willing to trust him and take the chance on a future with him and our baby.

I sat there, mouth gaped open, but the words never came out. Dennis hadn't been dead for even one whole hour yet. It would be tasteless and inappropriate to say that now. Besides, I couldn't be sure that he would forgive or even believe me anyway.

"Would you take me home?"
"Of course, I will," Ray said earnestly.
"I mean, to Charlotte?"
"North Carolina?"
"Yeah."
"Today?"

"Yes. There's something I need to do."

Safety in Lovers

Devian Nikei

Gone to Carolina

"Continue straight for 0.2 miles then turn right."

It was after nine at night, when Rayshaun and I finally reached Saydhe's house.

"Turn right, now."

We made the quiet ride to Charlotte relatively quickly, however we spent the better part of the last hour lost in the city. The landscape of Charlotte had changed so much over the years that I barely recognized even the permanent landmarks. I didn't know that it would be so difficult for me to find the way back to my childhood home.

"Your destination is on the right."

I didn't call Saydhe. I needed the ride to figure out what I would say when I saw her. I hadn't spent one night in that house in over ten years and I had not spoken to Saydhe in over three.

"You are now at your destination, 6113 Mockingtree Court"

My stomach turned in knots as the house came into view. Rayshaun pulled into the driveway and turned off the engine. There it was— Saydhe's same ranch-style house with its same maroon shutters and same beige vinyl siding and the same flower pinwheels spinning in the front yard, as the wind blew. Not one thing had changed. It was as though the house had been preserved in time.

"No pressure, but I can stay if you want me to," Rayshaun offered.

Rayshaun didn't know very much about my relationship with Saydhe, except that it was non-existent. I never gave him so much as an inkling about the secrets that this house held.

"No, Ray. It would be better if I handled this myself."

"I guess I can respect that."

"Are you going to be alright for the drive back? How's the shoulder?"

"It's pretty stiff." Ray winced, as he made a circular motion with his elbow. "The doctor told me to keep the sling on, but it's messing up my swag." Ray popped the collar on his long-sleeve, black and gold striped Polo shirt.

"Whatever." I rolled my eyes. "I'm serious, Ray."

"Nah, I'm straight. I got a line brother up here in the *Queen City* and I told him I was gone be in town. He said I could crash with him tonight. We're going out to pick up some females. You know women are into bullet wounds and shit like that." He leaned in close to my face. I did know Rayshaun, at least well enough to surmise that he was baiting me. He wanted to see if I still cared. I wasn't ready to bite just yet— for now, I had bigger fish to fry.

"That sounds very nice. I hope y'all have a great time," I added courteously.

"Do you need a ride back to Atlanta?" Ray said, looking deep into my eyes.

"I'm going to stay here for the weekend, so I can get back on my own."

"Okay, love." Ray kissed my cheek.

To say that Saydhe wasn't expecting me would be a gross understatement. She wept when she opened her door to find me there. She hugged me so tightly that I almost suffocated. She and Rayshaun exchanged brief introductions, as he helped me with my duffle bag.

"It's kind of late, son. You're welcome to stay here, Rayshaun, if you want to." She demurely extended the invitation.

He shot me a playful glance, rubbing his palms together, then graciously declined. "No ma'am. I'd better be going now."

Saydhe got me settled in on the pullout sofa bed in the den. My room had been converted into a daycare space. The guest bedroom had become home to Uncle Snoopy after his stroke, so this was the only space available at the inn. Saydhe and I agreed to save any in-depth conversation for the following day, as I was exhausted from the trip as well as the events of the day.

I don't think it completely sank in that Dennis was dead and in this newly unfamiliar environment, I could disconnect from the woes I had experienced in Atlanta. This place presented a different kind of discord. Throughout the years, I held an obstinate belief that even the sight of this house and Saydhe would grip me with such insurmountable anger and terror that I never returned to it. My fears, as I was now finding out, were completely unfounded. It was actually quite a comforting relief to come back home.

Saydhe made a decadent turkey sandwich with warm milk for me, before retiring to her bedchambers. I sat alone at the kitchen table, eating the snack under a dim, flickering fluorescent light. I rifled back through a myriad of childhood hopes and memories as I ate. I looked around, from wall to wall, at the evolutionary chart of family portraits. I am rarely sentimental, but I was admittedly affected in this place. After I cleaned my dish, I eventually found my way back into the den, and then off to sleep in front of the blinking lights of Saydhe's 60" LCD television.

The next morning, I awoke to the aroma of bacon and buttered biscuits. I almost forgot what a home smelled and felt like. Home cooking is an art form that I did not acquire before I left home, so this is a very rare treat. My baby began to flutter within me. I was enthralled by the sensation of tiny bubbles popping in my tummy. I lifted my fitted sweater and rubbed the little knot that twisted within me.

"Denae, are you pregnant?" Saydhe appeared in the doorway.

"Yes ma'am," I said, returning to that same little girl, caught with my hand in the cookie jar.

"Ohhh." I wasn't familiar enough with Saydhe to know whether her expression conveyed gladness or disappointment. Either way, she appeared concerned. "You're not," she paused, "in any trouble, are you?"

"No, not at all. My visit is purely social."

Relief flowed into her face as the alarm drained out. She took a seat on the sofa bed beside me. "It's special, isn't it?"

"What exactly?" I asked.

"Being a mother," she replied with a hint of nostalgia in her tone. "There's nothing else quite like it."

"Yeah. There's nothing that can prepare you for it either." We both nodded simultaneously in agreement.

"Come on. Let's get some food into you and that baby." Saydhe ushered me into her Country Kitchen. We were talking and laughing over a heaping bowl of cheese-flavored grits and eggs, when her face took on a somber expression.

"I know that I may be the artist formerly known as your mother, but you are still and always will be my only child. I missed you, Denae."

To echo that sentiment would have been completely artificial, so I smiled genially. "Look, Saydhe. I don't want to be fake with you. The relationship that we had in the past is long gone." I said, spreading jelly on a biscuit.

"I got sober while you were gone and I gave my life to Christ. Addiction can turn you into someone that you don't even recognize sometimes. I have lived with many regrets for years, but there's something that I've wanted to tell you for quite a long while. It just never seemed like the right time until now." She paused and put her hand over her mouth.

"I honestly don't remember that night, but whatever happened was awful enough for you to leave our home—"

"Look, I didn't come here to hash out the past. I'd rather not talk about that," I said as politely as I could.

"This isn't for you, it's for me. This is something I need to say and something I think you need to hear." Saydhe's brows knitted together with the weight of burdensome contrition.

I motioned dismissively for her to continue.

"After you left, Vaughn moved in with me. His wife kicked him out. I asked him for days what happened between you two, but he gave me some lie—claiming that you attacked us. He said that you were in some drug-induced trance. I guess I always knew better, but what other conclusion could I draw without your side of the story. Besides, I was so lonely without you here, that I just accepted the lies. To make a long story short, over time he became terribly unbearable to live with. He was distant and moody one minute, then aggressive and violent the next. He smacked me around almost daily." She sniffled as tears began to roll down her face. Saydhe squared her shoulders, patted her cheeks with a napkin, and then continued.

"I thought I would never get out of that nightmare with him. Every day he just pulled me down lower and lower until I thought I couldn't do any better. Then one day his wife called the house. She asked for him, but he wasn't here. She and I struck up a conversation about him. She told me that she threw him out because she caught him in bed with their thirteen-year old Spanish-speaking foster child. 'I know Vaughn ain't worth a damn, but he's all I got,' is what she said to me. She told me that if I would kindly send him on back home, she would continue to turn a blind eye to our affair." Saydhe began to laugh, almost hysterically.

"What did you do then?" I asked with wide-eyed wonderment.

"His shit was packed and waiting on the doorstep for him when he got back from work. I had all of the locks changed and went to stay with my sister for the weekend."

Saydhe had a dismal countenance, as the tears stood on the rim of her eyelids. "I could never be with someone that I knew for sure could do something like that. I tell you the truth, honey. I never would have believed that he was capable of doing that... to a child."

"Obviously," I replied with a smirk.

"Look, I know there's nothing that I can say to undo what's been done, but you need to know that I'm sorry for what I did. It didn't go unpunished either. God is not mocked, whatsoever a man soweth, that shall he also reap."

Dennis's words flashed back in my head, as she spoke.

"Well, I can forgive you, if you will forgive me too." Saydhe appeared almost astonished by my request. She opened her mouth but the shock and amazement stole her voice. "I just want to start over with you—a new thing. If you're up for it, Ma?"

Saydhe... my mom... smiled and nodded.

* * *

It was over in the evening on the second day, after hours of shopping, when the probing began.

"Who is the baby's father, Denae? I haven't even heard you say even one word about him."

"Rayshaun is the father." I answered lackadaisically, with a mouth full of Strawberry Cheesecake ice cream.

"Well, he is very attractive," my mother mused. I gave her a contemptible glance, before returning my gaze back to the television.

"What's the story there? He seems like a very nice, young man."

"We're not together, if that's what you're asking."

"Well he brought you up here, and helped you with your things. It seems to me like he cares."

"It's not that simple, Ma."

"Well, tell me what's so complicated. Is he a decent man?... Does he want to be with you and that baby?"

"Yeah... I mean... I don't really know. Rayshaun is a bit of a player— no, scratch that! He's like the MVP extraordinaire of pimping."

"What man isn't? What does that have to do with anything?"

'That settles it. The whole world has gone crazy.' I thought, as Mama stared at me blankly.

"Do you love him?"

"That's not the point."

"Hell, if it ain't."

"Look, Saydhe... I mean... Mama. Everyone can think what they want to, but it's going to be me who walks in on Rayshaun with some blonde skank one day." I huffed, pointing at my chest.

There it was.

I said it.

I laid my heart out on the table. That was my biggest fear and greatest anxiety. It sounded so ridiculous when verbalized.

"Okay... So what happens until that day comes, or what if that day never does come?"

I was awestruck by her questions. I was drawing a blank. I had no answer for them—the idea of that had never entered my mind.

Could Rayshaun be faithful?

"Baby, love is like energy; it's neither lost nor destroyed, only transferred. All of the love that you give will find its way back to you. Love is already a second-hand emotion. You can come up with eighty thousand reasons why you shouldn't be with someone, but you only need one really good reason to stay."

I was still speechless.

I would never have known that my mother was such a wealth of wisdom by the way that she lived her own life. She continued, "If you love him, then that should be a good enough reason to give it a try with him. I can guarantee that you will regret it if you let him go."

"But Ma, I can't let him make a fool out of me."

"It's the love— not the man that makes a fool out of you. There are lots of women walking around here with egg on their face and they didn't even really want the idiot they were with." Saydhe frowned and pointed at herself. "Denae, you're being selfish and that's not fair to Rayshaun or that baby."

"You don't know the whole story. I was with him for four years and he never told me that he loved me even one time until a couple months ago." I sighed with frustration. My head was spinning.

"But he did finally say it— that he loves you, right?"

"Yeah, but-"

"Denae—"

Whenever my mother uses that tone, I know she is getting ready to drop some heavy knowledge on me. I felt like Wylie Coyote standing under the anvil.

"Still waters run deep, baby."

"What on earth does that mean?" I threw up my hands.

"The external appearance of a body of water may appear calm, tranquil, even motionless, however far below, there are mighty rushing currents churning down deep, which never even disturb the surface. Some men are that way and you have to be patient with them. Sometimes when a man really loves you, he can't just say it like that. If those words come from a really deep place inside of him, then it might take a long time for him to say it, but you should be glad to be bestowed with the rare honor of hearing them. Anybody can say they love you, but I have found in my experience that it's usually the man who can't say it—that really cares for you the most."

Saydhe paused for effect.

"That is the most... ass backward advice that I have ever heard." I gawked at her.

Not the effect she had hoped for, I'm sure.

"Look, all I'm saying is that you get one ride around the sun. Tomorrow's not promised. You would rather have used your time to give and receive all of the love that you could possibly muster than to live afraid." She shrugged.

I didn't want to continue the conversation any further, but Saydhe forged on, "The most divine purpose that you can fulfill in your life is to allow yourself to completely and selflessly love another flawed, imperfect human being—the same way that God loves us, and girl you know we a mess."

We both nodded emphatically. "You will find that out when you become a parent. It takes courage to love." My mother said, staring at me. I knew what her look insinuated.

"Well, Denae baby, I'm gone turn in now." My mother stood up stiffly and started out of the room.

"Hey Ma . . ." Saydhe turned back to face me. "I love you," I said authentically.

"I love you too, sweetie. Goodnight."

The following afternoon, my mother took me to the Greyhound bus station on Trade Street. Driving through uptown Charlotte brought back vivid memories of my childhood. The addition of several towering skyscrapers to the Queen City created a skyline similar to Atlanta.

However, Charlotte is different in many ways. So vibrant and colorful—not as I remembered it at all. This city has become quite a Concrete Wonderland.

My mother embraced me, as we said our goodbyes. "I am proud of you," she said suddenly.

I was astounded by the words. It's so strange because, up until that point, I never knew that I needed to hear my mother say those words. Those words... resolved something in me that a thousand apologies could never right. Before that moment, I believed that I had divorced myself from any concern for how Saydhe viewed me. However, hearing those words proved to me that not only did I still care, but I would have forever remained incomplete without the puzzle pieces of those words.

'I am proud of you' I played her words back in my head, like my favorite scene in a movie, as she hugged me.

Every child, young or old needs to hear their parents say those words. I filed that lesson in my Mommy Notes-To-Self. Saydhe held my face in her hands. "The Lord put it on my heart to tell you this," she smiled through her tears. "Do what you love and what makes you happy. Don't be upset and bitter no more, okay? If you give up on love and let that pain fester, then everyone that ever tried to hurt you will win. And when you lose, you lose alone, honey." My mother kissed my cheeks. "Don't ever let nobody steal your joy, baby."

"I love you, Mama."

"I love you too."

I have heard it said that bad things happen in threes. Me, I never put much stock in superstition and wives' tales, but just because you don't believe in something, don't make it no less true. After the death of Maw-maw and Dennis, I never thought that tragedy would strike again and so soon, but that was the last time I would ever see my mother.

She died that very same night.

It would be another two weeks before my family could reach me with the news. None of my relatives had any contact information for me, so locating me was virtually impossible for them. My aunt Karen finally tracked me down. She told me that a pilot lamp on my mother's gas stove ignited a dishrag that dangled from the hood. Because my mother had taken sedatives to sleep, Uncle Snoopy got out, but the house burned to the ground with her inside.

Aunt Karen said, "When the Fire Department got there, it was too late. Saydhe was charred beyond recognition, but they believe, based on where the fire started, that smoke inhalation killed her long before the flames ever reached her body. At least, she didn't suffer."

My aunt told me that I missed the home going service, but she would send me the urn containing my mother's remains.

The grief that I will feel at the passing of my mother will be so devastating as to plunge me deep into a debilitating depression for months. However, that news won't come for weeks, so in the meanwhile, I was on my way back to Atlanta to pay my last respects to Dennis.

It was late Sunday night, when I arrived in Atlanta. Lanelle was waiting at the bus depot for me. By Monday afternoon, I had decided not to attend the viewing of Dennis's body. By Tuesday, I had consented not to go to the funeral on Wednesday either. I didn't want to see him that way. I wanted to remember him the way he was: full of life and charisma—irresistibly infectious. I imagined that he was somewhere in a white leisure suit, frolicking in a field of sunflowers like P. Diddy in the "I'll Be Missin' You" music video.

I never knew I would miss Dennis so much, that his death would leave such a giant void in my life. I regretted that I spent what little time I did have with him on such frivolous matters. I wished that I had not been so afraid of what other people thought. I wished that I had been an unconditional friend to him.

Meditating on human mortality caused me to long for Rayshaun, even more. We hadn't spoken since he dropped me off in Charlotte. I wondered what he was doing... and if he was thinking of me, too.

* * *

"Denae, you really ought to go."

"I don't think I should go. I don't want to go."
"I will be disappointed if I don't see you there."
"That won't be a first, now will it?"
"Look, this is an important part of the grieving process. You might regret it if you don't go."
"I've shed my tears and put the past behind me. I'll be fine."
"I don't know why, but his family has asked me to say a few words at the funeral." Rayshaun's voice softened. "I would appreciate it if you came to support me, Denae."

Rayshaun had been trying to convince me to attend Dennis's funeral all morning.

"I'll think about it."
"The funeral starts at three, so get going."

* * *

Lanelle and I arrived at the church late. We slid into the back row just in time to hear the last of the eulogy given by Dennis's younger brother, Stafford. He was tearful, as he returned to his seat aside Simone and a gentleman that was undeniably Dennis's father.

Rayshaun took the podium next. He stood in front of the pulpit, attired more modest and informal than I have become accustomed to seeing him in these settings. He wore a ribbed gray turtleneck under a black sport coat. He still managed to exude a confidence that compelled the focus of the congregation.

"I didn't know Dennison very long," he began," but in that short time he and his family have made a profound impression upon me. I am standing here before you now, only because of Dennis."

Rayshaun went on to describe how a partially paralyzed Dennis struggled across the convenience store floor, to seize one of the gunman's two weapons, only to be shot in the chest before he could fire a round. Rayshaun recounted that the assailant turned the gun on him and fired a bullet into his shoulder. Rayshaun motioned towards his right arm, which was back in the sling. "Before he could finish me off, Dennis gathered what strength he had left and shot him through the elbow—enough to disarm him."

Rayshaun paused. He appeared visibly disturbed, but maintained his composure. His piercing jade gaze darted around the room, surveying the various faces. "I had hoped that he would be here with me to share this story, but God had other plans for him."

Rayshaun continued on to praise Dennis's courage and character. He commented on their shared zeal for revitalizing the community. Ray remarked on Dennis's resilient spirit, even when confined to a hospital bed. It seemed bizarre, but at the same time refreshing, to hear Rayshaun speak, with such vehement admiration and respect, about a man with whom he shared more than just camaraderie—but also a lover.

"Dennis was an exemplary role model for rehabilitation and transformation," Ray's eyes found mine. "I can see why he was beloved by so many people..."

Following the service, many of the attendants mingled amongst themselves. Lanelle and I made our way out of the church and to the parking lot.

Simone was waiting outside for me. "Do you want to ride with the family to the gravesite?" she asked. Simone wore a grand, elegant black hat and veil. Her face was almost completely obscured by it, but her eyes still shone brilliant and vibrant. Today, she had found her Rock and was clinging on with determined tenacity. Her strength and restraint was admirable.

"No ma'am," I replied. "This is where I say goodbye. Just coming here has proved to be too much for me."

"I understand." Simone offered a dignified nod. She gave me a polite hug and climbed into the long, black stretch limousine.

By the time the vehicle pulled away, my eyes had already found him in the crowd.

I studied Rayshaun—with his debonair carriage and graceful mannerisms. Our eyes met, as he bent down to embrace an elderly woman. We stood far apart, but caught in each other's sights from across the parking lot—All of the people, space and time between us disappeared. It seemed as though he was reaching out for my hand, when another slipped into his. A small ginger-colored female with Asiatic features snuggled up close to him, wrapping her other hand around his elbow. I sensed the rage welling up inside of me, but I abated it quickly.

'Don't jump to conclusions. It may not be what you think.' I told myself as he opened the driver side door of his New-Money green Jaguar for her. He circled around the vehicle, then threw a wave in my direction before hopping into the passenger seat.

Devian Nikei

Table for Three

'Maybe she is one of Dennis's relatives.'

"Probably not."

It had been three days since the funeral and I was still obsessing over Rayshaun's mystery woman. You'd think that I would have something— **anything**— better to do on a Saturday night than this. I paced around my living room, mulling over all of the possibilities.

'Maybe... she is a relative of Ray's?'

"Definitely not. We've never seen that midget before," Alisha fumed.

Alisha was just as distraught about this situation as I was. I chewed Lanelle's ear clean off about the topic for days. After I told her on Friday night that I wouldn't be joining the weekend *Party Express*, she stopped answering her phone.

"Look, you didn't ask for my advice on this one, but if you had, I would say that I think it's time for you to go and get your man back."

'I think you're right,' I assented, as I slipped into the only pair of jeans I had in my drawers that still fit—my baby jeans. I stretched into an oversized, celery-colored cashmere sweater.

'Where are my keys?'

I glanced around my coffee table and sofa, then reached into my pockets. My fingers did not find keys, but did however, graze over a small, familiar square of paper—

Dennis's note.

My hand trembled slightly as I withdrew it. I sucked in a deep breath and blew it out slowly, as I unfolded the paper. It read:

> He is still in love with you

"Thank you, Dennis." I whispered, clutching the note to my chest.

* * *

Finding Rayshaun proved more difficult than finding my keys.

I went by his Brownstone. Not only was he not there, but this curiously, effeminate white guy, named Dayle, answered the door.
"Do you know where he is?" I probed.
Dayle puckered his lips as though he was sucking on a lemon. "No, I don't know," he tapped his chin. "I would say that you could wait here for him, but Ray didn't tell me that he was expecting any company."
"That's fine. Do you know when he'll be back?"
"Hmm," Dayle pulled his chin-length brunette hair behind one ear. "I can't say for sure, but knowing Ray, it'll probably be late." Dayle gave me a playful grin. "I'll let him know that you came by Deena."

After that, I got resourceful.

I figured that Rayshelle wouldn't know where Ray was, so I called Rayshaun's closest homeboy. These two are so tight that their relationship borders on a Bromance. If anyone on the planet knew where Ray was, he would:

"Hey Marcus."

Marcus Mayhew, a cinnamon colored Egyptian god and former Atlanta Falcons' tight end turned business attorney. He and Rayshaun were childhood friends, and at one time, the Heavyweight Tag Team Champions of Pimping. They became inseparable pals after pounding the tar out of each other in middle school over a little light-skinned cutie, who ended up dumping them both for another boy...

You'll never guess who?

Nope.

Curtis "Curtisha" Jones. Even back then, he was prettier than either of them would ever be.

Small, strange world, huh?

Anyway, that day they learned the first rule in the Players' Code that they would live by for many subsequent years:

Bros... before Hoes

"What's up, Denae," his smooth voice flowed through the telephone receiver.
"I'm looking for Ray... Know where he is?" I asked casually.
"Now, you know I'd be violating the Code, if I gave you any information on Ray's whereabouts."
"C'mon Marcus. You know me better than that. Besides there's nothing between Ray and me now, but the baby."
"That *is* right," Marcus said enthusiastically. "How are you and *the baby?*"
"We're fine."
"I thought that you were officially wifey by now?"
"Nah, not really."
"Denae, you can't con a con-man. I know that you and Ray keep each other tied down tighter than Al-Qaeda hostages."

"Not unless you know something that I don't," a dash of bitterness salted my comment. Why did everyone else, except me, get the memo that Rayshaun was in love with me?

"It's not like that anymore."

"Don't shut my man down. He's really got it bad for you."

"Oh really. That news comes as a complete surprise to me... So how do you know so much?"

"Rayshaun has been my niggah for a long time and there ain't much that I don't know about him and what he does. But when it comes to you, he's like Fort Knox."

"That's my point, exactly. He never talks about me to anybody. He keeps me away from all his friends..."

"Denae, you gonna turn me into a bitch-ass, snitch-niggah, today. It's against the Man Law for me to divulge our secrets to you, but I will have to take one for the team, because I can't have you putting Ray on notice."

Marcus sighed. "That's how you know Ray loves the hell out of your ass. Men only brag about sluts. He respects you and what y'all got enough not to tell us a damn thing about you and not to parade you around in front of them hound dogs we hang out with. He's very protective of you. Ray is closer to me than my own blood brother, but he would probably kill me, if he knew I was talking to you right now.

That's how serious he is about you. We don't talk about y'alls relationship, but at the same time, I ain't heard no other woman's name in his mouth since y'all hooked up neither. For somebody like my man Ray—that's huge."

I huffed in frustration. Suddenly, everyone is an expert on love.

"I just need to get something from him and I don't know where he is."

"Does he owe you some money? You know if you need anything, I got you, right?"

Before I could answer, Marcus whispers, "You didn't hear this from me..."

"I never do."

"He's at that Taurus Restaurant, but that's all I can say."

"Gotcha'. Thanks, M-n-M."

"Hey, Denae. Do me a favor, please? Keep his ass straight, before he ends up like me with kids all over the place and up to his neck in child support payments higher than a mortgage. I love my babies and everything, but I guess you got to pay to play."

"Oh, don't worry. I got him covered."

* * *

When I arrived at *Taurus*, Ray was sitting cuddled up in a booth with that same little Miss Rae Dawn Chong.

I wasn't sure how to handle the situation. I had found what I hoped I wouldn't.

'Just breathe,' I said internally. 'There's an excellent explanation for this.' My steps were hesitant at first, then increasingly confidant, as I breezed casually up to their table.

"Hey, Ray."

"Oh hi, Denae." Ray smiled slyly. There was no shock or anxiety evident in his expression. Kimora Lee, on the other hand, was a different story. She looked as scared as a pedophile in prison. "Excuse my manners," Ray said, being the consummate gentleman. "Ahn, this is Denae—my child's mother. Denae, this is Ahn. Ahn was one of my nurses at the hospital."

"Sooo, is this some kind of check-up dinner appointment or something?" I drawled out the words, hoping for an affirmation.

"No..." Rayshaun gestured between Ahn and himself. "*This...* is a date."

My heart felt as though it had been smashed in a head-on collision.

"Look if there's a problem," Ahn whispered quietly in Rayshaun's ear.

"No problem," Rayshaun said assuredly. He wrapped his arm around Ahn and focused exclusively on her. "Denae and I are just friends. As a matter of fact," Ray turned back to me. "Denae would you like to join us?... My treat." He motioned towards the empty seat across from them.

"No thanks, Ray." I replied sardonically. "I just need to borrow you for a second." I pulled Ray to the elevator and took him downstairs to a quiet alcove in the restaurant lobby.

"Ray, what are you doing?"

"Well, the doctor says that I have to wear this sling for at least four more weeks or there could be permanent damage. Surprisingly though, I pick up more females with it on—"

"Don't play with me, Ray. Now is not the time."

"No, now is not the time for your bullshit." Ray shocked even himself with the sternness of his tone. Ray caught himself and took a brief timeout, then said quietly, "You've got my child inside of you, so I don't want to be disrespectful, but unless you've got something important to say, I need to get back to my date. This is really inconsiderate, Denae."

'I deserved that,' I thought to myself.

"No you don't, no one does. Just tell him how you feel." Alisha said encouragingly.

Ray was stepping back into the elevator when I grabbed his elbow.

"I love you, Ray." He rolled his eyes and continued into the elevator. I placed my foot in front of the door slot. "At least give me the same chance to be heard that I gave you," I pled with him.

Ray slowly stepped back out of the elevator. "Go ahead then," he sighed, watching his feet with disinterest.

I took his left hand in mine. "Ray, you know I'm not really good at this. I don't have fancy words, but I want to open myself up to you." I licked my lips. "You were right. I wasn't ready to trust you. I thought that you would hurt me."

"Denae, I've done right by you. I've never given you even one reason to doubt me." Ray snapped defensively.

"I know. Just let me finish," I consoled him. "I'm not blaming you. This was my fault. I made a mess like a toddler with finger paints. Deep down inside, in a place where I wasn't even willing to admit this to myself, I thought you were too good for me. I never believed that you could truly love me and so I sabotaged our relationship, because I would rather push you away than have to deal with you leaving me."

Rayshaun seemed pained by my confession. "That wasn't fair to me, Denae. Where was I at in all of your self-preservation? Where is your faith in me?"

"You're right. It wasn't fair to play with your heart and I'm sorry." I kissed the back of Ray's hand.

"Don't do that." He pulled his hand away, but I could detect the vulnerability in his voice.

I went in for the kill.

"It was you that I chose that night at the hospital. It was always only you."

"You can't be serious?" His tone denoted a hint of sarcastic amusement. "You got a funny way of showing that."

"I know it's hard for you to believe me right now, but it's true. It was just bad timing. I didn't know how to tell you and I was afraid that you wouldn't forgive me for the whole Dennis episode." I slid my hand up around the back of his neck. "Ray, I love you. Let me prove it. I just want to make it up to you."

"You've been in my old playbook again, haven't you?" Ray smiled slightly. "Game recognizes game, Denae." He pulled my arms from around his neck. "You played yourself, Dee but I got a sure thing upstairs. So you can just think about what you lost out on, while I'm remodeling her pussy and knocking some walls down tonight, a'ight... I'm over this."

Ray turned from me and pressed the elevator button. My heart sank. I almost couldn't breathe as a tight, stinging knot developed in the center of my chest.

"Can you guess which hand?" I extended my closed fists towards him.

"Come on, Dee. Be original." Ray said, turning to face me.

"Just . . . humor me," I could not disguise the desperation in my voice. Rayshaun squinted his eyes and groaned with irritation, but I didn't let him off the hook. I remained steadfast with my hands outstretched until he caved in.

He touched my right hand.

I opened the empty hand.

Ray tapped the left.

I opened my hand to reveal a platinum band adorned with twin white diamonds.

"Marry me, Rayshaun. I'm ready to love you the way you deserve. Please forgive me." I bit down on my bottom lip, as tears began to spill from my eyes. "Please," I wheezed through quivering lips.

A slow, hesitant smile stretched across his lips.

"Okay," he replied simply, taking the ring from my trembling hand. Rayshaun wiped the tears from my cheek and threw his arm around my neck, giving me an almost brotherly hug. He leaned over, but then stopped short of reaching my lips. "Wait... First, I have some terms and conditions. I don't come that cheap, ya' know." Ray tapped the tip of my nose.

"Say on," I obliged him.

"If I take you home with me tonight... can you guarantee that I'm going to get some ass?"

"Ray!" I exclaimed, smacking his good shoulder.

"Don't get uptight on me now. That nurse upstairs is a freak and she promised me a game of Doctor tonight." Ray shrugged nonchalantly. "It's been over a month since you gave me some action, and now even righty is out of commission too. I'm only human. A man has his needs," Rayshaun said diplomatically. "So you gone let me beat it up, or what?"

"You'd better shut your mouth, Ray."

"You'd better open your legs, Denae." Ray mimicked in a squeaky voice. His lips caught mine, as he put his arm around my waist, hugging my body to his. Ray pulled me into a concealed corner behind the elevator shaft and pressed me up against the wall.

"You know how it turns me on when you're mad." Ray kissed along my collarbone. "You gone give me some warm milk-and-cookies, Mama?" He was building a fire between my thighs and I wanted to strip him down right there in the lobby. He slid his hand under my sweater and squeezed my breast.

"That's a sure bet," I moaned lowly.

Ray stopped to calm and adjust himself in his slacks. Ray grabbed his package. "Down boy," he told the raging serpent in his pants. "We wouldn't want an accidental discharge later on."

He smiled, looking me up and down. He took a deep breath in, and then shook it out. "Alright, let me go get this blow job from Ahn— right quick, and then I'll meet you at the Jag."

I leered at Ray angrily, as he handed me his car keys.

"Yes!" he cheered, pumping his fist. "Keep it hot for me, babe. I'll be right back."

* * *

Rayshaun, the gentleman— right?

After giving Ahn some line about his sick child and leaving enough money with the waiter to get her "whatever she wants", Ray met me at his Jaguar outside and we sped off down the highway together, bound for his place. By the time we reached Ray's Brownstone, we were on fire for each other, and melting from the blaze. We had already started the foreplay in the car.

Ray sucked on my earlobe as I drove. He licked my neck and kissed my lips at stoplights. Once we reached the front door, Ray stood behind me biting at the back of my neck and reaching his hand into the front of my jeans, as I fumbled with his keys. I thought that our erotic interlude would ensue right there on the hardwood living room floor, just as soon as I opened the door...

Instead, Dayle was sitting on the couch, watching T.V. "Hey, Ray. You're back pretty early?" he asked, still watching the television screen.

"You've got a house sitter now?" I asked, quickly buttoning my jeans and fingering my hair back into place.

"Oh, hi Deena. I see you found him."

"Yeah Dayle. Let me holler at you, my man." Ray took him to the side. They exchanged a few whispered words before Ray stuffed some bills into Dayle's hand.

As I looked around Ray's place, I saw cardboard boxes everywhere. Ray took my navy, double-breasted pea coat along with his brown leather jacket and scarf, then placed them over the arm of his sofa. Ray and I both stood, side-by-side, staring awkwardly at Dayle.

After a few silent minutes, he finally downloaded a clue. "Oh... I guess I'd better be going now. Well, y'all have a goodnight." Dayle screeched, grabbing his jacket and man purse on his way out of the front door.

"Okay. We're back on," Ray said, unfastening the sling strap from around his neck.

"The doctor told you to keep that on, Ray." I fussed at him.

"I'm sure one hour won't hurt anything."

I gave Ray a crossed look.

"Okay, fine... two hours." Ray grabbed me ferociously. He kissed my neck and chest, as he yanked my sweater swiftly over my head. I undid the buttons on Ray's tangerine collared shirt, with such frenzy that I popped off a few, before tearing it off of him.

"Upstairs... Our bedroom," he panted in my ear.

We left a trail of clothing along the stairs and rails, as we reached his room, completely naked and fully aroused. Ray closed and locked the door behind us. The glow of a street lamp shone through the curtains and blinds, casting tiger-striped shadows over our bodies. Ray touched the button on his remote and a soft Chris Brown melody dispersed throughout the room.

"All night... We can do it, all night..."

He walked over to me and embraced me. Ray allowed his lips and hands to wander over every inch of my body. His touch was like electricity, making my hairs stand on end. He wrapped his hands around my head with his thumbs under my chin, as he tilted my face up to his and kissed me deeply. I put my hands over his, as his tongue caressed mine. He sucked on my bottom lip, before releasing his grip.

"I'm going to do it for you tonight," I murmured softly, kissing on his chest.

"Do what?" he breathed, as I licked his nipple.

"You know... it. I'm going to do *it* tonight," I said, with a gentle caress of his balls.

Ray's expression turned giddy, as he realized to what I was referring. "You don't have to, if you don't want to. I know how you feel about it."

"No, I really want to. I want you to have something that I've never given to any other man."

I pushed Rayshaun down on the edge of the bed. "I love you, Ray." I spread his feet apart, and then kneeled down between his legs. He sat back on his elbows, observing me as I took his manhood (or at least what I could fit of it) deep into my mouth. A long, low moan escaped his lips, as I ran my tongue along the shaft.

His body tensed as I blew cool breath on the tip. He pulled the clip out of my pressed hair, releasing it to cascade down over my shoulders. My moist lips caressed his member, as I sucked on it. He gently put his hands around my head, not pushing but guiding me. "Just like that baby," he breathed softly. I allowed Rayshaun to show me how to pleasure him. His member felt good as it slid down into my throat. Fellatio wasn't what I thought it would be. No bad memories here. Only Rayshaun— My Love— was in my thoughts. It wasn't degrading, either. It was actually quite empowering. I was gratified to see how much satisfaction I was giving him.

Ray returned the favor.

He pulled me up on his lap, then rolled over on top. He took his time, sucking and nibbling on my lips, my neck and then my breasts. He lingered for a while, paying special attention to my small, round belly. I ran my fingers through his soft hair, while he caressed and nuzzled my womb. He looked up at me with tender, viridian eyes as he kissed both of my palms. He, then, continued down to my Happy Valley. He hoisted my thigh over his shoulder and parted the petals of my flower.

Rayshaun ran his tongue in slow, circular motions over my clitoris, and then sucked on it. "Ohhh," I moaned out in ecstasy, as he slid his fingers inside of me. His tongue was an apt paintbrush to my anxious, throbbing canvas. Ray created toe-curling, calf-flexing, back-arching artistry. He lured me to the brink of lip-biting, leg-quivering ecstasy several times—teasing me, before bringing me to a spasmodic climax.

As I lay there, sighing and twitching, Rayshaun kissed a sticky, wet pathway up my body, before reaching my lips again. He gently rubbed the head of his python over my kitten, driving me crazy with an anticipation that he refused to satisfy. Instead, he stood up and grabbed me behind my knees, yanking me forcefully to the edge of the bed.

"Come here," he grunted, grabbing me under my arms and lifting me up to my feet. I knew what he wanted.

Rayshaun is **The Boss** in the bedroom and I am his secretary. He gives the orders and I take his *dicktations*. He wants all the control and I give it to him.

Ray used one hand to pin my wrists tightly together behind me. He turned me around and placed his other hand in the middle of my back. Ray bent me over, pressing my chest flat against the mattress. He rubbed his hand slowly over my buttocks, as though he was polishing them. He smacked one cheek roughly, absorbing the bounce against his palm. When he was sufficiently satisfied with his progress, he separated them and penetrated me.

"Oh yeah, baby," I sighed, feeling the pressure inside of my walls. His strokes were long, slow and deep. I purred and cooed with delight as the taut flesh of my *Pretty Wings* opened to receive him.

Ray gripped my shoulders firmly, like a steering wheel. He knows just how to handle my body. Like a professional driver at the helm of a high-performance vehicle, Ray hugs the curves and drives it hard down the straightaways. Ray clinched the top of my buttocks tightly, as the tempo and intensity of his thrusts increased. His smacked my butt cheek again, but harder this time. It stung so good to me. I was overwhelmed with spine-tingling ecstasy.

He wrapped his hand around my throat and lifted my face to his. He licked along my jawbone, as his other hand delved down between my thighs, and simulated my clitoris. My warm nectar oozed out over his penis and rolled down my legs. I could feel his excitement as he panted against the back of my neck. Ray grabbed my hips, digging his nails in.

He roared loudly, and then suddenly pulled out. "Damn baby, you feel sooo good... too good," he huffed bewilderedly. The juice from my passion fruit glistened on his engorged organ. It thumped and throbbed in his hand, as he massaged it slowly.

"Can I get a ride?" I asked seductively, smiling my mischievous, come-hither smile.

Ray laid down on the bed and propped his back against the pillows, as I straddled him. This is his favorite position, he says, because he loves to see the expression on my face when I cum. I could feel his penis pulsing, as I slid it inside of me. Ray cupped my breasts, pinching my large, chocolate-drop nipples, as I began a slow bob up and down on top of him.

Rayshaun is a watcher.

His eyes are ever alert. He studies me in the darkness, like a night predator stalking his prey. He smiled at me, enjoying the sound of my moans.

"Damn baby..." He's blowing my mind right now. Rayshaun is a perceptive and receptive lover. He asks me what I like, and responds to my requests. After four years, we haven't tired of each other yet. Ray treats my body like a challenging Rubik's cube—every twist reveals a new pleasure for both of us.

"You love that D, don't you?"

"You know it, daddy."

He reached his fingers up into my hair and pulled my head back forcefully. I cried out from the painful pleasure. Then, his hands slid down my back and encircled my waist. He led my hips, in a winding motion as I rode him hard. Even from the bottom, Rayshaun has to call all of the shots. Ray's head dropped back. He began to pump his hips up forcefully against mine.

"Hold up a minute, babe." He stilled me, pressing down heavy on my thighs. "Don't move," he exhaled.

I rubbed my hands slowly over his stomach.

"Damn it, Denae. Stop moving." He growled, fighting back a laugh, as he tried to curb his enthusiasm.

"Is it feeling too good for you, Champ?" I breathed, placing his finger into my mouth. I taunted him, slightly swaying my hips.

"Okay, I see how you want it," Rayshaun grabbed me tightly around my waist. "I'm gonna' get your ass."

I giggled, as Ray flipped me over onto the bed and pounced on top of me. He is about to unleash what he calls, "The Beast." I love it when he turns into a savage in my pussy.

He owns it... and he knows it.

He placed my ankles on his shoulders. Warm sweat dripped from Ray's face, as he gathered his momentum and charged for the finish. Ray thrashed against me, drilling his rod down in deep. I was enthralled as my hands slipped along his lean back, feeling the thick muscles on his lower back constrict and flinch with his thrusts. As he groaned and convulsed, I could feel him erupting inside of me like a volcano. The hot lava spewed forth, flooding the valley and running down my cheeks.

A few sharp jerks of Ray's pelvis signaled the halt of the Carousel. His eyes rolled back, as he collapsed—exhausted and winded—on my chest. He kissed my neck and rubbed the back of my thighs, as he lay between them resting.

"Baby, you the best. Up top—" Ray sighed, throwing up his hand for a high-five. He rolled over and slumped down beside me in the bed. "I love you," he kissed me gently, before laying back against the pillows.

"I love you too, babe." I said, rubbing his chest. I permitted my fingers to stray over to the tiny scars developing in the red-and-white Superman tattoo on his shoulder. "Does it still hurt?"

"Not that much, anymore," Ray said sleepily, as he put his left forearm behind his head.

"Can I ask you a question?"

"Uh-oh. That doesn't sound good." Ray sighed, closing his eyes. "You can ask whatever you want to, but I might not answer. Okay?"

"Have you had another female in this bed?" I inquired reluctantly.

"Yes."

"Do you love her?"

"Do you really want the truth?" Ray peeked at me with one emerald eye.

"Yeah, I can handle it," I said coolly.

Ray laid silent for quite a while. His breaths became so heavy that I thought he had fallen asleep, until he said—

"Very much... Next to you, she's probably the only other girl I've ever truly loved."

Okay, I lied—

I couldn't handle hearing that. I rolled over, turning my back to him, as my lips began to tremble. "Denae, I think you're asking the wrong questions. None of that should matter." Ray said in an irritated tone.

"Then tell me what does matter?" I tried to control the quivering in my voice.

"I haven't sexed any other females since the very first night I made love to you, and if it matters at all, you're first in my heart." I flinched away, when Rayshaun kissed my tear-streaked cheek. "Don't be upset with me, Denae." Ray squeezed my shoulder.

"I'm not mad. Just a little disappointed that's all, but I'll get over it." I turned back to face him. "I love you and I'm not going anywhere, this time."

"Me, neither." Ray lifted my chin and kissed me lovingly. "How about another round?" he breathed in my ear.

* * *

I awoke to the smells of home. The aroma of toast and some other sweet floral fragrance filled my nostrils. When I turned over in the bed, there were a dozen long-stemmed, pink roses in a vase on the nightstand. As I pushed my hair back from my face, I realized that the pink-diamond engagement ring was on my finger. I beamed, feeling like a kid in a candy store. I got my man back and now my whole world was right. I felt like a queen as I slipped into my coral satin robe. I hopped out of bed and pulled my hair up into a bun, before grabbing a towel off the rack in his bathroom. I took a swift shower, splashing water everywhere and messing up my press, in my eagerness to get downstairs to Rayshaun. I quickly slipped into one of his oversized gray sweatshirts before blasting out of the bedroom.

He was in the kitchen, when I came hurrying down the stairs. It was the strangest thing to see him in an apron, gliding skillfully around a room that I didn't know he had ever entered. I wasn't sure if his food would be any good, but it was certainly a treat to watch his sexy ass cooking in his sleeveless, red t-shirt.

"I didn't know that you cook?" I asked with bright eyes as I approached him.

"One of many things that you don't know about me." Ray flashed a sneaky smile with a pan in one hand and a spatula in the other. "How do you want your eggs?"

"Scrambled… hard,"

"Don't say that to me right now. You might get attacked."

We both laughed aloud. My relationship with Ray has always been so casual. It was a new and exhilarating feeling to stand here with my heart racing like a cheerleader at his championship game.

"Why didn't you get me up?" I mused quietly. "I don't want to miss even one waking minute with you."

"Really," Ray groaned seductively, then bowed his head to kiss my lips. "Well there was no use trying to wake you. You were dead asleep, snoring and drooling all on my arm. That baby sure has turned you into Sleeping Beauty, huh?"

"I guess so," I yawned, stretching my arms overhead.

"Thanks for the flowers. They're really beautiful." I sat down in a bar chair, eyeing his every move closely.

"Don't give me that look. We've got to eat some time." He winked at me. "Let's save some energy for our honeymoon."

Ray said, placing a delectable plate of golden French toast covered with strawberries and whipped cream in front of me.

"It looks delicious," I said, digging in anxiously. The first forkful of brown-sugary goodness made me "Mmm!" with delight. "If you're such a great cook, then why are you always eating over at your mom's house?" I asked, wiping syrup from my chin with a paper towel.

"I let her cook and take care of me because it makes her feel important. I wouldn't want to burst her bubble. She needs me to need her, so I let her have her way, but I have kept this a secret for a long time, so don't tell her."

Ray sat down on the bar chair next to me, rubbing his hands on the apron, before removing it.

"Well, your son definitely loves his daddy's cooking."

"My son..." Ray's shock turned to excitement. "Are we having a boy?"

I nodded sheepishly.

"Yes!" Ray bellowed, sweeping me up in his arms and spinning me around. He sat me back down, and kissed my tummy. "Eat... eat. You better feed my little man." As he patted my stomach, his huge smile began to fade slowly.

"What's wrong, Ray?"

"Look, I don't want to blind side you, Denae. We didn't really get a chance to talk last night." Ray said with apprehension.

"Blind side? What do you mean? And what's up with all of the boxes?" I muttered with a mouthful of fruit.

"I bought a house."

"Why? I like it here."

"We need more space."

"Not really. We can convert your old whoring room into a bedroom for the baby. Of course, we'll have to bomb it for fleas first, but I'm pretty sure we could make it work."

"Well, it's a little more complicated than that." Rayshaun looked nervous, which is very rare for him.

"Good morning, Daddy." A tiny girl, in pink-footed pajamas, appeared in the doorway of the downstairs bedroom.

"Good morning, lil' mama," Ray smiled brightly. "Hey Bunny, do you remember that lady I told you about?"

She nodded her head.

"Come over here and meet my bride— Miss Denae." He said, beckoning for Deity to come to him.

Blind side was an understatement.

Rayshaun pulled her up on to his lap. "Denae, this is Deity— the love of my life and my other sleep-over buddy." He said, smiling with a wink. It was then that I noticed my ring on his finger. I felt warm inside. The picture of the pair of them was so endearing.

"Hey, Deena." She chimed.

Deity is a beautiful meringue-colored little girl with a mass of sandy blonde coils and her daddy's green eyes. They sat down together on the bar chair, staring at me and I at them.

"Your hair looks like mine." She said quietly with her fingers in her mouth. She made an astute observation, as both of our heads did look a fuzzy mess.

"It's nice to meet you Deity. Will you let me make your hair pretty, after we eat breakfast?" I said, finally managing to assemble a sentence.

She nodded excitedly.

Devian Nikei

A House Is Not a Home

"Madgey, the Mouse... is the tiniest creature in the house."

'Here we go, again'

"She scurries in a hurry, without a care or worry..."

Once a week, Family Movie Night is my one ascent from depression into a condition that somewhat resembles normalcy.

"She's Madgey... the Mouse!"

It was Deity's turn to pick our movie selection. She curled up, to get her hair braided, on what was left of my lap. Rayshaun and Preston were stretched out together on the recliner.

It's been about two and a half months since we moved out of Ray's Brownstone and into our new house. Rayshaun did an excellent job of choosing a property that would meet the needs of our growing family.

The four-bedroom, three-bath split-level was constructed of multi-colored bricks with a spacious balcony deck behind the house. Rayshaun has now added grilling to his top-secret culinary repertoire.

It's taken many personal touches to turn this house into our home. We're not completely unpacked yet (may never be from the looks of things), but we made quick work of settling in as a family.

Every week, we have three events dedicated to the family— Movie night, Game night and Meeting night. Chores are easily divided. Preston and Deity are very helpful and considerate children. They go back with Treasure every other weekend, so those are date nights for Rayshaun and me. Extremely structured and predictable, I know, but it relieves a lot of the stress that this situation can cause in a relationship.

I was surprised by how quickly Deity took a liking to me. It's astonishing how sharp and keen she is at only six years old. She has the profoundly mature conversation of an adult tinged with the, sometimes brutal, honesty of a child. We have developed a deep affection for each other in such a short time. She's my little sweetie, and since I am expecting a baby boy, she and I represent the Minority Party in the house and will, therefore, remain undivided on all of the pertinent political issues.

Nine-year old Preston is different. He is a quiet, introspective boy. It's hard to know where you stand with him. He is polite and mannerly, but somewhat reserved and distant. Preston bears no resemblance to Rayshaun. He is a handsome child—short, stocky and chestnut-complexioned with small, slanted black eyes, but very evidently not from Rayshaun's stock. Ray and Preston do, however, have an extremely close bond. They have this odd, unspoken language, in which they communicate with each other through a complex system of gestures and grunts. They pride themselves on having inside jokes that Deity and I cannot decipher. We've got a little Girl vs. Guy rivalry going, but it makes for an amusing family dynamic.

I admit I was taken back, initially. I had no idea that Preston and Deity would be living with us full-time. I wasn't necessarily opposed to it, but it just took me by surprise to be thrown into the middle of circumstances I had no knowledge of.

After we got back together, Ray explained to me that one day, weeks before the convenience store ordeal, he was contacted by Social Services. They informed him that Deity had been brought into the Emergency Room. Treasure left the children with some irresponsible girlfriend, who placed the kids in front of the television, while she went out to get some "groceries".

After being left alone and hungry for hours, Deity tried to make some grilled cheese sandwiches. She sustained severe second-degree burns on her palm. Preston, unsure of what to do, took her to their cousin's apartment downstairs. Their seventeen year-old second cousin Shanice wrapped Deity's hand and took her to the hospital. Rayshaun came immediately, but it took several hours before they could locate Treasure. Despite all of Treasure's ranting, she could not provide a compelling enough excuse for her negligence, so the social worker gave temporary custody of the children to Rayshaun.

After that, Rayshaun and Rayshelle worked together to ensure that the children would have constant supervision. Following the shooting, Ray hired Dayle (the nanny) to help him with the kids and chores around the house. He did his best to keep me out of the drama, but having the kids around changed many of our plans.

After I received the news of the fiery death of my mother, this instant family proved to be an immeasurable asset to me. Before I regained the strength to get out of bed, Deity was Dayle's attentive nurse's aide and gopher. Her enthusiastically optimistic well wishes served as my inspiration to continue the fight to improve each day. Even Preston took on extra chores to help alleviate my load. Through everything, Rayshaun was the best. He remained, at the center of it all—the Master Delegator. He managed to never drop the ball and continue his constant support of me. Rayshaun bestows more love on the kids and me, than I knew he was capable of—especially Preston. Sometimes, I wonder if the boy knows that Ray is not his father. None of it matters though, when we are all together. Despite the overwhelming (but functional) depression, which beclouds and eclipses my days, we have created a blissful environment that is brimming with love. It feels warm and fuzzy; like something I've never had before—

A family

The den is my favorite place in the house. The vastly spacious room drops down a few steps within the main level. The walls are covered with wood paneling, creating a cozy, cabin-like atmosphere. The newly installed brown Berber carpet is perfect for walking and laying on. We have a plush, beige-leather sectional, with recliners at each end which almost wraps around the entire span of the room. Our very own, brand-new 60" LCD television was a welcome addition to this space as well.

'And they call this good hair,' I thought, struggling to part Deity's hair into sections for ponytails. This child has enough hair for three heads. It's soft and curly, but it tangles like a tumbleweed when I wash it.

"Owww," she whined.

"Sorry, baby." I said, pulling her hair through an elastic band.

KNOCK, KNOCK, KNOCK, KNOCK

Rayshaun, who had fallen asleep on Madgey, was startled awake. "Who is that knocking on my door like the damn police?" He groaned, hoarsely. The doorbell began ringing rapidly like an alarm.

"I don't know," I shrugged with my hands still full of Deity's tangled hair. "But at this time of night, it better be the police or whoever is at the door is gonna' need 'em?"

Ray rolled Preston, who had also passed out on Madgey, over on the couch and stood up. Ray tightened the tie on his black basketball shorts, as he staggered groggily up the steps and across the living room floor.

KNOCK, KNOCK

"Hang on a minute, damn." Ray said, rushing to the front door. "Who is it?" he huffed, peeking through the peephole. "Damn it," he said, instantly recognizing the late night visitor.

Rayshaun cracked the door. "What the hell do you want, Treasure?"

I strained hard to tune out the movie, but I couldn't make out all of their conversation. From their tone, however, I could tell that the discussion was heated. I generally stay out of their business. I trust and respect Rayshaun, so I give him a lot of privacy within our relationship. I remained there on the couch, until Deity jumped off my lap, to run to the door. That gave me an excuse to be a little nosey. Here's a little bit of what I caught before Deity interrupted:

"Treasure, you know that you don't get the kids until tomorrow."

"Well, I can't get 'em in the morning. I got something else to do."

"I thought I told you not to **ever** come by my house," Ray said in a seething tone.

"That's fucked up Ray. I ain't never say shit 'bout you constantly hanging around my place when I had them babies."

"We have a deal. You pick the kids up from Rayshelle. You should have called me. I could've dropped them off for you there."

"Fuck you, Ray. I ain't have time to call. I was already out. You got control over the kids, but you don't fucking control me. I can go wherever the hell I want to. My kids shouldn't live in a place where they own mama ain't welcome."

"Hey Mama," Deity swung the door open and clasped her arms around Treasure's waist.

I had never seen Treasure before, so this was the— **Moment of Truth**.

I stood back at the edge of the den, but she was clearly visible, standing under the porch light.

Okay, I hate to give it up for her, but Treasure is an extremely attractive woman. She had full, pouty lips with refined features. Her face was heart-shaped with chubby, dimpled cheeks. Her long, curly, possibly naturally colored, copper hair and large hazel eyes, made it easy to see her in a modeling agency catalogue. She had that cafe-crème complexion that I call "Triple A" (ambiguously African-American), because you're not sure if she really has any Black lineage or if she's just a perpetrating white girl with lip injections and a tan. Treasure is just as tall as me, (which is unusual) maybe even taller. I could tell that her body, even after two kids, was still flawless—perky, buxom breasts, and a small, but firm, round bottom. She wore a cropped, dark-denim jacket with a neon-green baby tee that revealed her flat, toned midriff.

'I hate that skinny bitch,' I thought to myself, looking down at my immense, swollen belly, which is developing stretch marks even as we speak.

I thought that Deity's intrusion would taper the flaring tempers of her parents, but- I was wrong.

"Come on, honey. Getcha' shit, so we can go?"

"Hell no. They're not going anywhere. If you can't respect our arrangement, then you're gonna' have to stick to what the order says."

"You only pull that custody order bullshit when it benefits you, Ray. I don't give a damn about no piece of paper."

Ordinarily, I wouldn't intervene, but the commotion had awakened Preston, who was standing beside me at the entrance to the den. Deity cried out as Ray pulled her away from her mother. There didn't seem to be any civil end to this squabble in sight. Treasure had a long, purple manicured nail pointed in Rayshaun's face, when I said—

"Hey Ray . . . I think Treasure is right. She should be welcome to come here and get her children."

They both paused in mid-sentence and stared at me blankly.

"And who the hell asked **you**?" Treasure scowled with a raised eyebrow.

'Okay, now I really hate this skinny bitch.'

"Who are you, anyway?" Treasure said, stepping inside of the doorway and into the living room.

"You're not going to come up in our house and talk to my lady like that Treasure." Ray's jaw clenched as he tried to subdue his anger.

"Our house?... Our house!" Treasure amped, wagging her head from side to side. "You got this hoe up in here 'round my kids! You can fuck whoever you want to Ray, but don't be having them sluts 'round my kids!"

"Not that it's any of your business, but Denae is my fiancée and you're not going to talk about her like she's yo' momma."

'Dang!' Ray was hurling fighting words.

Treasure stepped up to Rayshaun. They hollered at each other until both of their faces turned bright red. Deity started screaming and pulling at her mother's arm. In the heat of the exchange, Treasure accidentally slung Deity to the ground. The argument ceased abruptly, as Treasure knelt hurriedly to pick up her daughter.

"I'm sorry, honey," Treasure said, gingerly lifting Deity back to her feet. She inspected the girl thoroughly. "Are you okay baby? This will be some more shit for yo' ole' no-good ass daddy to blame on me."

"Treasure, you need to watch how you talk in front of these children." Ray shifted Deity over towards me. "Denae, please take them upstairs."

Treasure eyed me malevolently as Deity wrapped her arms around my thigh. "I know you like Ray's dick," she said addressing me. "But you just remember that I had it first. I got the best of him and he's gone always belong to me." Treasure flipped me off with her left hand, to display that she was still wearing her wedding band.

'That confirms it. This bitch is completely delusional.'

"Treasure, if you don't leave now, I'm going to call the police," Ray said calmly. He remained at the door with his hand resting anxiously on the knob. I ushered the children up the stairs. I turned off the television in the den then started up the staircase myself.

"And she's pregnant, too? I thought she was just fat!" Treasure wailed seemingly to herself, throwing her hands up into the air. "Just because Ray knocked you up, don't mean you can play mommy with my kids too, bitch . . ."

I disregarded Treasure. She is obviously a deranged lunatic. I started to scale the steps, a task which has recently become even more difficult with the introduction of numb toes and swollen ankles to the growing list of pregnancy-related ailments.

"I heard that you were slummin' Ray, but I didn't know you were scraping the bottom of the barrel with that baboon. I guess you'll stick your dick in anything these days."

'Alright, that does it.'

"Treasure, I've tried to be respectful," I said lowly, as I double-stepped my way back down each step. "But you got one more time to call me a name before— "

"Before what, bitch?" Treasure yelled, waving her hand in the air.

"Before nothing," Ray interrupted, pulling her elbow. "Treasure, that's enough. This is between us. You need to leave Denae out of it."

Squish, squish

"Ray..." I moaned.

"Just go upstairs, Denae. I'll handle this..."

Squish

"Ray..." I groaned. I had withdrawn from the verbal sparring contest. I had a bigger issue developing, in the form of a puddle at my feet. My soggy socks sloshed in the warm liquid that saturated them.

"Get the hell out of my house, Treasure," Ray fumed at her.

"Ray!" I shrieked.

"What?" He yelled, turning towards me. His face dropped as he beheld the dark, wet spill extending down the legs of my green cotton lounge pants.

"... Well, Treasure. I guess you can go ahead and take the kids tonight."

PART VIII

THE PROCESS

Safety in Lovers

Devian Nikei

Dearly Beloved

"If there is anyone here among us who wishes to object to this union, speak now... or forever hold your peace."

"I dare any of y'all to say one word," Lanelle huffed, eyeing the crowd.

Hushed Silence

"Well then, by the power vested in me, I now pronounce you, husband and wife. You may kiss your bride."

Uproarious applause erupted from the audience.

"I, now, present to you all... Mr. and Mrs. Stafford James Millsaps."

'I guess complete opposites really do attract,' I thought handing Lanelle her bouquet of white and fuchsia tulips. Lanelle had finally landed her man—and a good one, at that. She met Dennis's younger brother Stafford, a pharmaceutical researcher, at the funeral. They went out a few weeks later and became conjoined twins after only one date. Now, almost six years from that first date, here we all are.

I was Lanelle's **Matron** of Honor.

Yes, me—**Mrs**. Rayshaun D. Bivens (but we'll get to that later).

Stafford and Lanelle do make a genuinely gorgeous couple. A new curvy, not chunky, and unnoticeably pregnant Lanelle made her debut, in a strapless ivory Christian Dior wedding gown, beside her tall drink of black coffee. Though slightly shorter and leaner than Dennison, Stafford, with his dark brown eyes and goatee, is the more attractive brother. The only feature he has in common with Dennis is... you guessed it, the dimples. He was pulling off his fuchsia vest (Lanelle's choice), like only a man that fine can.

Simone sat on the front row, decked out in a giant, exquisite ivory hat, aside her husband, Dennis. She was gleaming. Simone's face displayed a transcendent serenity.

"God works in mysterious ways," Simone said to me, days earlier, at the rehearsal dinner, "The Lord giveth and He taketh away." Her words were precise and poignant. Although she had lost her eldest son, she felt blessed to witness the addition of a daughter-in-law and soon her very first grandchild, the little girl that Simone never had.

I had lost Maw-maw, Dennis and my own mother—three generations gone, almost within weeks of each other. I started to believe that someone had a personal vendetta against me. Some days, I even questioned what the purpose of life and love was. Was this just some wicked experiment gone awry in some celestial laboratory?

Everyone around me seemed like expendable, obsolete board game pieces that could be dispelled at any time. Life couldn't be that arbitrary and trivial— could it?

That was all before I understood my Process.

Some of you are going to be upset that the story didn't end in the previous section. I gave you the romance, the drama, the sex, and the scandal— every ingredient for the perfect stew. But what is it all without any heat to cook it?

My life was thrown into a furnace and, although the flames were painful and destructive, a miracle came forth as a result of the fire called Tragedy.

God truly gave me beauty for my ashes. So if I am going to give you the truth, the whole truth, and nothing but the truth (God help me) then I cannot omit The Process.

Understanding the purpose of suffering is one thing, but the process is another. It is our individual process that defines our purpose. If you experience much catastrophe, but you remain unchanged, then your purpose does not change and your suffering was in vain. You continue on as selfish, vindictive, indifferent or even complacent as you were before calamity consumed your life. For those, however, that allow adversity and affliction to transform and reform their lives, they transcend and excel their original purpose and attain unto a higher calling.

Many are the called, but few are chosen.

How you endure your Process determines your blessing. Three people had been taken from me—their lives cut like loose thread from the fabric of life. Those deaths were not God's doing— not His will, but still I couldn't see that at the time. I did not know that I was being positioned to receive his favor. My foundations were removed, those I loved the most and everything I trusted in— until only God remained.

He bestowed his love on me until I understood Grace. That's what Simone had that day at the funeral, what my mother and Maw-maw had attained before they died, and what Dennis gained in prison and gave to everyone he met. It made them seem heavenly and unencumbered by this world.

The understanding, then acceptance, of the knowledge that all experiences— whether good or bad; joyful or painful; uplifting or devastating—are the instruments of your enlightenment (so long as you resist bitterness and invite growth) is both the purpose and the plan of life.

It was Rayshaun Daniel Bivens Jr., or baby Ray Jay, (as we call him) who helped bring me around to that revelation. He was born in late May. He was a beautiful, bouncy almond-colored baby boy with my brown eyes and his father's cleft chin. He brought me back, seemingly from the dead, and gave me purpose again, reaffirming my faith in true love—

Before his birth, I was on the brink, just about to give up completely on life, love and God. Rayshaun gave his best effort to hold on to me, but all the death around me had drained my affections and left me weary. I was like a ghost. Ray could see but not touch me.

After Ray Jay was born, Ray and I found each other again, but what I didn't know was that irreparable damage had been done. Rayshaun had lost his confidence in me and our relationship, but Ray— being the kind of man that he is, buried it all away. We were married at an intimate ceremony in Rayshelle's backyard, a little over a year later. Ray walked down the aisle following Marcus, his Best Man, and his two sons, ten year-old Preston and fourteen month-old Junior, his groom's men. All of them looked so handsome in their matching gray and coral (my choice) three-piece suits with striped ascots. Lanelle, Juniece and Deena were my bridesmaids, but the star of the event was seven (going on twenty) year-old Deity, the little flower lady.

Rayshaun was breathless when I appeared on the lawn, alongside Bishop Simmons, in a flowing, pearlized satin, off-the-shoulder gown. I wore a large pink Camellia blossom in my elegantly intricate up do. Rayshaun smiled with flushed cheeks when he took my hands in his, and peered deeply into my eyes.

Our event was lovely, not nearly as lavish as this Millsaps' wedding, but still wonderful and private all the same. I hung on every word of Ray's personalized vows to me. Tears welled up in both of our eyes, when we kissed for the first time as husband and wife.

The wedding reception was beautiful. Rayshelle and her sisters out did themselves with eccentric, yet sophisticated, decorations. The wedding party and guests blew thousands of bubbles as we entered the reception hall.

The deejay was great, mixing a few new school songs with the oldies. We all enjoyed a riveting round of the Electric Slide. Rayshaun, who is not a dancer by any stretch of the measure, felt content to stand on the sidelines. He bobbed his head and sipped on a flute of white champagne, until he saw Marcus engage me in an upbeat two-step, which aptly he cut in on—demonstrating his duck shuffle. Everyone was having an excellent time, but before I could toss my bouquet, Treasure showed up most-uninvited.

Rayshelle caught her at the door, attempting to do damage control, but Treasure was completely irrational and hostile. I have never seen a girl that pretty, act *so* ugly. She caused such an embarrassing scene, cursing and raving in front of all the guests.

Ray was next to take up the cause. He dragged Treasure, by the elbow, out of the hotel to the parking lot. That decision proved to be unwise, because the altercation intensified into a full-scale disaster. Treasure attacked Ray like a wildcat, jumping on his back and tearing at his eyes and face.

Breaking up the fight was just about as wild of an event as the fight itself. Marcus grabbed Ray, before he could choke the consciousness out of Treasure, and brought him back inside the hotel. While I attended to my husband, Rayshelle and her sister Adelle *"subdued"* and *"restrained"* Treasure until the police arrived. The whole incident ended with several wicked scratches on Ray's face and a demolished driver side window in his Jaguar.

Needless to say, Treasure spent quite a few days in jail and received a stringent Restraining Order barring her from **any** and **all** contact with Ray. He was later awarded full custody of Deity, as well as Preston (of whom Treasure still swore under oath, to her own chagrin, that Rayshaun was the biological father).

Since we had a full house, we decided to postpone the honeymoon. However, I realized shortly after the wedding that the honeymoon was already over before it began. Only a few months in, Ray started hanging out with frat brothers and stopped coming home at night. Sometimes days could go by and I would have to go by his office just to make sure that he was still alive. He wasn't the only one who was keeping a secret though.

Shortly after the wedding, I was contacted by an attorney, Mr. Jeffrey Garis. He advised me that he was responsible for overseeing Dennison's estate. According to Mr. Garis, Dennis willed his house to me with implicit instructions to liquidate it upon his death and transfer all assets over to me. With all of Dennis's renovations to the house, it sold for around $250,000.

I didn't know what to do with the money, so I decided to do what Dennis had urged me to do and pursued a career in clothing design. I resigned my position in Probation and Parole and enrolled in The Fashion Institute.

Around that same time, Rayshaun likewise received an *"anonymous"* Community Revitalization Grant for an amount in the neighborhood of half of a million dollars to found the establishment of a Youth Development Center in Clayton County. Rayshaun jumped at the opportunity to spearhead the project, promptly enlisting Marcus as his partner. Although Ray had the Marketing Degree, he assumed responsibility for the accounting and bookkeeping, preferring the office work (and hours) to the field operations.

Marcus was placed in charge of recruitment and public relations. Marcus employed his "Each one, please one" philosophy in order to lure, I mean, entice-sorry, that's still not right either... encourage (yeah, that's better) single mothers to enroll their youths and teens in the Center.

The Dennison John Millsaps Youth Center became a huge success. Many young people in the Clayton County area were able to take advantage of resources that were previously unavailable to them. Rayshaun poured all of his energy into the Center and it exceeded expectations.

The facility offered many different disciplines, including educational enrichment, sports and fine arts (like poetry writing). I was glad to see Rayshaun find fulfillment in his work. He was finally able to trade in the three-piece shark suit for a sweater vest with rolled up shirtsleeves and relaxed fit khakis.

It seemed as though, the Wheel of Fortune that had crushed us the year before was hoisting my family and me up to new, unimaginable heights. I still couldn't ignore the warning signs, flashing in my rearview mirror. Ray and I were straying off into different directions, even the children were being affected by it. Deity's constant questions, "Where's my daddy?" and "When is daddy coming home?" were breaking my heart.

Finally, one night, I waited up for a disenchanted Rayshaun to come shuffling through the door. I bombarded and accosted him with questions. I told him how disappointed I was in the fact that he could mentor other children and not even come home to his own. He exploded and a horrendous argument commenced. He blamed me for an assortment of problems and threw up my relationship with Dennis... again (as usual). However, everything came to a head with his admission that he had an affair.

I didn't handle the news the way I always promised myself I would. I always vowed that if Ray cheated, I would pack up and dip out, instantly— no conversation, no hesitation.

However, things were different now. It wasn't just about me anymore. I had children to think of and— despite the fact that he messed up, I did still love Rayshaun very much. I was surprised when he broke down, bawling and begging my forgiveness. He told me that it only happened a couple of times, during my depression, with some female attorney that he met at the Sports Management Firm, shortly before he resigned his position to open the Center.

"I just missed you so much and you kept rejecting me. I needed someone and I didn't want to keep pressuring you when you were already going through so much."

"You didn't do me any favors, Ray!" I shouted at him. "What you did only caused more pain. You practically tore this whole family apart with your lies and selfishness . . . And all for what? . . . A piece of ass." I turned my back to him, but he came around to face me.

"There's no excuse for what I did, Denae— only an explanation, if you want one... It started out as innocent companionship. I thought I could handle a friendship with her. I thought I had it under control, but it was too late before I realized that I was wrong. Then, I felt so bad afterwards that I couldn't look you in the eye anymore. That's why I stayed away from home."

I waved my hands, signaling him to halt his confession. Every breath I sucked in scalded my chest with searing heat, as I wheezed out painful sobs. Ray pounded at his head with his fists. "I'm sorry . . . I'm so sorry, Denae." He dropped to his knees in front of me, hugging my waist tightly, "Baby, please don't leave me." He drenched the front of my robe with his tears. He said that he didn't want to lose me or his family, so I finally consented to defer all decision-making until after we attended counseling. Rayshaun readily agreed to participate.

In hindsight, I ask myself, 'Why on earth did we do a thing like that?'

Marriage counseling was like war, no **Armageddon**—but with referees. It was like a three-ring circus with lions and tamers. In those sessions, we built fortified battlements and hurled emotional artillery at each other for an hour. At times, we would wound each other so deeply with our subversive criticisms in counseling, that the following week in session would be our first words to each other since the last meeting. Other times, we would enter our consultation already engaged in a raging combat that ensued days prior. Rayshaun tired of sleeping on the sofa bed and moved out after just a few months.

About eight months in, everyone was ready to give up on our relationship. The marriage counselors refused to schedule another session with us. They told us that we were not compatible and they believed that a divorce would be our best resort. Ray agreed and filed a motion for separation.

It was then that I had my Awakening.

I realized that I loved my husband and all I wanted was for our marriage to work. The following week, I went to his apartment. I came this time, seeking to understand my man. I didn't come to be heard anymore, but to hear. I didn't come to speak, but to listen.

At first, it was like walking out into the highway during Rush Hour or diving headfirst into an empty pool. I had to take his verbal blows and lashings without any defense, and it was excruciating. I surrendered to my love for him and let God be my strong tower. I didn't retreat; I embraced Rayshaun and all of his defects. I let go of what I needed from him and gave him all that I had. I humbled myself and submitted to him.

Guess what happened next?

He responded.

He met me there, right smack in the middle of love. He learned the art of submission from me, as I yielded to him. My defenselessness disarmed him and he opened up to me again. We began to educate, instead of compete with, each other. He taught me how to respect him in how he honored me and I showed him how to love me in how I cherished him.

We finally took the honeymoon that we put off for three years and boy did we get our *groove* back on. I spent ten days at a beachfront paradise in Lamu, Kenya (yes, Africa) with my husband. The landscape was stunningly breathtaking, unlike anything you see at beaches in the United States.

We invented new ways to make spontaneous love to each other, exploring desires that we didn't even know we had. I knew that Ray was a **Champion Lover**, but he made me feel things that I didn't even know were physically possible. The sliding doors to our suite opened up directly onto the white sands of the beach. During our stay, we spent countless hours enveloped in each other's arms, rocking and rolling with the cadence of the waves outside our window. It wasn't all fun and sex, however.

For the first time, Ray and I took an odyssey into each other's heart and mind. We trekked skillfully into the intimate depths of all our insecurities, fears, hopes and dreams. Armed with a heightened zeal, we dissected each other down to the barest essence of our beings. Once there, we divided the real from the counterfeit and renewed our vows of honesty and trust.

Our last evening there, we went out on the beach and built a small bonfire. It was late in the fall season, so the coasts were, literally, clear. After awe-inspiring *sex on the beach*, Rayshaun and I bundled up together, naked and gratified, in a huge comforter. We sat by the shore, holding each other and gazing out at the stars for a long time.

"Thank you, Denae," he said softly, over the peaceful rustle of the waves.

"For what?" I asked, studying his beautiful face.

"For not giving up on me." He continued to stare off into the distance, as he spoke. "I never had a man in my life to show me how to be a good one. When I was younger, all I had were superheroes to learn from, and that didn't do much good. The superheroes were never who they appeared to be. They always had an alter ego, a whole other persona that was completely opposite from their Herculean nature, but my question was always which character was the real man? When I grew up, I leaned on my friends to teach me, but hell, that was the damn blind leading the stupid."

Rayshaun picked up a shell and threw it into the waves. "I was one of the only men in my family. Can you imagine being the only one?... All I had were women, my aunts and cousins around me all the time talking about how men wasn't shit. They made it seem like it was a bad thing to be born male. And I didn't have no role models, no male perspective to balance it out, so having all those women depending on me put a lot of pressure on me. I thought that being a man meant being strong and perfect, all the time. I didn't ever want to be weak, so I tried not to feel anything for anybody. I conditioned myself to live that way, and just got colder as I got older."

Ray shivered slightly from the breeze. I pulled the cover up on his shoulder and snuggled in closer to him, placing my head on his chest, as he spoke. "I thought I was doing it right 'cause women seemed to love it. The more I dragged them, the more they were into me. That made me feel like the fucking man for a minute, but everything I did started to leave me empty after a while. I was dead inside when you found me, but now, for the first time, I think I am beginning to see what being a real man is about. Now, I realize that I have a chance to break the cycle. I have children, my own sons and daughters, as well as others, who are looking up to me, counting on me. I have to teach my sons to be men and show my daughter how she is supposed to be treated. You are doing a great job teaching her how to be a strong woman and still remain a lady. I'm the one who needs to step it up and I think I'm finally learning how... from you."

He smoothed my hair back from my face. "You taught me about love and strength, because you stayed with me even when the pressure broke me down and had nothing left to give you. You were my rock when I was in pieces and you never left me alone. I didn't have to be perfect for you to love me, and I thank you for that—for sticking with me, even when I fucked up."

Ray kissed the back of my hand. "I'm only human . . . and sometimes I will make mistakes, but I don't ever want to be anywhere else, but with you— if you'll have me back in your heart," he said bringing his gaze to meet my eyes. Rayshaun placed his hand behind my head and laid me back on to the sand and into the comfort of his embrace. I drew my knees up alongside his body, and crossed my ankles over his buttocks. He pulled the covers around our bodies, creating a warm, snug cocoon. I could feel the erection of a huge monument in my honor.

"I won't hurt you again. I need you. Please trust that," he whispered in my ear, before kissing along my neck. I wanted to lose myself in the cool breeze that blew over our bodies—but I couldn't. I tried to release my inhibitions, as the surf broke sending tiny ripples of water rolling up to lap at our feet, however in the back of my mind, I felt a sense of foreboding. I hoped and prayed that our ardor for each other would not dissolve as soon as we arrived back at home.

Nevertheless, like a transplanted flower, our affection bloomed and blossomed when returned to its native soil. The passion that flared in Kenya exploded in our home. The laundry room, the basement, the bathroom, and even the attic— Rayshaun and I found every place and occasion to (as we call it) "exercise" in private, away from the roving eyes and ears of all the children. We soon realized that we had returned from Lemu with a souvenir.

A few weeks later, my gynecologist confirmed that I was pregnant again. The following year, we welcomed a sweet, quiet green-eyed boy named Denzel Marshall Bivens into our family.

Over the past two years, Rayshaun has become the kind of husband that I never knew how to hope for. He is considerate and kind; thoughtful and romantic. Ray has renewed his dedication to the children and me. We are an exceedingly happy family. I thank God every day that He gives me the grace to show my husband and children the same patience that He has shown me.

My mother was right. The love that you give always finds its way back to you. What she didn't tell me about was the concept of seedtime and harvest. The love you sow comes back triple fold. My sacrifices were menial compared to the gift that I received from having Rayshaun, the kids, Maw-maw, Mom and even Dennis in my life.

Many times, Rayshaun and my family overwhelm me with such abundant love that I never seem to have room enough to receive it. I learned through My Process that life and love are blessings— not curses. They are God's gifts to us and not a taunting game that He plays with us. When we imitate and mirror His character, then we understand the renewing power of selfless love initiated by God, intercepted by us and dispersed to the world through our lives. He doesn't waste anyway. He doesn't throw any of us away and we should never give up on people either; no matter what background, educational level, complexion or other superficial division may exist between us.

I also came to realize that life itself is just an outline. We are born, develop and abandon various relationships, live a certain unpredictable number of days, and then die. That is common to everyone, thus making all of our pictures the same, but life is not cut and dried— it's never just black and white. Although there are some gray areas, not even those color our lives. We all have the free will and basic colors to decorate our own existence.

Love, passion, religion, beliefs, convictions, desires are just a few of the pigments found on the palette of life choices that we can make. There is only one colorant that we can't choose, but are most often esteemed by, and that is the color of our skin.

However, all other blank spaces are open to our own artistic interpretation. As decisions are made and different colors combine, an assortment of diverse hues, tints and shades are created. The way that we use these various colors to paint our murals is the only factor that differentiates us from one another.

As children, we are all taught to paint in different ways. However, none of us are the product of arbitrary or accidental circumstances. Every shade on your canvas is composed of pigments standard to everyone, but shaken together in the paint mixer of your own choices. However, it still remains, that all the fanciful colors we can contrive will distract and even delude us— if we let them— into thinking that we are flawless artists.

Dennis once told me, "No one else can judge your work in progress until its finished. And even then, all opinions are subject to imperfect interpretation.

So often, we judge others around us for the way they choose to paint their portraits. Criticizing them for putting orange in the place where we think that purple should go. Since none of us, who are evaluating, have ever completed even one entire painting, I don't think that any of us are qualified to be professional art critics.

Some will occasionally color outside the lines, but that is all a part of the process, just as it is with children as they learn to paint. It's just a small, and oftentimes, unnoticeable blemish in the grand scheme of the Big Picture, which is constantly changing and evolving with each brushstroke. Remember that just as we have our own paints, we likewise are paints in the hand of the Creator (that's why we come in so many beautiful colors), and thus part of an even larger portrait than just the one we are individually responsible for.

I'll bet I sound pretty deep right now, huh?

That's the interesting thing about life, just when you think you are swimming in the ocean, you find out that you're only wading in a pond.

Safety in Lovers

Devian Nikei

The Gun Line

Here's what they don't tell you in the ***Follow Your Dreams*** brochure:

- They don't tell you that your dream of being a famous fashion designer may not get you to Milan or Paris or even Fashion Week in New York.
- They don't tell you that after seven years, you may have only had six local fashion shows and a few custom pieces hanging in a boutique on Auburn Street.
- They don't tell you that you can bust your ass every day, but people will still treat your work as though it does not have the same aesthetic worth as Louis Vitton or Vera Wang because it is not a brand name.

I didn't feel like a failure, though. The adventure was success enough for me. I had dared to ride the comet until it disappeared. I was collecting sufficient funds from the sale of individual dresses and jackets to continue to finance my small business venture, but not to build a fashion empire. I received praise at least once daily for the fit or ingenuity of my clothing. I had attained some local celebrity clientele. I was content with that, so after a handful of years, I closed up shop.

After only a few months at home, I began to develop a bit of Cabin Fever. Once Denzel began Kindergarten, I had no reason to stay at home anymore. A kitchen floor can only get so clean, and Preston had developed into quite the teenage sous-chef under the tutelage of his father. Even Deity has joined the cooking ranks this year, so I was completely obsolete at home. I visited the children often at school, but soon even Denzel had to ask me to get a life.

Rayshaun, on the contrary, didn't mind the office drop-ins so much. I'd say he rather enjoyed them, as his desk was seeing more action than our bed. When I told Ray that I was going back to work, he was vehemently against it, stating that I didn't have to. Our family didn't want for anything. There were many youths enrolled in the Center. Marcus's campaigning efforts were going well, picking up more sponsors and donations from local celebrities and foundations daily. Rayshaun offered me a position as his secretary. He told me that the position would come with *benefits*, but I declined. I enjoyed the enthusiasm he had at the dinner table, recounting his day of reaching this or that child, so I didn't want to impede upon his Man Space.

As much as Rayshaun aired his protests, he told me that he would support whatever decision I made, the same way I had supported him across the years. So where do you think I ended up?

Three guesses.

Nope.

Not even close.

Okay, you got it.

Back at Probation and Parole. I'm glad that I didn't torch any bridges (like I wanted to) by cussing Sgt. Bledsoe out before I resigned. Luckily for me, I got to work under Sgt. Davis Ludlow's supervision this time. It felt strangely good to come back to work for the Georgia Division of Probation and Parole. It was my routine— cozy and comfortable, like old, broken-in shoes or your favorite pair of jeans.

"Look alive, Richmond... I mean *Bivens*." Sgt. Ludlow said dropping some case files on my desk. "Sorry to drop these on you like this but, Smythe is out with some bird flu virus or mad cow disease... I can't keep track this time."
"Ewww," I stuck out my tongue.
"Yeah, I know. He's a terrible liar, but whatcha' gonna' do?" Davis smiled with a shrug. "It's inconsiderate and inconvenient too, because one of his parolees is here right now. Ordinarily, I

would reschedule him, but this is his initial consult, nothing but paperwork. Can you handle it?"

"Yeah sure. You know I got your back."

"Thanks, I'll send him over to you."

I threw the file open. I barely had time to find his name before he was seated in front of me. I am always mystified by how amputees can commit crimes. This guy's left arm, from the bicep down was missing. I didn't have time to get into his story right then, so I reached across my desk and shook his right hand.

"Mr. Thigpen, I presume. Terrence— is that right?" I said, taking my seat.

'Thigpen. That name rings a bell,' I thought as I sat back in my chair, surveying this scar-faced "client". He donned the standard issue mad-at-the-world scowl. Eye contact is my new thing now, but I couldn't place his face.

He leaned back in his chair. "Yeah, I don't answer to that slave name, no more. You can call me Hassim Khalid Mustafa... or Tig."

Devian Nikei

The End

Devian Nikei

**If you loved this book, also check out
The newest Nikei Novel**

Just in Case

By Devian Nikei

Available now at Amazon and Kindle

Devian Nikei

Safety in Lovers